# the calaboose epistles

Other Books by R. T. Smith

FICTION

*Faith*
*Uke Rivers Delivers*

POETRY

*Waking Under Snow*
*Rural Route*
*From the High Dive*
*Birch-Light*
*The Cardinal Heart*
*Trespasser*
*Hunter-Gatherer*
*Split the Lark*
*Messenger*
*The Hollow Log Lounge*
*Brightwood*
*Outlaw Style*

# The Calaboose Epistles

Stories

R. T. Smith

Iris Press
Oak Ridge, Tennessee

Iris Press is an imprint of the Iris Publishing Group, Inc.
www.irisbooks.com

*Book Design by Robert B. Cumming, Jr.*

Library of Congress Cataloging-in-Publication Data

Smith, R. T.
The Calaboose epistles : stories / R. T. Smith.
    p. cm.
ISBN 978-1-60454-209-7 (pbk. : alk. paper)
1. Appalachian Region, Southern—Fiction. I. Title.
PS3569.M537914C35 2009
813'.54—dc22
                                        2009029929

## Acknowledgements

The author would like to thank the editors and staffs of the following journals for publishing these stories and for all their encouragement and assistance:

*Appalachian Heritage:* "Against a Sea of Troubles," "Sugar" and "Ruminants"
*Arts & Letters:* "'Sang"
*Blackbird:* "Wishing"
*Chattahoochee Review:* "Correspondences"
*Connecticut Review:* "Fig Honey"
*Elixir:* "Aloft with Grief"
*Fugue:* "Cockers for Christ"
*Louisiana Literature:* "Tastes Like Chicken"
*Nantahala Review:* "Rampskin"
*Nebo:* "Independence Day"
*Prairie Schooner:* "Orin" (as "Story") and "Red Jar"
*Quarterly West:* "The Calaboose Epistles"
*Southern Humanities Review:* "The Pig Is Committed"
*StorySouth:* "Flurries"
*South East Review:* "Since Doby Ran"
*TriQuarterly:* "Luna"

"Tastes Like Chicken" and "Orin" (as "Story") were reprinted in *New Stories from the South: The Year's Best* (2006 & 2007 editions).

"Tastes Like Chicken" was presented onstage and recorded in Richmond, Virginia by the James River Writers and Barksdale Theater.

"Against a Sea of Troubles" received the Denny C. Platner Fiction Award from *Appalachian Heritage.*

Thanks also to Sarah Kennedy, Hank Dobin, Suzanne Stryk, Kent and Claudia, Ann Pancake, George Singleton, Bret Anthony Johnston, Sheriff Blaine Sherburne, Faye Dunaway and especially Bob and Beto Cumming.

*for Sarah, my only*

# CONTENTS

## I

## 2

## 3

## 4

Raze out the written troubles of the brain.

*—Macbeth*

I

# COCKERS FOR CHRIST

THANK YOU FOR INVITING me to share my faith with you this evening. In Jesus name, praise be. First off, my own name is Charity Henrietta Stark, but people call me "Roo," which is short for "Rooster," which as you see I am holding here under my arm. His name is Bedford Forest, which I spell with one "r," but it is still after the Confederate hero, and you may not know, but the South put gamecocks on some of their money because they are fierce and beautiful and true.

This June I turned fourteen, and I expect most of you out there are wondering why a tomboy girl like me has been invited to speak to the True Breath Methodist Men's Club about being saved, but in a nutshell it is this: my whole family—which is Charles Wray, Tommy, Momma and my daddy Walter Stark (known in gaming circles as Windy) have been through the Valley of the Shadow. We have been the Devil's instruments, and have screamed and cussed and sassed each other right down to flinging household items and knocking holes in doors, though I'm obviously not the one who did that last item. We were not in the Word and the Spirit, and we got so bad to spat that Momma (who was born Lucy Dartry) packed a grip and ran off for six months, which led us all to suffer the affliction of guilt after we drove her from our door, but Daddy mostly.

But that is not the faith part of my story, which is this. You may not know how big the chicken business is around these parts, but the coolness factor this far up the Blue Ridge makes for good training weather, and my daddy Windy Stark was so deep into breeding and raising and selling and pitting cocks and making wagers that he was about to run us to the poorhouse, as a man who goes to the whiskey well too often does not make for a careful handler or gambler, and you know about money-love and the root of evil, and that was what set them at each other and brought Charles Wray—he's twenty—in on Daddy's side, as he loved the pits and the betting and the loose women he'd find at the derbies. Tommy is nine and given to fickleness, swapping sides on a regular basis, but as I had learned early how to shurl and dubb the roosters and already had complete charge of feeding and keeping the water cups full and leading the cheers, I threw in with Daddy.

So Mama lit out. You see, it was gamecocks that drove us deep into the ditch of selfish worldly meanness toward our own precious kin, but it was eventually gamecocks that lifted us back on the path of righteousness, and that is what I am here to testify. You may not know that of our fifty states only Louisiana and New Mexico held out to allow legal chicken combat, and even that could change any minute, so now you will understand why many of the tournaments are held off in secret places, and anybody so much as waist-deep in this business is defying the law of the land on a daily basis, which is not the way things were originally ordained, as these birds are born to scuffle, and two cocks will fight each other or one his reflection in glass or even start scratching and hackling, if he so much as sees his own shadow wrong. It's not a thing we do to them, and God made them game, made them what is called "happily belligerent," though that liberal Discovery Channel will try to tell you otherwise. Fact of the matter is, birding is an honest and sincere part of our Southern traditions like the Stars and Bars and freedom of worship and to bear arms. If the Lord had not wanted them to spar and struggle, He would of made them different, and praise His Name that He didn't, because I and then my family finally learned from watching and loving the birds what it means to follow your right nature, and man's right nature is to be the master of all beasts and help them achieve their best work and surrender to the Spirit. Following Jesus is a discipline, and training up birds is a discipline, too, and I learned this from Cockers for Christ and brought it home to my hearth and kin, and now Mama is back and we are all in the Lord and in the business, and we have been rewarded with better handling practices and trophies and prize money and a good name on the circuit, but that is not so important as the feeling of joyous love He has granted us, for we are like the birds in how we have fought through the pain to seek Victory over the Devil, like Dixie itself, which was born of a quarrel but now lives in our hearts and shines.

You may not know this…excuse me a minute. I've got to put Bedford back in his carry case here, as he keeps kicking and squirming. He doesn't much like to be still and stays on the look-out for a rival, as he is a champion. If you are going to handle these birds, or anything that is blessed with beauty, you are going to get cuts, you are going to carry scars. It is the holy price, as you know. Myself, I do not mind the scars.

You may not know this, but you may: Despite whatever people like to say about the popular wild turkey, it was the gamecock that almost beat out our bald eagle for mascot of yours and my great country. Two votes. They almost knew what they were doing. And President Andrew Jackson was a bird person himself and fought cocks in a pit right there in the White House, and what some history experts just found out is that before each bout he would gather up all the owners and congressmen and slaves and whatever have you to hold a prayer to the Mighty Mystery before they started to bill the birds. If you've seen pictures of Old Hickory, as my history teacher Miz Percy says people called him, he should have been named Old Rooster, as he had a shock of hair that stood out like a poultry comb, and he was himself known to step out and duel when his honor was besmirched, which is like a gamecock in nature and is akin to a Christian who will not stand by and let some unsaved scoffer take the name of the Lord in vain.

This fact is maybe what made Wesley Morfield of Opelika, Alabama start a prayer group that would meet in the fresh morning before every battle royal, and it was real informal and word-of-mouth at first, everybody just holding hands and asking to be blessed and that the event would be not unruly but fair and clean without anger or anybody doping their bird or letting fly before the other handler was ready and that even the heavy betters keep in mind that it is the Lord Who has given us this day with its joy and the freedom to own and train and appreciate birds, even if we do have to evade around a bit to avoid prosecution, akin to early believers in the Savior. They would also pray that the state assemblies would see the light and legalize a perfectly legitimate business and hobby.

I know you want to get on with your scripture lesson and prayer call and the like right soon, and Bedford Forest is a little nervous up here before so many people with no other animals to point what his job is, so let me get on with how I got pulled in and give my testimony. Brother Samuel Lafferty of Iron Station, Tennessee is just one year older than me, and he would come to the big matches with his Uncle Lovell. We got to be friends hanging out at the campground areas, and we would go off to look at flowers or catch frogs, and he could always sneak a Bud Lite or two, which we would drink, with the result being a little giddiness I took to like a pig to mud, but I might also get sick and upchuck, which I didn't, as you can understand, enjoy at all. I liked to be with Samuel, as he has always been sarcasm-funny and good looking despite a wall-eye, and because by this time, as I said, my family had been sundered, and I was restless and reckless, too. So of course the beer turned us to fooling about, and pretty soon we were touching each other in the unspoken parts and doing everything but *It* off in the woods or in his RV when Uncle Lovell (who is ordained himself) was in the pits. I kind of liked the body rubbing and kind of didn't, not all that much, as it gets creepy even when you're tingling, but I was picking up habits, straying far, which you might not know is not much of what goes on at the big derbies, most people (excepting Charles Wray and a few bunk bunnies) being so deep into the birds that it fills up their minds. But deep in my heart's heart, what I most loved was not the licking and wrestling so much as being with Samuel in a trusting and sweet way, walking out under singing robins and big leafy trees, just holding hands and learning some of the thousand things he knew about game birds.

He'd say, "Roo, you can't work a white chicken the day before you pit him. He needs his leisure. But a red rooster will appreciate a good exercise and a hen to tread, as well, then about rip his cage apart when he lays eyes on another cock." Or he'd just tell me ways to smarten up a bird's attack just before release or how to shift the feed mixture every year after first frost. This was when he showed the most pep and pleasure, and I could just stroll and listen to him till the cows come home.

Well, just last September when I hadn't seen Samuel in a couple of months or even swapped letters more than once, we met up at an event down near Danville, and when I saw his RV and ran over to latch onto him, Samuel was striding fast toward a big white tent, and when I got close I could see his blood-red T-shirt said across his chest in white "Cockers for Christ," and I asked what that was, though I was crude in the way I asked it. You see I was picking up the wayward ways like a magnet, not even asking how far I might have strayed from a true path.

What Samuel said was, "Roo, I have turned over a new leaf." He had been baptized when he was a lap baby, but now he'd been re-saved in South Carolina by Wesley Morfield, who I have already mentioned as the first spark of this new fire slowly running through the ranks. I didn't want to buy into it at all, so deep was I into the worldly mire, and I traipsed off to go look at some Arkansas Travelers who were big favorites in the betting book because people had bragged on them over the Internet.

Next morning, though, he came after me, Samuel, and coaxed me with his croony voice to the prayer circle where about thirty mostly men but of all adult ages were holding hands in a big ring, and they shared a prayer in which it was said that roosters behaved too loyal and gallant to not have souls, and men are their keepers to train them for excellence and dedicate every word and action to the Lord. It was a little hokey at first, but then Mr. Morfield, who has bad acne scars but a big old welcome grin, had a few thoughts to share, and they hit me hard. They made deep sense.

What he said was how we all have to carry on our beliefs in every corner of our lives and that white Christians were particularly bad to "pigeonhole," he called it, our convictions away from our livelihood and recreation. Cockfighting is mostly white people, as you might not know. Coloreds, Uncle Lovell has said, once were more likely to go off in a swamp and cut a rooster's throat to throw a curse or read his liver, but that is most likely pure hen crap and Lovell's personal blindness problem, if he still holds to it. But Wesley Morfield—who knew me on sight and said, "Proud to have you with us Miss Stark"—then reminded us how the Big Fisherman Peter was tested when Jesus was tracked down, and the soldiers—Romans, and wall art in Pompeii proves they fought birds—asked him did he know the man they caught. Well, Jesus had told his friend the night before, "You'll deny me, Peter, before the cock crows thrice," while Peter stomped up and down and swore, "I'll not do it." But he did, and it was all a symbol, as Sweet Jesus knew the rooster calls out to the sun to dedicate every day to light, and God is Light and Jesus, and without Them we are in darkness like the disciples fumbling around in actual night or the night of turning away. It hit me so true, I started to shiver and feel all giddy in a way better than any beer or that other stuff. Wesley Morfield was glowing like an ember while he spoke, and it was plain as your nose on your face I had been like as one who embraced the night, enjoying the birds for what they could give me and not for the message they were born to bring, the message of letting go and letting the light pour in. And I had also flirted with sins of the flesh and bad language.

That was our lesson, to turn away from the darkness, and I started right in to believing that the Stark family had mis-heard the calling to sport with birds all along. We had let gaming sink us down into the blood sports just so we could have fun and be excited and make a name and hope for the big payoff, but the real reason the Powers had steered us to chicken fights was to eventually locate our path back to the Holy.

While that man from Opelika spoke and glowed, my cheeks were damp, and my palms had turned hot as pokers in the hands of Samuel on one side and a big-bearded Kentucky breeder named Roy Toy on the other. After a spell of bowed heads and silence, we broke up the ring and everybody took turns embracing and sharing the Holy Kiss, which was pure and more rewarding than anything Samuel and I had done in the shadows. Then I walked with Samuel over a field of wet clover and under new growth pines with thimble-sized cones, and while we talked it all out, I could hardly feel the earth under my feet or the breeze that made the leaves all shake, letting the sunshine wash down on us. I was beginning to understand how a Greater Purpose was starting to fill me, and I could speak of it openly and marvel with this sweet boy I liked and not have to sneak around about sharing a glow and a common purpose. Maybe, I thought, this was a secret that should be shouted out. When we went into the barn where the battles were held—not the drag pits where the wore-out birds go to fight their last throes, but the main event with the crowd and the excitement—I saw the fury and glory of sacrifice for the first time in its true righteous light.

We had a Claret named Hammer who had won twice already because he was a high flyer and a good cutter and was our money bird. Daddy had been tossing him on the tether several times a day, just conditioning, as you don't really have to train what's natural, and he was up on all his black drops and tonics, peaking in his energy and zest. Daddy had got him used to his new boots and had whetted up a pair of Ruff Tuff briar gaffs, and Hammer was ready as a bird could be.

When I got in and inched my way up to the rim, Daddy was billing our hero bird against a Kelso name of King Kong who was six pounds if he was an ounce. They might as well have called him Goliath, and you near about expected him to roar. In the handling area both creatures were eager for it, size differences aside, and fully obedient to both their owners' wishes and the messages in their blood and tiny brains. Well, I'll tell you: They came together in mid-air like two balls of fever, all squawk and wing-flap, feathers flying and blood slinging out. It was fast and wild, slash and stab, peck and lunge and tornado spin, but I saw it like somebody had put the speed on wrong, for they were nearly about frozen before my eyes, their own eyes sparkling and white fluff, red feathers and a green plume from Hammer's tail all whirling in the slowed motion.

Their spurs gave off the honed steel light—flash and gleam in the floods—and I could grasp the world's bewilderment and weirdness in their pose, holding on, then touching the damp dust of the pit and then rising again and giving off light like a will-o-the-wisp, but now I felt as how I had never witnessed this before. And even after they were handled because they both had spurs deep into them and Kong was lung-punctured, with their men blowing along their ruffs and saddles and kissing their bloody crowns, well, both cocks reared back at the same time almost and crowed the kind of call that speaks out to dawn and the first verse of every day's glory. It was so beautiful and fulfilling, I suddenly didn't want either bird to lose, as their passion was like unto the angels themselves, and I could feel the tears stinging my eye corners, but on the release they charged again fresh as all fire and double-struck, not one ounce of bird fury held back. Cut and cut—in thirty seconds Kong was a goner, his eyes clouding like mist on a berry, though it wasn't much better for Hammer, who took about four weavy steps and let out a feeble cry and dropped on his own face, dead as a doornail.

Sacrifice is sure enough what it was. Hammer gave us what we needed—to see devotion and the whole-heart effort—and then he had to give up the ghost, but there was a dignity in it I knew right then was divine and everlasting. By then, the tears running over my face were tears of joy.

But I don't want to paint too rosy a picture for you here tonight, as most owners didn't ever come around to our conversion. They can be a rough bunch and set in their ways, belligerent as the birds they prize, so pretty soon the Cockers for Christ shirts didn't show up that often, as the rank and file scoffed and talked about shunning people who couldn't keep their religion separate from bird business. In my heart I believe this was also the influence of the big-money organizers, who always fear the common man when he gets inspired. But some of us hung on to our new understanding and purpose. We'd all been persecuted before by the outsiders who scoff at rooster fighting for their own blind reasons, so I could take it from the insiders, too. Here's the reason I had to.

When I met Daddy back at the trailer and showed him the sense of it, how the birds were a sermon meant to draw us back to the straight path, he looked me straight in the eye and said, "Roo, I can see you are changed. You are flushed and shining to beat the band." And even he could see the clear fact of it, because he said then, "Girl, you look akin to some thunderstruck twice-born!" So I told him about the prayer circle and Apostle Morfield's words and how they shook me. Sobbing it out, I gave my account of Hammer's becoming a martyr, and he looked riddled at first, but then his breathing got fast. Pretty soon he broke down and cried like a wet baby and said it was a sign, it was out of the mouths of babes, and he could not live any longer in vanity nor without his Lucy, and Hammer being gone just made it worse. It was truly moving, as he's a hard man not prone to showing weakness, but he confessed he'd been guilty of pride and self-preening like a rogue cock, and he'd been striking out in wasteful directions for greed, out of nature and not at all with the Heavenly Father. He placed his hands on my brow and said I was charged up as an altar. And that was how we started climbing the higher path.

The next Sunday we all took Preacher Dobber's invitation down at Rehoboth Chapel and rededicated, and in his witness Daddy asked Jesus to please bring Mama back swiftly as the weaver's shuttle, though he didn't deserve to kiss her hem or precious feet. Because her sister Lace was in the congregation and had a cell phone, the rest is history and bliss. Mama, who had been living at the Peter Pan Motel, came back that very night, and we all fell down on our knees in the front room and thanked Jesus, not to mention Hammer, Samuel, the Apostle and the other providers and guides along the Way. I was in my red "C for C shirt," and Charles Wray held the Living Word above his head and swore to seek the narrow path and self-control in the company of harlots, which on account of his new hormones is a big sacrifice.

And this is what we've done, us Starks, becoming His instruments, overcoming the temptations to bile and haughtiness and greed sins of the flesh and now bringing the Word to anybody with ears to hear and a heart to understand. That is why I have this chicken with me this evening, Bedford Forest, who has—with all our Stark hands being guided in conditioning and pitting methods and the general overall attitude of thankfulness—won out in the main four times, and despite all his scars and a permanent limp he is a legend now and an example of what you can do if you put your mind to it and you have good habits and the backing of the Lord. And I'm here to speak for the whole family, all of us gaming with a new vision and in harmony, as Mama now mixes fortifying chemicals and helps clean out the brood pens. Little Tommy is learning how to exercise bantlings for a coming derby, and I am a cut man, if you can use that for a girl, and hope to be a handler myself some day, especially if fighting birds ever gets legal again in this land of the free and righteous. Now I am going to leave you with this last thing, as Bedford here can crow jubilation on command, since God has granted him the kind of understanding we used to believe was reserved for angels, and his goodle-doodle-do is in the service of the church and is God's pure instrument.

We would appreciate you to stand now, to bow your heads and raise a hand straight up to Heaven. That's right. Don't be shy. The Lord wants you to rise now and lift up your eyes to the ceiling. If Cockers for Christ have ever had an anthem hymn, it is the farmyard sunrise call—a *reveille*, they name it—and look out because here it comes, warning us every mortal one to "Wake Up!" as the Heavenly Father's trumpet speaks beauty-bright and clear from the beak of a blood-washed bird. Bedford Forest, raise your Ebenezer, give witness. Redeem us in the Blood now, O Mighty Lord.

# Tastes Like Chicken

ALL THESE HERE behind the screen wire—look out!—are your eastern diamondbacks, *crotalus horridus*, which are your most popular native snake, and as you see a little testy by nature. They've got the color pattern like Indian wampum or an hourglass, and those tarnish-colored noisemakers on the tail give 'em a musical impact, nodamean? Can't read the age by it, like some folks think, though. They'll not slough skin on any man's regular schedule. Woman's neither. Whoa back now. That's Darth, and the palish one twined with him is Michael for that Jackson freak on TV. Over there giving us the hard eye is Hillary. They all sense we're here through the infrared plan and some have to make their strike, but they're used to people, mostly. Still, you can't predict 'em. They can always marvel me, and everything they inspire I write down like their secretary. It's what you might call my passion, the scribbling. Some day, luck comes for me, I'll make a book and make a killing, downpay me a condo in some paradise. Jesse Turley's the name.

As for all these lazy boys dozing in the red crates, they are your copperheads, also indigenous to our Blue Ridge, which are more shy but prone to hide at the wrong place in the woods where you'll reach your hand every time. Truly. See the yellow tail tip? They favor your old sawdust piles and wild blueberry shrubs. The smell, I think. They have given me some near misses. Speaking of smell, they have other ways, and when a kingsnake in the area tells copperheads "make yourself scarce," they skedaddle. You have to love a kingsnake. Not mean, these copper rascals, but serious poison, even the younguns. Let me stir 'em. See those fangs? They fold up when the mouth is shut but pop out to needle in the hemotoxins and serotoxins and all those other strange aminos. Miracle, if you ask me, like the way a snake's jaw'll unhinge so he can swallow a rat or frog or even a kittycat. You just missed feeding. Females, I expect, are the worst. Mother instinct, maybe. Science don't know. You'd have to ask a permanently married man.

And this hermit over here is my only timber rattler, so I call him Herm, like a hermit. Big shakers on the end almost like a pine cone. He could be over a dozen winters old. Six foot long if he's a inch. That black back half like dipped in tar, that's his family sign. Herm's got a story. Guess he was sunning on the railroad bed when the Charleston freight passed over. Stunned, I reckon. He was an easy acquisition, truly. He was nearly demised. I brought him home in my bare hands. His kind, now, has the tendency to sull back and not eat. I've seen a many of 'em starve, but Herm has the old time life will, for sure. I wouldn't sell him for gold nor rubies. It's like we're a couple of old brothers running this outfit without another human hand.

I mostly catch 'em when Orion's up and they're dreaming under rocks. Groundhog holes and old fox dens or just a karst pocket in the dark. They's most always two holes to the den, and I slop some gasoline in the one, then snag them with a pincer on a pole when they rouse and make a sluggish run for clear air. Don't use the well-known forked locust stick cause I need to lift 'em into the sack, which you probably guessed is a step toward your heavy duty aluminum trash can. You get a bin weighty with them rascals, all snarled up—man, they can hiss some. Like a ladies' auxiliary gossip party at the Moose. Truly. That's women.

Course, my wife didn't take to the whole exhibition. She's farm raised and don't see them as nothing but trouble. "A deadly animal is not entertainment," she'd say. Fussy as a pullet, she was. Being in the Navy so long, I got to missing all the land critters from ticks to jennets. Coulda been anything, but snakes kind of came to me, as I was handy with 'em when a boy. I had some store pets—parakeets, kitties, a canary—but they didn't satisfy. In the Philippines I saw my first snake zoo, kraits and mambas and everything, right down to a bitty harmless gardenhose green. Out there on the Pacific, I'd dream of setting up a rattlesnake ranch for tourism just like this. Imagine. I schemed someday to marry till forever and settle in as a sort of ringmaster. I wrote down all my plans for years and read up what I could cheffing down there in the galley with the skillets and pans and barrels. Thinking of snake dens I'd pour water off the spaghetti and watch it tangle like a bunch of honest Injun albino vipers sharing a dark space in winter.

Buchanan's where I hail from, over toward Roanoke, little dying town off the path but perched over the James like a picture book. Blacksnakes was my favorite when I's a boy, Kings and ringnecks, racers and corn snakes, but the Peaks of Otter park was full of coppers, and once I got the surprise of my life from a jumbo copperhead under the push mower when I tried to yank-start it cold in April. That's another story, and you can bet I've got it spelled out in a notebook somewhere here. Mostly copperheads I yarn up. Plenty of time for that these days, batching it, nodamean?

I usta drive on down to Georgia and Alabama, where they'd have the famous round-ups. The wind bloweth where it listeth, the saved are prone to say. I'd take my notebooks and story pens, compete at harvesting with the locals on behalf of Kiwanis and my own wallet. Prizes for the longest, the heaviest, oldest, most. Deep Dixie is a snaker's paradise, nodamean? I've got some brassy trophies to show for my labors. Those were mighty fine times, the rodeos, for bluegrass and dancing. They'd carry on all weekend. Lots of bourbon turned to pure yee-haw and morning piss, lordy. Even had a beauty pageant in a one-hearse town called Opp. My wife herself was a beauty when young—sparrow-color eyes and hair long as a willow—but she went sallow and skinny. Worry, probably, putting up with me long as she did. My collection of slithers and all my windy stories. I promise you, though, they're mostly safe in the cages. Now I do my daily double check. That was her first ultimatum—at least twice a day, every inch of cage wire and frame, every possible escape. I was sure not a one would ever be a threat to us.

Course, there's more than a little money in the merchant game. Roadside restaurants way off yonder in the north and even overseas love to serve them up. Rattler fingers. Serpent on a stick. Reptile jerky. Probably sliver 'em into an omelet or pot pie. Being a former galley slave, I can just imagine. Usually they deep fry them, though, and you gnaw off the meat. It's mostly spine, truly, but a good eggy batter makes you think you've latched onto a genuine delicate delight. Pepper, some Texas Pete. Odd to the Yankees as grits, I guess. Exotic. It's the batter makes the taste familiar and not like snacking on evil. Some people will say snakes are evil.

Roving around to those festivals and reptile rallies, I thought myself part of the export world, a man with a profit mission, and Verna, she'd stay here and run the stand, hang out the flags and the plush tapestries, hose down the yard art. She'd get lonely since Feather finished school and moved to Staunton. She's a tooth hygiene worker, Feather is.

Anyway, most folks stop for the fireworks—Black Cat, Ting No, Wild Jack, Pirate—till a gnome (with a *g*) strikes their fancy or wind-flapping textiles of the faux Cherokee persuasion. A bird bath might grab 'em then or blue Buddha or even a polymer bear. They're native too, old bruins, and I have seen more than one rassling with trash barrels, but you can't collect them on account of the law. Once a she-mama tried to scramble into my car on the Parkway near Afton, but the rangers frown on picking up hitcher bears. Stone angels, pixies and nativity shepherds, though, I can move them all year.

Now, your wild goose in many postures is the present popular favorite. Dream-like, nodamean? We only see them mostly way yonder up there, majestic-like, sky-riding in formation like a ploughshare. Unless we shotgun them into a limp dinner. Myself, I've never taken to the hunt. I'd rather wave when they pass and write them into a fable or some such, a goose gospel, I guess. What if animals have got souls?

Yard ornaments was always okay with my better half and all these rebel caps, off-color bumper stickers and souvenir whatnots. No family battles. Come to snakes, though, Verna was a yellow-dog skeptic. "Virginia is for lovers," she'd say, pointing to the bumper sticker display. "Snake ranchers need not apply."

Here's the real deal. I know you know about milking fangs for the medical antitox, but the Holiness Church has run rife up here, hiding out in the coves and gaps, I spect, and they put faith in signs and wonders, tongue speaking and rolling about like they swallowed an Isaiah ember. Them firebrand congregations—End-Timers and New Lights—and I won't say a congregation's place name for legal reasons, but you've heard of the ones up to Jolo on *Sixty Minutes*—they almost always want a box of snakes to test their spirits on. The Word, they say, is their shield.

Even the best won't hardly last out a year. The brethren do what they can to rile 'em, kick the crate, yell down at 'em, shake the floor with their godly dance. Guitars, too, the Telestar Gospel. They call it Signs Following. They say they get anointed, say they are proving the Sacred Lord's Victory over free-range devils. Then they haul 'em out and speak directly to the creatures, snakes wrapping around their arms, crawling over their heads and shoulders. It ain't legal. Poison ones, I mean. Truly. The copperhead and moccasins, rattlers especial, all the pit vipers. Rattlers are the best, spearpoint with eyes on one end, tambourine on the other. It's like they're baptized members just lapsed since the Eden incident. I hear the true anointed like them up in Raphine'll pitch jumbo timbers about and even try to get cobras and corals and such. Plain crazy. They sing-say scripture in the eyes of a snake, but now and again a saved soul gets bit. Comes a swelling, retching and thirst. Myself, I'm more wary of the coppers, who will lure you and look so lovely, calling to your touch. That's the Eden trick. Hypnosis, like the way they charm a bird.

Talk about some writing. I've got all the handling stories, but second hand, nodamean? The faithful don't lay on ice but use blessed palms to try for healing, and prayers too. Some say it's just a jolt and then a bliss. Brother Horton swears by eating a bucket of sauer-kraut to fight the venoms. Lily Briscoe says she washes in coal oil if one fangs her. Come over here to buy replacements, you can see the swole up or dead places on their wrists and palms and fingers. Grown man usually makes it if he's caught on a limb. Neck or face or any place on a child—probably a goner. Not even Sister Sharon can save their bacon, and she's said to have the touch. Preacher Bannister himself is always trying to coax me over—now I've slipped and said a name—but I was Saved five times in my country's service until I was officially immune. What all that's got to do with Jesus is way outta my range. They will tell you, though, the crowned and born over, that more folks die from lightning in our country than snakebite every year. Divorce, I've heard, has also taken its share.

Anyway, when I got wind of the high demand, I thought I'd make the market here, close by my native ground, catching the devil's animal and trading in them. Verna was not keen for it an eensey bit, nodamean? Not from the start. It's like the way I'm telling this. Stories. She thought it foolish I'd ramble on with customers like I do, but hell, I'm colorful, the local genuine article, don't you reckon? Maybe that's too much, but on four different destroyers, I have seen the world so far as it touches salt water. A good story or a voyage is like a snake for suspense, nodamean?

Now for myself, I believe in due respect, and I know how to catch a viper behind the head, squeeze his neck and keep the tail from lashing about with my other hand. Been me in the First Garden, I wouldn't gone all swoony just because the creepy thing could talk. We'd had snake chili and cut the tree down, lived forever on long meat and Paradise peaches.

I milk them into jars I make sterile in a warming cabinet, then send the goodies to Roanoke clinics in a six-pack cooler. Licensed—there in that frame. Pursuing my chosen field, I'm close to danger, but I take precautions. I'm no daredevil. I won't have but one out at a time, and I won't let them holies handle their purchases here in the shop. They point them out, and I pincer the choice ones—the elect, I guess—with my three-foot gizmo, drop one by one in the box. They wanna be geeks or corpses, it's their own business, but not on the premises. Nothing crazy in me. And I keep their secret from the police. A little hush money, cold-blooded cash, and it's all off the books. Nobody asks. Retirement nest egg. Rainy day.

Verna, she didn't see it that way, and she thought even having them in the pens was foolish. What if one gets out? What if one comes snapping after us? Women, nodamean? There at the end, she was so arguey, I started calling her The Rib in my secret diary, my private version of the Word.

We did a brisk business from the get-go, but she hated the smell, which is like a mild reek. Everybody has his own description, but I'd say rotten cukes is close, the juice simmering with summer. Still, it's life.

It like to give me the giggles, selling those big velvets of Elvis, the ark, suffer the children with a lamb, Last Supper, also Gandalf and Nemo, but inside charging a buck to visit Jesse's Last Chance Hall of Reptiles. It had to be all snakes, like the Indiana Jones movie, nodamean? So they were writhy in the holding pens, waiting to get their day in church, and passerbys would see the sign and pay to watch them doing mostly nothing. I'd sell some star shells and whirligig sparklers, Big Blast and Roman candles. Verna said it had to be a sin, stooping to the lowest nominator.

Fella come in here from New York, he claimed, though the accent was wrong. Empire State, he said. "Let me see what you got." We had a full house, and it knocked him silent. "How'd you get so many?" he wanted to know. "Do you eBay? Do you breed 'em?" I had to laugh and answer back, "My friend, we let 'em do that themselves." Ain't that a holy hoot?

One time, I fried up a diamondback was so faded nobody saw fit to take it off my hands, not even discount. Wallflower, nodamean? I hate to think the creatures are stuck in this place more than temporary. I worry about being the host of Limbo. Sometimes, though, I will flat-out kill the overstock, skin them for the saddle-shaped cross bands and distribute to leather crafters, the folk art trade. Belts and boots, hat bands and guitar straps. I'd pickle the heads to go in plastic paperweights, keep the rattles to make keychains and other geegaws. That evening of the supper secret I was careful to spiral cut all the tender meat free of backbone and laced the batter mix good with pepper and cane sugar like a hush puppy. Verna, she ate hearty, said I was always a better cook than her or Feather. Want to bad enough, I guess you can fool anybody, nodimsayin? Tastes like chicken. Truly.

This geezer comes in here once, big Panama hat and one of them Rolliflex watches with a rusted out Cadillac hissing on my gravel. He says I'm so good at painting pictures with my words. Says, "Mr. Turley you should write down this shit. You got the gift." Them notebooks on the shelf behind me, every color you can put a name to, binders spiral as a snake vine, that's my brainwork, my library of stories. I was way ahead of the game. I started them somewhere off Australia. Not all snake tales, but I do have some special ones I made up with a Tarzan-like jungle man who has a pet python. No Jane around, though. Gist of it, all Tonga's—that's his name, my savage man—all Tonga's other pets keep disappearing, and he thinks the snake is sick too, count of it won't ever take the rats he usually gives it. Turns out, well, you can guess. Python is just real sleepy, all fat and smiling and sassy. Whole time, Geezer keeps snapping his watchband and grinning.

That old guy was having some fun at my expense, asking more detail information about poison and if they lay eggs, if a self-defense shocker on a bite will cure it. He was deep-eyed and deep country, and I made out the scars on his gnarly hands. I didn't let on, you see, but I knew him for a handler.

Once I get moving on a new yarn, I'll set at the linoleum table there and cursive my words for hours, like vines all looping. We live in the back. I do. All night sometimes, the writing. Missed the Super Bowl once just plotting out a detective mystery I never did figure how to finish. It had a villain type dosing kinfolk with venom. Verna said back then, "Put me in one," but she was not the story type, a dry country woman. And a temper. I couldn't trust how she'd react if I even tried to describe her on paper. She had that streaky hair, crow and gray, and a face that was good only in a smile, which was more and more rare. The snakes I reckon. Nossir, not the story kind.

She's long gone, of course, and I don't do much cooking. Not worth the grease to chef for one, so I like to slip on down to the Pedal Car Café at Berky's, grab some grub and listen to the truckers hassle with their dispatchers over the booth phones. Or pocket phones, lately. Now it's mostly cells, which seems wrong-headed, the booth phones just hanging there useless, no words flowing through the cords. Dead snakes, a man like me would say. Most everything is changing.

The Berky's crew still brews up a great mug of mud, though, and I sweeten it with Equal in the blue-sky packages. Black eyes and niblets, corn muffins, some mighty fine steak and gravy—make you wanna smack your mama and kiss a clown, nodamean? Kiss a snake might be too far, like that Roy guy out in Las Vegas. Born stupid in my book. Tigers. You got to keep to the borders of good sense. It wasn't an idiot invented the cage.

Diamondback got loose, of course, slipped free one night when Verna was gabbin at me. I was tending to the feeding, when I don't need distraction with those live mice scrabbling in the box. She got me flustered, and I couldn't get back my stride. Cage cleaning, I set him in what I reckoned a safe container, and he nosed up the unlatched lid of the basket. All she wrote, so to speak. He thought he was a cobra, maybe, but he was really my other timber rattler I called Timbuktu. I been there. Anyway, that was when the horrificant rattle sound commenced, Verna's high pitch like a skyrocket.

You never seen a woman dash about like that. And climb. She got up there, high rack of that star shell display frame with the sparkler sign on top yelling it was over, I was headed to hell and she was going to Richmond. Crazy snake was whipping about on the floor, addled, scared, looking for shelter. It was touch and go, but I snagged him in my catching instrument and whacked him at the neck with the hatchet. Tail flipping one way, head going the other, biting air. A waste, but I was hoping extreme rescue would settle her down. George and the dragon, nodamean? Dream on, Jesse, dream on.

I followed her about, making my plea and promises I couldn't keep. In the bedroom, she was stuffing her frillies into a zip-up bag. "I don't know what I'll do without you," I said.

"Write something," she says. "Make something up. You're good with words."

I knew what she meant, but even your best artist needs to get mused and worked up. Verna gone, I'm starting to yearn out for stimulation. The snakes do not make a whole life. Need to sing a new tune, find a new direction. I hear scuttlebutt the New Lights up to Raphine are planning a brush arbor wedding this weekend. Lots of lemonade and catch-as-can eats, a big spread, even if you place no faith in those dusty vows people swap. I saw Preacher Bannister, though, at the Food Lion, and he says they has a passel of satinback rattlers never before been handled, wild things just ripe for the Glory and the stroke of a hallowed hand. He's been working on me to get in the Word, to witness the Son of Man in action and watch believers bathing in serpents and not being bit for the Hand of the Lord hovers over. I might just go down and see that for my-self.

"And copperheads," he said, "I promise—copperheads a plu-plenty."

Canaries, though. Yeah. That would have been smarter from the start.

# The Calaboose Epistles

*October First*

Dear Mr. Blalock,

Greetings! You don't know me, but my friend Ouida Cooper has delved deep into the Ouija board, and it sent us to you. Personally, I had always thought such spook endeavors were hogwash, but when I tossed out my husband for trafficking in porn videos, Ouida insisted her board's powers would guide me, which I never guessed would lead me to correspond with a man on death row, but there you have it. Misfortune has led me to you.

It hasn't been easy, as Ouida's spirit entity Dr. Spoons does not care to work with strangers. We settled the board on Ouida's millstone coffee table and vigiled for over an hour, but the planchette just wiggled about and refused to scry up a coherent word. I grew fidgety and said the invisible was a waste of my time, but Ouida scolded: "Fran, you promised you'd focus your entire self. Work harder." About the time we polished off the second bottle of Tuscarora Red, Dr. Spoons said he was ready.

I don't know if you have much discussion of the supernatural in prison, but even a skeptic can be shaken by the Ouija. I mean, the planchette really does have a life of its own, like a self-pulling mower. The pointer shivered and jumped at the letters like magic. My fingers tingled. Then it jolted all through me.

They say you have to beckon from your depths, and I guess I was working from the soul by the time we got a bite, because I was bawling over the spilt milk of my life. Experts say the ouija actually wants to give you answers, to prove itself so even doubting Thomas will believe. Its name means *yes* in French and German—*Oui* and *Ja.* Anyway, all it would render was my initials, F. P., and then B-L-A over and over. Ouida says Dr. Spoons is fond of codes and tricks, meaning we'd have to cipher it out before he'd converse. At least, she's always suspected it's a he.

The next night, which was yesterday, as I was eating sushi in front of the "Valley News," the cross-eyed reporter with rat's nest hair interviewed your lawyer, Mr. Robin Bond. It's been a while since the shooting, so I hadn't given you much thought lately, but soon as I heard him say "my client Mug Blalock," I knew it was your name the entity was hinting, *B-L-A*. I was so distracted I overdid the wasabi and got scalded. I've still got the blister on my tongue, so it's a lucky thing I can keyboard this letter instead of having to call you up. I'd have to say, "Mr. Bwawock, pwease." (Joke!)

Anyway, here is my theory. A man facing death like yourself is said to develop second sight, pretty much like the Ouija, so I wanted your opinion on my situation. Also, I figure you might be lonely just now among all the crack-pot letters from the liberals of the Mercy Party and the Sweet Jesus cults. What I'm offering is to provide any luxuries the prison system will permit in exchange for your meditating on my plight. It could be a win–win arrangement, a yes-yes. If you are willing, I promise to stick by you to the end, whatever it might be, and this will give you a chance to do something meaningful, if worse goes worst, before you know....

Please answer if you will consider this arrangement. I have enclosed a roll of postage stamps. By the way, Ouida says (telephone) that technicians sedate capital offenders now with a slow drip, and when the lethal dose comes, you're already dazed and just slip from the little sleep to the big one. It's still no picnic, but there you have it. It beats that electrical shock they used to inflict, but it doesn't sound so bad just now to a woman who lapses into weeping fits in the middle of Leno.

I look forward to hearing back and hope you take this seriously. I promise to let you know if there's further word from Dr. Spoons.

Respectfully,

*Frances June Pierpoint, née Rushton*

*October 8*

Dear Mr. Blalock,

Business first. You should already have the C.A.R.E. box I sent with the items you requested, mostly. The Rex Stout and Grisham novels were easy to find at the Bookery, but the Stouts are not in A condition (still a steal!). I am happy to know you are a dedicated reader. While I could not locate a round holiday Claxton, I did send two bar fruit cakes, along with the carton of Swisher Sweets, and you will find the roll of butterfly postage stamps and the Mel Bay book.

This brings me to the guitar. Louise at Blue Ridge Music says she can send the Gibson in a week. And don't worry about the expense. I think it is brave and positive of you to begin music at this stage, and it most likely signals a strong burning of the life force, which will be a good sign no matter what. Optimism is one thing Ouida says Dr. Spoons insists on.

As to Stickney, here is the history in a nutshell. Sit tight. He was a non-trial attorney and low handicap golfer, but now he appears to be a porn shark. As a couple, we date back to when our parents were country clubbers. Stickney Martial Pierpont and I were sweethearts, chasing in the morel woods, conking squirrels with a slingshot, playing hide-seek in the VMI barracks all summer. To young eyes that institution is a haunted castle with battlements and miles of shadowy passages. His daddy was the superintendent, a stiff barking man in a uniform green as Tennessee spruce, but we clandestined about and knew all the secret cupboards and dungeons. We were pure mischief. Once we stole the Virginia blue *Tyrannis* flag from the tower and hid it in a howitzer barrel. Another time a Rebel ghost floated with his wounds still gory, real as Hell, if you'll excuse my French.

As anybody might expect, by the end of junior high we had played the tease games and discovered our bodily wants, so that summer while the fireflies were snapping like matches over the parade ground we took each other's virginity under a desk in the seminar room where they teach artillery. Between giggling at the chalk diagrams, I found out that, while Stickney was just a warning

shot and a shudder, I was designed for a full volley. He had to clamp
his hand over my mouth, and I rewarded him with a clear dental
impression. Before long we had performed our sweet deed everywhere from the chapel with its famous New Market martyr mural
to underneath the cannons on the lawn. This is public knowledge,
as I posted a memoir called *Gone with the Wild* on the web a few
years ago, and it raised a local stir. Maybe I should have kept it mum,
but there you have it. I was not taught to be ashamed of natural
urges.

Stickney picked UVA. and history, while I did music at Mary
Baldwin, and we kept our courtship hot while college changed us
into adults with cars and credit cards for motel rooms and julep
bourbon and all. You get the picture. After school, Stickney read
the law in Horace Littleman's office in Buchanan while he worked
lawns, and I was playing the organ at Devotion Baptist (I'm not one
myself!) and trying to fend off all the back-to-the-nest gifts from
Daddy, who was Lincoln Rushton, an over-achieving real estate
broker. His picture often appeared in the Roanoke paper, as he had
the ante-bellum look and dabbled in politics. Because six and a half
feet of white linen colonel with a spade goatee is not easy to vote
against, he served our commonwealth in Richmond twice, but his
dandy dignity spurred me to rebel.

For Stickney, the wheels were pretty much greased to join his
granddaddy's firm when the judge returned to practice. As newly-
weds, we were the toast of the Star City, and life was sparkly as a
cotillion chandelier. I wouldn't be honest if I claimed there were
early signs he would stray. I thought I had him tight in the love lock,
but there you have it.

I hope this is not boring you, but soon we had Frank and Fred
and my life went into a routine of cocktails, musical evenings and
European junkets. His mother passed, then his daddy, and since he
was an Only, we moved into The Cedars. Then, like everything, our
paradise slipped downhill. Plenty of parties and causes for the arts
and the unfortunate, you understand, new Jeep Cherokees and the
James River cabin, a battalion of bosom friends. We were frequent at

the Kiwanis, High Country Gun and Reel and the Tinker Mountain Club, but Stickney seemed to lose interest in me as flesh-and-blood. It wasn't a sudden thing, but his sweet nothings diminished, and he fell in love with the weather channel.

I don't really know why, as I never grew obese or shriveled, and working on my folk opera projects allowed me to stay home as much as any red-blooded man could crave. I can prepare haute cuisine and sing and tango and coax vintage roses out of any soil, but I guess it wasn't enough. His single-barrel bourbon played a wicked part, and I began to imagine Miss Georgia Dickel as his mistress, which was not quite on target, as you will see.

There you have it, in a manner of speaking. At least, that's all I can say about it today. I feel myself swirling back into depression, and I have to get perked up before my music appointment. I am trying with the help of Dora Longstreet to work out a harp version of my "Appalachian Spirits" theme, which I plan to market. You'll learn about that soon enough. Stay tuned.

What I do want to tell you person-to-person, new friend, is not to give up hope. Never. I have done research on the Internet and discovered why you shot him, and though I do not condone even a crime of steep passion, I can understand. It is like a Grisham story with pieces of the jigsaw missing. I know your lawyer keeps saying "accident," how you and Lowell Moose were long-time hunting buddies and how his "entertaining" your wife only came to light after the shooting. I don't know what to say to that, but I recognize you are a man of strong emotions, which I am beginning to believe is the only way to be. I know you are sorry and have begged forgiveness from his wife Mary Moose and your own spouse, and maybe there will be a pardon down the road, though six bullets paints the mishap defense a little thin.

You know, temporary insanity doesn't mean you're totally off the planet, just that for a flash you unhinged over some crisis, like a petit mal—you know, the little death—and you could climb back on with appropriate therapies. It's what the legal eagles call "a viable option," and maybe the guitar will lend a hand. (Discipline!)

I have not seen Ouida today, but we are going to clean up Stickney's cabin tomorrow and see what needs tending to. She says Dr. Spoons suggested it and claims to have known about the videos all along. Stickney himself is still in the hospital and the dog house, but I have not roused a lawyer yet. Please dispatch your mind to the twilight zone and tell me if I should be a forgiving person or if I should get my legal ducks in a row, which the ouija has refused to advise. I suppose even an entity needs a coffee break! As soon as they allow non-related visitors, I will hasten down there and deliver some items. Meanwhile, enjoy the cakes.

Your friend,
*Frances Pierpoint, O.D. (Ouija disciple)*
p.s. I believe you should give up the smoking. You are smart enough to know why. And thank you for praising my writing style. I don't know if writing can communicate looks, but I'm not your average Plain Jane. p.p.s. Is this what they mean by having a pen pal?

*October 14*
Dear Mug,

I am thrilled you appreciate the guitar, and I'm hoping you'll see the frets as bars that do not a cage make. It would be cruel for them to limit you to one supervised practice hour a day, so I hope that changes. I don't know if they treat you the way prisoners are handled on TV, but I have seen A & E shows about "Big Stir," Parchman and Angola (also Grisham!), making it all quite alarming. It's too bad you are in with deviants, but I am amused that you call the jail "hoosegow." I've personally heard everything from "slammer" and "calaboose" to the "bar farm," but "calaboose" is my favorite, as it sounds like something on a train. It's always healthy to feed your sense of humor.

I'm still hoping to visit, but for now, can you send me a picture in exchange for the snaps enclosed. One shows me in the garden with hollyhocks, the other a little naughty at the beach. An old photo of you would do fine, as the newspaper ones are grainy and usually have a hand in front of your face. I like to look into eyes—windows to the soul and so on. That's one thing I regret about dealing with Dr. Spoons.

But back to my story. You're absolutely right. I adapted. The boys went off to Duke, and now they are the famous Pierpoint Brothers firm of San Francisco, where they support gay rights and are called the Peerless Pierpoints. By the time they relocated, the big house on Jeff Davis Drive (The Cedars) grew hollow as a gourd, and Stickney began to conduct his tort research in Blackledge or whatever out at his log cabin on the James. Not being particularly imaginative or silver-tongued, he has never been a stand-up lawyer but just did the research. When the judge passed, Stickney turned the whole office to real estate closings and living wills and trusts, no-hassle clients and clerk work. He still has that look of a fox hunter gone to seed, and since it inspires confidence in lost causers and old monies, he didn't have to put his nose to the grindstone. He hid out at the cabin with all his fishing gear, Ben Hogans and big screen TV where he could satellite up any sporting event in the world while he was gorging on pizza and portable Chinese. For a long spell I thought he was just redirecting his sex drive into junk food and bourbon. But the truth will seep out.

He also paid an old Teke buddy who passes as a landscaper to bush hog and lawn up three golf holes in the meadow for his private course, "Sub Par," and I endured it, distracting myself with music projects and my rustic costume designs which are akin to outsider art, according to the Charlottesville paper. We were "estranged," but Stickney never admitted to it, though he was daily into the George Dickel dance long before the evening gun. Everybody suspected he was a soak, but he kept that tidewater accent and noblesse manner, so who cared? He made a great ornament, and I never wanted for comfort nor material goods, though the nights were long.

For me, it was all going dark. There you have it—a dark time, a rising tide of sorrow. I had asked Sappho Ewbanks and Ouida Wilson, of whom you know, to help me with an intervention. I thought maybe Stickney needed abducting, to be hauled off to one of those dry-out farms, but Sappho, who has always been fond of

Stickney, disagreed. She even went to some pigskin tailgaters with him and one steeplechase when I was visiting Richmond kin. As for Ouida, she was deep into a twelve-step retreat under the guidance of Dr. Spoons, so she was too distracted to help me institutionalize anybody. What could I do?

That's where it was when I got the call from the hospital. (Cell phone! I was actually at a harp lesson). It was a Sunday night, and I assumed Stickney was safe in his lair, probably monitoring some soccer match from Bulgaria, if there still is a Bulgaria. The nurse said he was in emergency and seriously banged up from a severe automobile incident.

Stickney had rolled his Expedition over a bank along the Blue Ridge Parkway near Peaks of Otter. It was foggy both on the road and in his mind. When I got to the clinic, I lingered at his side and held his unmangled hand, swearing to Jesus (whom I've somewhat lost touch with since the VMI make-out days) that I'd set our marriage back on a firm foundation soon as my husband recovered. He had an awful wet cough from being sprawled out in Otter Creek, which is high this year, and I couldn't bear to look at the parts of his face with no bandage. He whimpered like a child. His shoulder was broken, collarbone splintered, as well as internal discombobulations. He was bruised blue as a heron.

Then Officer Rogers with a clipboard beckoned me into the hall. I knew it was DUI for sure, no way out of that, but he said there was a more complicated matter. The back of Stickney's black-and-yellow SUV that resembles a squared-off bumble bee had been loaded up with XXX videos of a sort that you can't legally purchase in this commonwealth. Things like *Butt Babes of Borneo* and *Cow Poke* and *Triple Booty Foxes*. Dozens scattered all over the rocks. It turns out that Stickney could possibly be the Appalachian black market czar of DVD sleaze.

All revved up with outrage, I stomped into his room—he was barely conscious—and announced that he'd not sleep under my roof again. Ever.

I know this has been slow, Mug, and I appreciate your patience. Indulge me one iota more. What I need to decide is this. If I divorce him in loud and public fashion, it will be a scandal to rock the social crowd and will be heard all the way from the VMI parade ground to the house chambers in the capital. After all, his great-great-great saw the last year of the Civil War from the governor's mansion. Not to mention my own mama still alive and in the Cotillion Ultimate Residence for Ladies, and even my sons out west would get wind of the filthy details. For those reasons, I'm inclined to think this marriage should have a funeral as quiet as its death, but in that case, everyone who's in the dark will say I have abandoned Stickney in his hour of dire need. He's a hopeless soak who surely won't ever golf again, and he's roosting over in the Lexington Hampton Inn. If I toss him now, they'll say I must surely be some royal bitch, though I'm not sure I can keep his DVD treasury a secret. The police are not drawing hasty conclusions but, I suspect, examining the evidence with professional attention.

Since I know you have suffered through all your private life being bandied about in the public eye, I need your common sense advice about whether I should let these issues sleep or raise a stink. I know that Stickney is probably headed for double trouble. He'll be dis-barred (irony!) and worse if he can't come up with a real circus of an explanation for all those DVDs, but it's a hard problem. How far from the blood-letting do I personally need to get? You know of these matters, and I can tell from your letters you feel an intimate sympathy with me.

Speaking of getting far from it, I saw in the *Washington Post* that your lawyer has some troubles over the probate of his father's will down in Texas. It all looks fishy to me, but when he is on TV advocating for you, he is every bit the gentleman, and I believe he is succeeding in rousing public sympathy for you. The more he reveals about that Moose's life, the more clear it is that either one of the deceased's drug customers or some other irate husband would have terminated him sooner or later. Dr. Spoons has no comment on Mr.

Robin Bond, but our friend from the other side agrees that Moose was bad news.

As for the Appalachian Spirits, how sweet of you to applaud my scheme. I have composed a music box tune and designed a doll in mountain homespun to merchandise to the nostalgia market. It's the sort of thing mothers would want to give their girls for a registered keepsake, and Ouida's husband Lowell has suggested I put a chip in it so that parents and daughters can record their voices at different stages and have an audio time capsule. This is my longtime dream but not my first creation by a longshot. For me, ideas always start with a tune in my head and usually lead to something with genuine market potential. As you have said, I am a unique sort of person. But with all the time on your hands, you might come up with some astounding ideas, too.

"Michael, Row the Boat Ashore," by the way, was a splendid choice, but I am sorry to hear about your fingers. I guess that is a stage everybody who wants to be a string artist has to suffer, and when your pads toughen up you'll be able to practice like a regular Ralph Stanley.

I was surprised that you work in the kitchen there, and didn't know you had been in the food services business all your adult life. I expect that explains why you liked to hunt so much, as animals are food, too. (joke!)

Dr. Spoons told us at brunch today while Ouida and I drank mimosas that you are the one to answer my Stickney questions and he hopes he will not be meeting you soon, if you get my drift. It still gives me the shivers to have a friend in the other dimension and one in prison, but there you have it.

May the Appalachian Spirits keep watch over you.

*Your friend Fran*

*October 31*
Dear Mug,

I am mad as a wet hen. I am on a bonafide tear. Damn that Stickney to hell's cellar. And that Sappho, too. As if the porn stuff wasn't bad enough.

We went out there, Ouida and I, to clean up his shack and see what he might need. Angry as I was, I couldn't abandon him after all these years, so we planned to spruce it up. I was also thinking that maybe I could investigate around and do away with incriminating evidence on the porn question. After all, I am still his lawful wife, and I decided to follow your advice about doing things discreetly, especially in light of the back-sliding nostalgic moments I have late at night. No more, Mug, no more.

Ouida was the one who found them, all bowtied neatly at the bottom of a drawer. I was Comet-scouring the sink and figuring how the pipes could be wrapped against the weather when she walked into the kitchenette with her shoulders slumped and these pastel packets in each hand. She had on the lavender crepe blouse I like, but it looked dead on her. Her eyes were as blank as bullet holes, which is rare for Ouida, as she is a redhead with bright green crab-apple eyes.

She said, "Fran, you need to look at these."

They were not literature, exactly, but they were poems, sexy poems written in a prissy hand on expensive stationary folded and sewn into little booklets, wrapped in silky ribbons like straps snipped from camisoles, and addressed to Stickney or referring to things unique to him. They were signed by Sappho Ewbanks, the actress and my own next-to-closest friend, and the first letter went back thirteen years. They had breasts rhymed in them with bed fests, and nipples and love vines and palm licking, not a poetry I can appreciate, and those poems made it crystal clear my husband's interest in off-color videos has never been a solo avocation.

You might know who Sappho is, who was an over-the-hill belle in "Gods and Generals" most recently but has been on TV and played everything at the Barter from Maggie the Cat right down to Cordelia Lear herself. She is married to that Chance Ewbanks who teaches the creative writing at VMI and by-lines himself "Colonel Ewbanks," as all the faculty there are required to swear in as officers in the Virginia Militia. He wears a goatee like my late father and parades about town with his hands clasped behind his back like a person swimming deep in semi-thought.

He has plenty to contemplate now, I'll tell you, as I sent him photocopies of the whole collection. Worst of all, he and Sappho have been couple friends with Stickney and me for almost twenty years, throwing parties and taking dance lessons, and I have been to Europe with her twice. Once even to Finland.

I went ballistic, I'll tell you, and Ouida had to entreat me to stop when I started flinging the Pierpoint family Spode at the windows. The face of betrayal is always closer than you think, as you are well aware, Mug, and I was ready to murder them both. We have shot-guns, too, lovely Parkers, all inlaid and hand-tooled, and I have been afraid to unlock the gun cabinet these last couple of days. You can't get much darker.

I can't direct my mind to your situation right now, but I am sending the Stetson you asked for in a separate package. I will re-connect with you soon as I can, but already the sedative is taking over and the monitor screen is wiggly as a river. Damn him.

F.

p.s. Here is one of the damned poems, just so you can get the idea.

*Sweet Sweat Kissed on Your Back Broad as a War Horse*

*My silk, my cream, my roe satyr like satin,*
*I come at once maid, muse and bruise-bashful bride.*
*In your bower by the river's lisp-whisper*
*your Greek and Latin*

*are wind in lashed branches. I shiver.*
*My tongue is useless to protest your divine*
*sighs. Will the goddess make you my Rubicon,*
*my Caesar, my Rome,*

*my lush freedom? In this Eros-riven rush*
*I chant your peerless name as we burn skin*
*on russet-rubbed skin. You are my only law.*
*I obey and thrash*

*when we touch blushing flesh, womanly bone brash*
*against man bone, the swaying cradle and staff.*
*Under the sky bear made of stars, I savor*
*your surging maleness         the color of Mars.*

p.s.s. He doesn't know any more Greek than Balaam's ass.

*November 18*
Dear Mug,

I want to say how much I appreciate your indulgence of my rants and raves. It has provided solace to know you're there for me, and I hope to return the favor once your situation sorts out. You are sweet to ask how any real male could be less than passionate about me, and it makes me sadder that a man like you is locked away from the world.

I am also sorry for the silence, but Ouida and I have been working with Dr. Spoons on the legal complications, and we almost have it plotted out. It is not a revenge issue for me, but just how to survive with dignity. I have to respect all those years we were partners, and whenever I would get myself exercised about Stickney and Sappho out there in the stag cabin cavorting in front of a big screen TV with those "oh-baby" blue movies playing over and over, I remember he was always tender with me. What went wrong is likely something in his blood, as a couple of early branches on his family tree wind back around into itself worse than wisteria. Lawyer Littleman arranged probation and has him enrolled in a twelve-step program to move beyond both the porn addiction and the bourbon thirst, and Stickney has offered a generous settlement, financially speaking.

It's best to move on, isn't it? I expect you have times when Eula comes to you in the imagination just like when you were young and she was still pure. Stickney was always able to comfort me when the world got under my skin. We had a Pawley's Island string hammock, and he would gather me up in his long arms and pull me into it, then sway us while he sang "Fair and Tender" or "Jimmy Brown." He even had a little tune about me that went, "You know my Fran is so swift and intelligent and always as elegant as an Irish swan." I know he's fallen far since then, but it would be wicked to forget those evenings with him running fingers through my hair and humming the calming notes.

Besides, Mug, I need to channel more of my energies into your appeal, which as you say will be coming up "before you can say Jack Robinson." I hope your learning to perform that gloomy "Streets of Laredo" is not a sign of despair. With any luck, we will prevent you from being "wrapped in white linen." Life has too many prospects.

I hope you don't think this is just a mood swing on my part. The doctor has given me Paxil, but it's just a reality drug to help you understand that nothing is so bad as it appears.

By the way, I have met a new gentleman friend named Zell, and Dr. Spoons says I should give him a chance. He's a fishing guide and something of a primitive (joke).

Here are more Swisher cigars, as you see, but I still think you're too big a man to be dominated by a cheap little roll of leaves. I have also deposited money for you with the warden. I hope it will keep the wolf from your door.

*Your pal Fran*


*Thanksgiving Night*
Dear Mug,

I was excited and relieved to receive your letter. I had seen about the fire on TV, and when they said it was near the D block and in the dining area, I got concerned and tried to call in to the warden. No luck, so I was nervous as a foal. Thank the Lord you are safe and can attend your own appeal.

Right now I am getting in on a wonderful plan that will doubtless amuse you. Zell has an idea better than any of mine. Did I tell you that the local nature re-enactor Darnley Wolfe was honored at a book-signing party at the Ram's Head Bookstore? That's when I met Zell. The two of them have a scheme for a wilderness resort called Explore Bound, and I can invest on the ground floor and be the administrator-hostess.

Did I remember to tell you Zell's past? He is also writing a book and will reveal all about when he was a hermit in the Yukon, panning for gold, shooting grizzlies with an authentic black powder musket, evading the system and generally being against the world of foolish convenience. He didn't even pay taxes back then, and for a while in the eighties he was smuggling Korean brides across to Canada in a Cessna he flew himself. He says it is the Roosevelt adventurous gene in his system that sparks him, though his name is not now Roosevelt but Zell Rosen. He is on Viagra, and you'd think he was closer to sixteen than sixty. (Secrets!) He says the pills make everything look blue, so I guess we are in a movie of our own. I feel like a girl.

*Aloha,*
*Fran*

*December 1*
Dear Mug,

I am sorry to hear that you can't share my enthusiasm about Zell. If you could meet him, you'd understand why I am so be-dizzled. He has wavy silvery hair that used to be blonde and is tanned like an Indian. "Stormskin" he calls it. Even after all those years on a snow ranch in Alaska, he has clung to his Delta accent, and when he speaks, it is sourwood honey without the bees. He gives me more attention than I have ever craved, and I just know you would admire the way his eyes light up when he's telling a story about Eskimo wisdom eaters dancing for the sun to come back. At first, Dr. Spoons wouldn't say anything about him, but Tuesday Ouida and I had a long session in which he (it is *he!*) predicted her husband would take early retirement and the president would not be in the White House for long. Then he gave Zell a sterling silver endorsement and advised me to trust him in all matters financial. He also said Explore Bound was a splendid idea and to bet on the Spurs, but we don't know what that's about.

I don't have as much time for Ouida, for I have signed up with Phoenix University to earn a degree in Lodging Science, and Zell believes that our pooled nest eggs and what I'll earn from selling

The Cedars will get the ground broken when the first jonquils open. We plan to create a private park on the James where they now have Wilder Water Excursions. If you've ever been this far into the Blue Ridge you'll know that place, as the present kayak-rental building has a steeple. It used to be a Baptist church, in fact, but land tax drove off most of the congregation, so the Wilder Water people bought cheap.

What we intend—and it gets me so excited I almost want to tell all our hush-hush—is to build a hunting lodge-style conference center with authentic log cabins all around. What will make it unique and appeal to all walks is that we will hire rugged individuals to attract the flatlanders (Zell's word!) and give them a luxurious view of the famous mountain delights. They'll bird watch and canoe and fish stocked water, along with craft classes and mountain culture lectures. They'll learn to identify hemlocks and whitetail leavings while acquiring survival skills in relative comfort and safety. Sound like a brochure yet? As you can tell, it will be a kind of extravagant year-round camp for families, people who do not want to see the natural ways lost. The Wilder Water people have decided (real hush-hush!) to retire, but the property isn't listed yet. I don't know how a newcomer like Zell could be aware of this, but he has his wily ways.

It's really lucky that The Cedars is fully paid for, and I can thank Stickney's ancestors for that. And Sappho? Well, she and her husband have moved up to Staunton to escape the whisper virus. But it won't work. A quorum of the local garden club ladies have agreed to shun her, and she's be-smirched forever, which is what such a self-smitten person deserves, don't you think?

Of course, I have no intention of deserting you, my friend. It's just that I've been caught in a whirlwind. Now that I'm routine with my studies on the Phoenix course (custodials, liability, décor!) and Zell is attending to the bank matters and bookwork, I can redirect some of my focus to you. As a peace offering, I hope you'll accept the homemade fruitcakes. They contain abundant pecans and candied green cherries, filberts but no filé (Louisiana joke from

Zell!), and the new strings I sent are most likely in the hands of your nemesis trustee who keeps the guitar and taunts you. Ask him.

Have you given any thought to hymns? I wouldn't normally suggest that, but Zell was an answer to my prayers, even the ones I didn't know to utter, so He's still up there keeping his eye on us sparrows. The Bird Watcher-in-Chief!

There you have it. If I get a buyer, Zell says we could break ground in the spring. He's a whiz with figures and has worked out ways to attract loans and grants. "Weasel work," he calls it. You wouldn't expect that from a man who smells like woodsmoke, but there you have it. He's a walking contradiction, and I have put myself in his rough but tender.

I have the letter from your lawyer, and he is confident, which is a sign. If things go right here, I am sure Zell and I will drive over for the holiday, so you and I will have the opportunity to meet at last. You're going to hit it off, I know. We'll all be soulmates.

*Your pal Fran, E.O. (Ever Optimistic)*

*December 23,*
Mug,

I'm so mad I could spit. Again. Anybody would think a woman with a spirit guide and a Death Row correspondent would be harder to fool, but you were on the bullseye about Zell Rosen, who has folded his tents in the night like the Arabs and departed for parts unknown. This whole Explore Bound was a flim flam. Ouida says he's likely played the gallant beau over more than one lonely belle with a healthy savings account. I'll tell you, a woman alone is in naked peril these days. Detectives are looking into what they call "the sequence" as we speak (write). As for myself, it's all I can do to sit still and type. I'm hitting every letter like a missile button to blow that bandit off the map of earth. Thank goodness for men like yourself.

At least (stroke of luck!) I hedged on sinking my total assets into the lodge, but even with my suspicions not completely asleep, he made a generous profit. I go dizzy thinking what would have happened if Stickney had already written me his check and that shady Tiny Allison had found a prospect for The Cedars. I could have lost everything from ribbons to rifles!

I found out through the answering machine. It's a mystery why his henchman Darnley Wolfe would not call Mr. Cassanova on his cell, but he left a message at my house, where Zell was parking his shoes at night. The culprit was on his way back from Charlottesville, making some last minute Yule purchases, he said, and I was at Ouida's bent over the board to hear what Dr. Spoons had to say about happiness. She claims the spirit world is always chatty around the festive time, so we had planned to pose some big questions. That didn't turn out so well, as I spilled wassail on the board, and all we could manage after that was the planchette dowsing toward the corner like it wanted to escape. I am now beginning to wonder why Dr. Spoons was so far off on Zell. Was he hoodwinked too?

Anyway, Darnley Wolfe was a little tipsy, which might explain his confusion, and he said, "I think the old hen knows. Grab what corn you can and scram."

That didn't compute to me, but it had an ominous feel, so I called Ouida, who was in bed, and she said to ask Zell when he came in.

I fell into Ambien sleep, so I didn't see him till the next morning. He was feeding the woodstove when the coffee fumes woke me, and I came up behind him and said, "What old hen?"

He startled and turned, then smiled, swearing he didn't know what I meant, but when I hit the replay button, his face went redder than a Santa suit. It was the first time I had seen him lost for words, and he sputtered and stuttered out something about a scheme he and Wolfe had to raise free range poultry. But, Mug, I could see into his eyes. Drugged over as I was from the Paxil and Ambien, I could discern he was not expressing truth, so I played cagey and shrugged, "Oh. But won't you have your hands full with Explore Bound?" Well, you never heard his slurry Creole accent so sweet nor saw him smile so wide, as he explained that we needed a sliding schedule of collateral capital and supplementary cash flow while we got the company incorporated and solvent. But I could still see the eyes, and I noticed that he smiled like a fox, a big toothy one with a snarl lurking behind it.

I made excuses and went to town, where I called Stickney (cell again), who is almost always out at the cabin now, since he's not mobile, and he said to sit tight while he checked which way the wind blew. I perched in the coffee shop and stared at the faux sugar packs, all the while hoping I was wrong, praying it was just over-suspicion on my part. We get that way, don't we? Just when everything looks rosy, we smell a rat, even if there's no sign of one. I hoped there was no rat nor fox nor weasel in this, but despite the Paxil floating feeling, I sensed some species of vermin.

Stickney called back to report that the proprietors of Wilder Water had applied for a loan to expand. You see, he's not a complete monster (a porno addict, though!), and he does know his field. Anyway, the Wilder Waters have no plans to sell, as they have a son who wants to step into the float business and hire out trout guides as well.

That settled it. I knew I was being fleeced like a spring lamb, so I called the police and spoke with some difficulty (tears and sobs) to a Detective Wasco. Do you know him? He's been on the TV news a few times himself. Wasco was very sympathetic and told me a cruiser would meet me at The Cedars in exactly seven minutes. We pulled up at the same precise moment from opposite directions like a movie with the snow beginning to stick on the wet street, but there was no Zell, no Zell clothes, no Zell sporting gear, no Zell truck nor real estate folders, nor yellow scratch pads he'd scribbled on. No Fran family jewels, either, as I discovered in the bedroom. And no surround sound Bose. I felt exactly the way I did when Ouida showed me those poem letters in November. I had to sit down and take some ice water.

The officers say there are multiple fingerprints, some of them likely Zell's, and I have given the number of his Oregon plates. The sergeant was a gentleman, and he fresh brewed some coffee to keep my hands from shaking so much. It didn't take.

That's where I was, and not even giving you one thought, until I heard on TV (for company) that the high court would hear your side of the appeal right after Christmas. That must be a positive, Mug, and I know you are due some luck, if for no reason other than being the only man to stand by me while I have been tormented. What is it that makes you different? Neither Zell nor Stickney displayed one iota of heart-felt interest in my folk operas or angel project, but you have been ever steadfast. I know the Lord or the spirit world or whoever is out there won't allow you to go unrewarded. I am planning to attend court myself and speak up if I get a chance. I will wear a festive candy cane sweater, and I have brown hair with a mature stripe.

Meanwhile, I hope they give you basted turkey with all the fixings. I'm going to eat with Ouida and her hubby and see if there's a Christmas message to us from Dr. Spoons, who has lost some credibility in my book, but don't worry yourself about that now. Merry Christmas to you, my rock, and expect a big present when I think one up.

*Your devoted friend and Santa Fran*

*Millennium New Year's Eve*
Oh Mug!

I was shocked they would not let me speak to you, and the way they had you all trussed up in chains was a crime. That pumpkin jumpsuit, too. I couldn't tell if you were able to see which one I was in the peppermint stripes (two others!), but I waved and hoped you would be comforted.

It was all a sham, and anybody could see how you were being railroaded, your lawyer (shifty-eyed, I thought) Mr. Bond always having his objections denied. And that shark-looking D.A. with his voice like a filleting knife. Heavens. Still, I refuse to be discouraged by that bald judge's harshness. That was nothing like a fair hearing, though I was troubled somewhat by the lab evidence that Moose had powder stains on his scalp, as if someone had stood close to shoot him that last time. The more I ponder, the more I need you to explain.

Here is the idea that struck me as I was driving home, which took some time (snow!). I know Virginia puts a lot of people to death, even whites, and I believe it's important we not leave you at their mercy. I am willing, especially if Dr. Spoons (doghouse!) will rise to the occasion and approve my scheme, to break some rules and sneak you out, because aren't we two of a kind, both burned by scum? I've had a lot of bourbon (Stickney's cache) and Co-Cola this evening—though less soda than Dickel—but it's making me clear-headed for once, and if they don't see the light when the whole story is laid out before them, maybe there's some way to free you from a twisted system. I know that the laying low is just as important as the getaway, but here's my idea for keeping you ahead of any bloodhounds.

I saw in the obituaries that Roy Bass originally from Roanoke has died. The article said he was the handicapped veteran who played Captain Hardy at the Riverview Inn fish camp down in South Carolina. Stickney and I used to stop for catfish and sweet hushpuppies when we drove to Atlanta, and I remember Cap Hardy with his handlebar moustache and that hook where his hand was blown off in Korea. Big pirate jacket, little hoop in his ear, lots of kids wanting to pet his parrot. Now, since he has passed, they'll likely be looking for a new eye-patched pirate to strut around and be jolly with a bird on his shoulder. Not Santa jolly, though, even if the coat and plume hat were scarlet red. Here's what we could do, if we could get you out: rent a bungalow at the Catawba's bend (on my VISA!), and you could apply for the pirate job. The rental cabins I know about are Pilot's Cove or Cave or something. I might be able to find them in the directory. I'm not sure yet how we could spring you, but it seems that trucks bringing food might be key, and remember, I am talking about a kind of restaurant job here, in harmony with your professional background. (The Paxil helps me see problems as opportunities!)

Now here's the major ruse. First, we would have to amputate one of your hands, to guarantee you the job, and I know this sounds extreme, but just think of the cleverness of it. Nobody would suspect that you were the escaped convict, as who would cut off a hand just to hide? And isn't a free man with one hand better off than being incarcerated with two? Or terminated? Even if it means the guitar hours with Mel Bay are wasted, that's one more thing that would shift any suspicion away from you. That idea puts us about two steps ahead of everybody—police, court and all. We could get you the job, and I could market my Appalachian Spirits plan from deep cover. The Internet makes things possible in a clandestine way, as I learned from that serpent Zell, and I could get a Gateway laptop. You would have to give up those cigars, though—a dead giveaway.

There you have it, my desperate plan, outrageous and crazy, but give it some thought before you say no. I need to spread this plan out before Dr. Spoons, but I am a little nervous about letting Ouida in on it. There's no way to solo on a Ouija, though, as your single subconscious mind might just arrow up answers you want, and besides, maybe I'm just nervous from the bourbon and pills now. I do feel a weariness of the brain and will have to rely on my spellcheck to clean up this letter.

The report on Zell, by the by, is this: no sign. They have an APB on him, but in the snowstorm, all trucks look pretty much white, and the collision rate has kept the state police busy with skids and whangers. That's something to write down. If you're going to flee something, use a snowstorm.

The one item worrying me is the powder burns on that Moose, so please write and explain how that happened. You know I'm not really doubting you, as I'm your first team fan, but I do crave an answer.

It's midnight now, and since my Ambien, the letters on my screen are wiggling around like party streamers, so I'm going to print this out and kiss it. I wish we were already as hidden as a buried treasure down in South Carolina, but I have confidence that it won't be long. Maybe the police will catch him and return some of my own treasure. Sleep tight, my Mug.

*Your rescue,*
*Fran*

*January 10*

Dear Mug Blalock,

I am sorry to resort to the formal, but our road has taken a sharp turn, as you must have expected all along. Shame on you, but I suppose it's understandable that you would lie, considering that you are incarcerated, to find a confederate on the outside. Still, it makes my head spin to know you are no different from the rest.

It was Epiphany Day when Detective Wasco and Detective Hollis brought me the Bose (left at a rest stop, probably a decoy). They said I might as well have it back, as there were no fingerprints. They lifted some partials at the house, but they haven't made a strong match with anything on the national computer yet, and Zell Rosen likely has numerous aliases. His kind always makes a mistake, though.

They also wanted to talk to me about my recent correspondence with a known felon, that is, you, and they were very curious and made pages of notes. At first I didn't want to confess, but when they said I might have to turn over my computer if I wasn't straight with them, I broke down and spilled it all, cried and admitted to not thinking straight due to family distress, and Detective Tom Wasco was very understanding.

They brought your file, and now I have seen your history, much of which they couldn't use in court. It was a horrible list, bearing out what Detective Hollis said, that you were "nefarious." All the way back to the army and the dishonorable discharge, even though you weren't convicted of poisoning any soldiers and they didn't actually die anyway. And it shook me to see you had been the guitar player in a band called Mystery Pizzle and were deceiving me about even your music.

Well, I have lost all respect for you, so I am not very upset to hear that Governor Kane says they will stick by their guns against mercy, no matter how many appeals. You're probably guilty of a lot more than they're punishing you for. This does not mean, however, that I wish you to suffer, and the procedures suggest you won't. By the way, Ouida and Dora contacted Dr. Spoons, who said he never meant *Blalock* anyway, but was trying to spell *Blake*, which could mean my neighbor Billie.

I'm also willing to take responsibility for my part. I was so desperate for solutions to my problems that I turned to a game board for answers, and now in that proxy session, since Dr. Spoons denied you, I know how foolish I have been. Ouida trusts in crystals and hand reading gypsies and anything else more shadow than fact, so I have to get some distance. You know how they say a coyote that's caught in a trap will gnaw off its leg to escape? Well, I have been that desperate, but the truth is, I have been gnawing at the wrong leg and have got to give up people with no respect for rules and professional behavior and common consideration. That is what these months have been trying to teach me, and I have finally learned. There you have it.

Tom Wasco has promised to tell me more about prevention, show me the warning signs to beware, and we're having coffee tomorrow at the Sir Walter where they have that delicious peanut soup and chicory drip coffee, so this is the last whisper you'll hear from me, and I just hope the Lord will show Mercy and let you go quietly before you latch onto some other lonesome heart, unless you would like the address of the porn poetess Sappho Ewbanks, which I can supply.

*Frances Rushton, W.U. (wised up)*

# Independence Day

I TOLD LARRY I personally would not care to eat an exotic misfit like emu, but then my boss Faith Rudisell strutted up and announced she personally didn't care if I went vegan, soupetarian or starved like a famine; if I wanted to stay head chef at the Pink Cadillac Café, I would by-God cook that gawky bird for our July fourth staff picnic, and I would make it delicious and beautiful, and what's more I would smile straight through, from the plucking to the pot licking. She is a woman on a mission: to get her heart's way.

Now I do love my job at the Pink on account of the plush Elvis decor and the neon juke box flashing like a Spielberg space craft filled with Presley doughnut wax singles, and since I've been going by "Chef Pelvis" for two years now, I figured I didn't have much choice if I wanted to stay who I was and where I was.

Faith herself isn't anything like a fan and sees the whole nostalgia diner set-up as a bald-faced but effective merchandise gimmick, but I just love being surrounded by the lore. It makes me feel sort of electrical inside. "All shook up," I guess.

Also, the Pink has a jumbo stainless steel kitchen under the faux-brass ceiling fan, and I get a kick out of the laminate dinner menu with every dish named for an Elvis connection—the Love Me Tenderloin, the Fools Rush In Chili, even Tupelo Fries, the Double Trouble Burger, Gladys Grits and the Foot Long Hound Dog. And who wouldn't appreciate the idea of a shrine restaurant dedicated to the people's grass roots entertainment hero, who could be either cruel cool or full of fire and knew all about the bruised and broken heart? I can't say enough about the atmosphere he gives a place and the way it raises my goose bumps just stepping in there with all those pictures of him and vintage movie ad placards and actual album sleeves framed and hanging on the walls.

Besides, our special Elvis theme lures strange people with even stranger lives over from the interstate, and I love to listen to the Yankee golfers and gawkers snicker at the Vegas bloat posters of Presley while their wives drool over autographed photos of His Majesty in tight leather and swiveling his hips back when he was a fresh find. "Hunka hunka burning love," you know. Sometimes somebody who actually met him will stop in and sort of minister unto us, because everybody has a favorite memory of his famous life. Even kids get a grin out of the toilet doors saying *Kings* and *Kingettes,* and there's always the Pepto-pink El Dorado slowly rusting out front. I enjoy looking out my window at all manner of travelers perching on the fenders to get snapshots grinning all happy and dazzled.

People who care for what Elvis represents have always had a special bond, so I come out in my *Elvis Forever* apron to swap stories with customers when the kitchen isn't too hectic, and I get a lot of compliments on my pompadour hair and glitter boots. Faith and Larry, on the other hand, wouldn't know "Blue Hawaii" from "G.I. Blues," but they pretty much keep out of the way when there's a need for elbow grease. They'd rather sit back in the office guarding the cash box and listening to hat acts and cleavage divas on the new country FM stations. It's drivel, and they're too busy conniving new ad flyers and scratching Mighty Ball lottery tickets to hold the reins real tight, so a lot of the time Ray and Glenda and Rochelle—our waitstaff and washers—and old Chef Pelvis himself keep the diner running without a hitch. We sink plenty of our tip quarters into the Wurlitzer just to let the King set the tone, and after my own years of aimless harum-scarum drifting, I have come to like this life.

That's why I would even consider compromising my beliefs and roasting the bird, but still, even if management has the final say about the menu, closing time and other policy things, I do not consider emu a game bird nor honest yard poultry, and at first cooking it seemed like just another Larry Rudisell wild hair nobody else would buy into. He brought it in slung over his shoulder and flonked it down on the butchering table like the hunter home from the hill. What he said was, "Roast my super chicken, Chef Pelvis."

I recognized from the get-go what it was, having petted an emu at a traveling zoo years back and off-and-on seeing Bradley Gilbert's hobby flock galloping behind the shock fence a little ways out highway eleven. That was where it came from. Bradley's emus had been hassled and snapped at for so long by ridge coyotes that a couple of males had finally pioneered a way to scramble over the fence, and this particular terrified fugitive fowl had run a rampage.

Of course, I didn't know the details until Larry explained his catch of the day.

"It got over there into my corn and pole beans," he said, "and it trampled my Better Boy tomatoes like a mongrel horde had passed through. That's why Bradley had to give it to me, to settle up. Least he could do."

Larry is Faith's cross-eyed third husband and likes to let on that he runs the Pink, but he just greets and seats and grins and slinks around in his heel-flashing Addidas, sneaking Pomona peach brandy in the pantry any time he gets half a chance. Faith is the actual brains of the outfit, which is not saying much, unless just making the cash register sing or squeezing the silver out of every nickel is a sign of intelligence, but that rube she hitched up with would gobble down Big Bird, I swear, if he got enough brandy fog in his noggin. He also quotes Limbaugh radio jabber and laughs with a shoat snort.

"So, Larry, how did you all conquer this dangerous bird?"

"Wellsir, you know Rabbit Rodgers is the local Robin Hood, alongside of being the county's animal control cop. A meter maid followed the bird to the public golf field and Rabbit's deputized drovers herded it toward the ninth tee where their archerman was in the chinaberry tree with a compound Shakespeare bow. The creature was quick as a hiccup, as Bear Bryant would of said, and grown men had been flanking and circling and running their armpits wringing wet for two hours when they finally scared it the right way, in spite of Bradley being so sure he could lasso it with a jumper cable. Thorne Brashear squatting behind the tree trunk caught the bird in a jacklight beam and made it freeze.

"'Zing,' Rabbit told me. 'Full draw, a deep breath, kiss the button, line the sights, easy release, perfect shot, a oneness.' Said he was in the Zen zone. Him and the bow and the cedar arrow were one true thing, because you know a down-sloping shot is never simple, and night makes it even harder. You have to be at the center of everything to make that kind of kill, but that Rabbit has true outdoor Indian skills and can even name maybe sixteen different animals in Cherokee."

Larry is a perfect candidate to fall for that mystic mischief, since he is half bull crap himself and never too clear-headed. Fact is, "Zen" is just a dorky hunter word for cold luck, which is the best Rabbit and his ilk could ever hope for.

The only pot at the Pink big enough to boil and loosen the feathers was for Fool Chili, but while I was deciding if I would roll my sleeves up to start dealing with the sad dead thing, I noticed the pitiful way the emu's head dangled like a snapped flower. Since that time when I touched a live one and felt its fuzz, their long necks and downy hair-dos have put me in mind of a scotch thistle. I mean, they have a goofy prettiness.

Anyway, Larry, as usual, didn't pitch in but started rattling on about how Rabbit wanted to take it home and make emu jerky, which is a real diet item the Au Natural Foods Co-op tries to sell to the local counterculture vultures. I guess we'd have to call it something like Flaming Star Pemmican if we served it at the Pink.

Hitching his trousers, Larry said, "Yeah, he was wanting to claim the white hunter's rights that come after any safari, but old Bradley thought it should be buried with honors for the fine chase it had led everybody on. Myself, I got a cartoon lightbulb in my head and thought why not have it tomorrow instead of fried chicken with our Silver Queen Creole Corn and Lisa Marie Ice Tea and your special hot Priscilla Peach Cobbler before the light rockets and other festive sky celebration stuff to honor our being the world's best country. I won the argument because I suffered definite personal property loss from the emu's jailbreak behavior. My rows are wrecked, and I'll be a lucky dog if I harvest another unspoiled Better Boy this year."

It's hard to sympathize with a dog brain like Larry. I pretty much hate him, but just about the time I stonewalled, saying our role model Elvis would not partake of such a meal, Faith waltzed up in that aqua halter top that always scares me a little because she is not a skimpy-built or overly firm woman. When Larry reported me for refusing, she pronounced her ultimatum—"delicious and beautiful, or else."

At that point it looked like my road was mapped out. With a sigh nobody could miss hearing, I set in to work with all my culinary craft and art, wondering why didn't somebody think to field dress the thing and at least save me the ugliest gore duties.

I'm a chef, though, and it's what I do, so I dug in, wielding my blades, seeking out the joints in my personal zen-like way, while those other two rattled around in the dining room and yelled at each other for a while about which one of them took a bad check from a tourist who looked Pakistani. I just hummed "Are You Lonesome Tonight?" and kept concocting.

When Faith and Larry finally stormed out the front, headed to their deluxe trailer which she calls a "doublewise," he turned to the window where I was standing, waved his *MORE BUSH* ball cap and stuck out his tongue like the local playground goober. I didn't realize before that he had gotten his waggler pierced for a gold do-jigger, but it did not improve his general looks nor endear him to my humble heart. He also has a tattoo of a Virginia Tech gobbler on his butt, which he once showed me before I could avert. It does seem a perfect brand for him, though he's never been closer to college than a tailgate party.

It's funny how a night of working alone in a July kitchen dressing and baking a bird bigger than a White House turkey will encourage you toward the beer cooler, and the more longnecks I drained, the more I wondered if the King would have let these creepoids push him around, if even old Colonel Tom could have bullied mighty Elvis into betraying his tasteful instincts and turning one of nature's curiosities into a Fourth of July picnic for half a dozen drunk-as-a-skunk yokels, especially Tongue Dope and Halter Monster. Elvis always had a streak of mercy in him and did not take advantage of the misfortune. You have to admire that in anybody who has been kissed by fame.

I do this sometimes drinking alone, but I wouldn't want a soul to see me. I was holding a Michelob bottle like a microphone while I danced around the kitchen shaking my tail and crooning and quavering for all I was worth. I have never seen myself as an impersonator so much as a follower, an apostle maybe, but even if I am too lanky and fair-skinned to fool an expert eye, I have the sound down solid, and on the radio, I could bring it off. I could do that for fun or get paid to be on commercials down in Roanoke, but that would be cheap. It would sully. I only copy the voice in private or for a few friends when they ask, just to honor the legend. Respect—it's in my skin. I can't help it.

"I'm just a roustabout," I sang, and, "Let me be yourrrrr Teddy Bear," all the while adding just another squirt of Texas Pete to the mix, just another pinch of peppercorns. And another. I could see my Elvis-curled lip reflected in the aluminum saucepan, and with my hair already dyed midnight, I was near about the spitting image.

I sang "Blue Christmas," then "Kentucky Rain" and "Return to Sender" all the while basting more cayenne on the emu and some Rock'n'roll Ribs, then sliver-slicing jalapenos and fierce onions so fine the weeping came out of my eyes like crying a river.

But it wasn't just that capsaicin chemical juice from my hands that brought the tears like a flashing flood, because I caught myself sobbing out loud, as well, thinking of how this noble beast which was just trying to be free had been brought down by a jack-ass bow cop and treated like so much roadkill by a bossy giggle-mind like Larry, who also treated me and most other people around Fancy Hill no better than a bunch of tick-ridden curs.

It didn't take long before I sorted out what my heart was actually driving me toward, and then I pulled the pies out of the side oven and opened them up to slip peppers in with the fruit slices. By the time I doused the Kid Galahad coleslaw with Tabasco vinegar and stirred a whole scoop of cayenne into the jug of Lisa Marie Ice Tea,

I had stepped into my Rubycon River and crossed at the ford. I had cast my fate to the wind and ponied up for the open road. Might as well go whole hog.

It seemed a waste of good Bic ink to leave those Rudisells so much as a note, and quick as a wink I cleared my gear, my guitar and my boxes of cassettes out of the Airstream I bunk in. It was time these imitation Elvisites learned a lesson about real respect, the honor due to a weird unflyable bird and to a bonafide first-rate Presley chef on the lam.

Grinning into the wind down 64 even now, as dawn washes into the rear view like sweet butter and the damp roadside pines lean out of the darkness, I can picture them gathered around the trestle table under the orphan sweetgum tree this evening, stropping the carving knife and cutting clean through the golden glaze and into the moist flesh, all the while praising my high-class chef art to the skies and wondering about my whereabouts. But about the time the first member of the Pink family, who will be Larry, as always, bites into the hyper-spicy dark fowl meat, he will lose that Don-Everly-loving feeling. I mean, he'll be screaming vengeance and red murder and weeping from eyes and nose and every sorry unclogged redneck pore, but by that time I'll be halfway to the pearly gates of Graceland, running hard, darling, feeling like royalty myself and what they call "anointed," or at least whirled into the pitch of mighty Elvis himself: "gone, Teddy Bear, gone and gone."

# Aloft with Grief

I<small>T MAY BE</small> that public radio is a mistake, because some out there will take it for the voice of truth. My daughter Hazel, for instance, sees those FM people as gospel speakers, because she has always put the classical music violins right up there with God. She claims she can't help me cook or wash without some German orchestra she can hum to. Now she's in Claney's black walnut tree with a thermos of white coffee, a survival Space Blanket and a croaker sack of my Pink Sultan tomatoes. Even Deputy Blevins over from Eep has given up trying to wrangle her down.

It most likely started with the news report on some California nutcase calling herself Remedy and bird-perching in a giant red-wood to stave off the timber company from toppling the humon-gous thing. The reporter went up on a rope, and Remedy said she'd been camping there for three months and planned to stay till what she called "corporate monsters" backed off. It's a touchy situation, what with all the press attention, and it looks like the lumber people will have to wait their trespasser out till winter, but if there's a just God in heaven, when the snow flies that young lady out West will be changing her name to Felony or learning about the shirt that fastens from behind.

That report's what gave Hazel the light bulb in her head. She's always appreciated Breece Claney's walnut tree back of that spinney of alders since his boy Luther had a rope swing there. Luther, he pushed Hazel in it and made teenage promises, but when the boy, who never could change a tire nor dig a plumb post hole, got him-self murdered in Iraq just after the Shock and Awe, Hazel fixed an attachment on the tree like she was a cult of one person. Mooning at it. Mooning in a trance.

Can't anybody swear if it was cash need or just being sick of seeing Hazel lallygaging out there every day after her shift at the

Mohawk plant, but Claney sold off the tree to a wood crafter from Fairfield—a Lipscomb, I think—who forked out a pretty penny behind calculations to cut it to planks and arrange them together again as custom vanities for the frou-frou shoppers. Claney was decent enough to send over a warning and say he'd save out a piece or two for Hazel. He offered to fashion her a yard chair of the wood, and this is what he gets—tomato bombs and Hazel shouting she is the remedy, he is the plague.

I heard the yelling just after first light and saw him out the window in his skivvies waving a toothbrush at the branches. "You get down, young lady" he said, and Hazel's voice from up in the green said, "Spare this tree, corporate monster." That was when she pitched the first Pink Sultan, which left a red splatter on Claney's chest, and since then she's hit several, including the Aubrey boy and, on the bursitis shoulder, me. I had to go in and change into a clean housedress.

So we called 911, and Harmon Blevins is what they sent us in his cover-alls and mucking boots with the bag balm still stinking on his hands, the brass deputy star pinned to his bib like a bull's-eye. He's a hefty specimen and makes an easy target, so he gave up pretty quick and called the fire volunteers. He had to be all hosed off to get de-Sultanized, and now we're setting here around the lemonade pitcher and waiting for the ladder team. I'm just trying to figure what drives a high school graduate and fan of Beethoven himself to hook onto every one-legged idea the world can come up with.

I could say it's on account of her being the only female of twins and the solitary one to survive delivery. Maybe it's because of her daddy's death by forklift or her appetite for raw catfish. I told her to let the Japanese menu stay in Japan. If it's actually on account of poor Luther Claney, I'll be a duck's uncle, because she wouldn't even be his corsage prom date last spring, and she passed up his funeral to eat a tub of Cherry Garcia ice cream and sulk in the pot shed. That was after she heard his personal effects involved a string of Arab ears and photographs of an army woman wearing nothing but combat boots and a possum grin. Now she is yelling she'll shed every stitch herself and resist stark naked to the death, if anybody tries to force her down.

Who knows why people carry on like that? Some would say it's their raising or natural defects or maybe a rattling calamity in their past, but personally I think it just comes down to what Dr. Phil calls psychological, which is, really, a complete mystery even to experts.

For the time being all we can do down here is enjoy the lemonade, which is fresh squooze and has a tart bite, while the wind slips down the draw and whispers to all the green leaves, including those in the black walnut where a stout branch holds that girl who's my only family, and not even the spirit of the tree knows how close it is to shaking and bleeding and smacking down in the bad racket of a chainsaw.

Now the siren is screaming in our direction worse than any noise from the radio, and I can tell Hazel hears it, as she's given us the bird finger and is commencing to peel. Blue Addidas and socks, then her brown blouse comes floating down, followed by the skirt I sewed her with musical notes on the cloth. Oh, lordy, and even if that wind is still kicking up enough of a fuss to blow her frilly underclothes about like kites, you can tell from the heat waves off Claney's shingles and the revving up of jarflies in the creekside pitch pines it'll be a scorcher to remember by noon.

2

# RAMPSKIN

*Who?*

He skulked through deep weeds with a june bug on a string. He pulled the nectar tongue of honeysuckle and whispered his song: "Lily by the greenbud, lady by the creek, laurels by the swamp path blaze the devil's flame. I will be a feather father. Dream yourself to sleep. You will never in a gillion guess my name."

From cypress beyond the Indian mound he fashioned a cradle. Mussed and wizened but rat-agile, he scrubbed in the crawdad mud amid the windfalls and spoil. He bleached croakers to diaper rags. He fashioned a doll from shucks, rattles from cooter shells and pebbles. He was mad as a snap but lonesome. He wanted a freshcut person of his own.

*But Everything Starts Somewhere*

It all kindled by the turnpike near Byhalia when the gaunt horseman spied a lurking girl named Lilatis between the cotton rows glowing white as camisoles and corn blades waving a green "so–long" to the whisper wind. He had been bargaining his crop at the Rabbit-ton market and was prideful and weary but awake. Her golden hair against the evening shone. His eyes were gray flint, absorbing. "Dip me the gourd, child," that one called, and up close, peering over the fluked creek water and the silvered pommel, he saw that she was thresholding, sure to awaken as a full-bloom woman some dew-dawn very soon. A little fretty, he could reckon in her eyes, shy but nearly ripe, with laughter coiled in her silence, a true trove. He dug his spurs and passed on.

Because her mother was under the wild roses, "ASLEEP IN JESUS," her dates hacked Roman into stone, Lily spoke to not one soul of the stranger and the smells of horse lather, mansweat and saddle, his eyes hover-hunting her form.

### *A Ransom*

That night, summoned from table by the mule boy with a lantern, her father stood uneasy on the porch to the big house. The evening star trembled. The master lingered, still in scarred riding boots, boards complaining as he shifted his weight like a bateau borne on the currents of the James.

"If she is fair match, I would marry your daughter, Mr. Jewel." He was more than colonel of the guard, and his voice was pitched to match the turning of a sorghum mill, the larch pole rasping against gimlet stone, the syrup dark. "What are her skills?"

"She can dance till the music breaks. She can trill the language of birds. I have taught her the weave and willow caning, soap-scolding, tallow draw, the art of the hoe. She can scald a hog and spice up sausage, save every morsel from snout to squeal. Swain hopefuls in Meatcamp and East Appleton stand in a line to swear under moonlight how she might could ballad the corn's gold to true silver. Her heart is a sparkle, her hands are surely magic in the back kitchen, at tanning, in the hyssop and mint and orchard fruit. Needlework and scrubbing. She don't hardly yield to nature's laws, but she's a root healer, a honey tender. She's a never-touched, an unsullied. She can scratch her history on a bead of corn, and for a wench, she can hold her tongue."

### *What the Father Got*

A fowling piece with powder, a Catahoula hound with one sapphire eye, six dollars, three pounds of sugar and one less mouth.

### *Made in Heaven? Enter a Stranger*

The banns followed, then the vows, a dollar in the wine-faced preacher's hand, but Lily was unready for the weight of a man; she was too frail and touchy to be torn. She spoke slowly, staring downward. One of her clear words was "no."

Two figures of stone stared across the wedding table as a servant shuffled and went. The groom simmered in wrath and disdained to speak. He locked her in the shadow attic. "If you are so much a marvel, if you are worth your weight, you must use this thread to weave a coverlet bright as a peafowl's feathers," and there in the wake of his going she wept alone.

Then that antic man from the deep woods climbed up the haw tree by the wall. Junebug in his fob pocket, rag cap from the rebel war on his fringey pate. His breath was the wild reek of swamp onions and rampion. She ceased her sobbing to say, "You are a curious, smallish man. You put me in mind of ginseng." He licked the air like a snake.

And when she raveled her plight, when she showed him the wreaths her husband's grip rubbed on her wrists, the gruff voice said, "I will take your spools of cotton to my bough house off yonder. I will work my work and fashion a wonder. Gal, you've only got to stall. I will save your bacon, but what will you sweeten for me?"

"I have a silken bridal scarf, its folds as smooth as skin, and other goods can surely follow. My husband will forgive and he is a right rich man."

A token, but ample. No wind, but dry leaves stirred.

### As Anyone Would Guess

When three days passed and she faced the glareful, thwarted husband with his riding crop smacking boot tops, with his spurs and moustache like a blacksnake, she unfolded the coverlet that was a wonder of ancient figure and device, of inexplicable sheen like a flower meadow in moonlight. Fish rinkling and bluebirds soaring, fox and wasp, Monacan women skinning a deer, smoke and spark, a red horse rearing, but only a moment was wasted in delight, and he thought to harvest more.

"Are you prepared to carry the weight of a man? Not just any suitor but this man, your lawfully joined? To feel his force and rush and shudder, his hot cry for a son? Lily, are you yet ready?"

But she was still girlish, too shy and frightened, so he locked her in the smokehouse where the hung shoat was still bleeding into a milk pail, the drops marking time like a clock. "Here is your knife, Lily girl. See if dealing in the grue and spill of meat will alter your mood. Waste not eye, tripe, chine nor bristle. Waste not the headcheese nor heart. Work me a wonder of carving. Be of some simple use, if you scheme to be wife only in name, which is to all my kindred abomination and shame."

There she sat with the candle and a blade nicked like war, and her tears were abundant, salt sparkling on the smokehouse floor. The flametongue hissing against the lantern glass was her meager comfort, the wax drizzle, the wick's wither, smoke's shadow on the door.

Just before midnight, he oozed through chinking. He entered like a fever. She smelled the scallion smell as he came to form before her. He was nimble and peppery as a skink. He was pussle-gutted, raw-palmed, his jaw already rough as emery just an hour after the razor moves on, and yet, she saw him as her ally and crossman.

"I am sore in need."

So the bargain was struck: He would whet and slice, skin and rend and hack, rive down to the bone, and she would pay penance, all she had left. In the corner she gawked while he danced and fenced with the carcass, singing, "O my bonie, oh my snout and brisket, my darling fly-summon, my pickling brine, my honey ham, my jowl." And she would give what was left for her to give.

"In three days I will make you the star of butchery over all of Sparrow Mountain, from misery to Tennessee. All you got to do is stall."

She cozened her angry groom through the boards of a spruce-wood door, "Dear husband, I am needing a trice of days again for to make my spell. When you return, all will be settled and well."

So it was, or seemed, and when the strange and goblin fellow brought his portion of the contract all neat and red from the ribs and giblets to a gourd of souse, Lily went back to her corner where the wicklight did not shine, and she reached up under her wedding skirts and stepped aside. She pulled out her pants frilly as fancy lettuce, and as soon as his fingers met the silk, he was smirky and gone.

### A Course Altered

Vigiling till dawn, she felt the hard air between her legs and wished to be sure, wished to be ready, and yet she was coming to understand the seam of cruelty that ran through her husband's cold veins. She had heard the mule boy whimper under the whip. She had heard the boar dogs howling. The sounds did not summon increase of desire. At daybreak, she was not yet ready. Her fear was aflame.

"I don't pretend to know the nature of conjure creature you are, woman, but long as you will not accept the recipe to be a wife, I will portion you work worthy of your pagan skills."

He led her, thonged at the wrists, to the barn where corn ears by the hundred, the kernel rows even as church pews, were stashed and binned.

"Here is your chance to work a greater magic. I don't care if you sing it or dance it or get on your fours and bark like a gut-shot hound, you will scare every kernel to sheer wealth for your lawfully wedded. This is the sun's best gold. Dream it to spending silver. It is a bride's task. I will be back from the Big Lick market in nearbout a week. Don't tarry. If you fail, you will be bent to the fields."

She tried to pray, to hymn God into a listening mood, but something had put the bile in Bible for her, something had soured the Word to woe. She wept to know the puck would come, and she had nary a trinket nor token to swap.

### Wherein the Moral Refuses to Arise

If she had been a skimp or fuss or straggle, a drudge or sass or dally prone to fritter, who could blame the proud powers for treating her such? But Lily was righteous and cheerful and kind, only afrighted of the act that carves a pain in marriage, that cleaving. So where does justice lie?

Easy as a weasel, he came. His arms like tent pegs, his skin like rickets, his voice like mill grist between the set stone and the one that turns. "You need a kindly hand, I reckon, deary dear."

"Not even you can help me now, old mister. I got nothing to trade with, and yonder is a mountain of corn he wants whispered to silver in just a week. I don't even follow what he thinks he means."

Flicking his eyes up and down the high summer corn, the creature grinned and offered up his pact.

"Only blood will lend itself to silver, and I law you will find the marriage bed softer than you expect, though an unsteady carriage. Promise me your firstborn chap to come and live with me where the owl hunts and the bobcat prowls in laceweed. I will swirl a cooling worm and cut the seasoned hardwood. The vat and passage that spirits it from corn to mist and drip as dew. I know a fire that can still corn to the staunchest silver, the shine called out of the moon to quench a mortal's direst thirst, to make him prance and giggle. That is my price, Missus Lily. Even such as I would crave a cuddlesome son to make the winter night shorter and less sharp."

She refused, but as he coaxed, she saw no other course before her. He told her to claim excuse after it breeched, to say how a fever came for the babe by night mist, as often happens. She could give herself to her man again and again. After the first, there could be other chaps. She would find it easy to repeat. He would be sated with the one.

There wasn't much she could figure but give in, thinking she might outwit this gnarl of a gnome once she was settled in her conjugals, once she had crossed over to be a full woman and maybe acquired night spells of her own.

*Thrift and Stealth: Blaze-eyed, He Cooks Shadow Whiskey*
In the hour between the hawk and owl when the vixen and hare bid each other farewell on the edge of a spent orchard amid a briarsnarl prone to host haints and misfit Senecas, just there the little man danced about pungent mash as it burbled and sang,

"I am the blacksnake in the bluebird box. I am the stillness behind the crickets' chitter. I will have a running mate for my tramp and traipse. I will raise the chap fierce and fitly bitter." When he smiled at the high moon, his teeth were a ripsaw's and his eyes were black as scorched spiders. His feet scuffled and jittered in the hepatica, in the bloodroot and plantain and rampion. He was a storm of pleasure.

What he brought to her barn in a tumbrel cart was prime corn squeezings in two dozen jugs, stump jump whiskey scald-bright and precious as any ore.

"I can't bear to abandon my own blood child," said Lily. "Give me a chance to wager back my own."

"A bargain struck is a promise to moon and sun."

"But I cannot bear the sundering with no hope. Surely you will not deny me some glimmer."

Her sobbing nearly moved him. He scraped his palm along his chin with a noise like matches striking. Then his eyes lit up like amber.

"One chance, missy, one resort. If you can puzzle out my natural name, I reckon I'll forgive the debt. All in the spirit of sport, you understand, but don't trust your hopes cause you can't, no more than you could skin a ram with your pretty fingers. I expect I'll see you again just a close bit before birthcry," and he faded like a rumor into the starlit fields.

### Another Bargain Born

With his teeth the Colonel pried the cork from its jorum and slung the vessel across his arm, then tilted his head and slugged. It was the rare silver of a full moon, cash crop of ridge walkers and shadow men, the cool burn of dream syrup. That owner of horses and breech-loaders, of a cider press, a race mill and a bellow forge set on hectares of valley with dirt as fine as gunpowder, that squire was so amazed he let a smile crease the leather of his face and said, "My dearest dear, you must be starved."

At the table she sipped sharp coffee and ate rolled biscuit with red beans and taters and chicken in bliss, knowing she was now ready to yes his question before he decreed another ordeal.

"And do you believe now," touching match flare to his Carolina panatela, "that you are ready to bear the weight of a gifted passion man? Can you bear my aspect, my flesh and caress? Will you give me a son?"

She averred she was ready, and all the servants were awarded furlough and ordered to make themselves scarce.

Wax and wane, the sky moved, seasons slipped, time raveled. But there was no pleasure in matrimony for Lilatis. She labored and ached but did not glow rosy. His love was cold. He was a barrel upon her, a thrashing of iron limbs, and soon even the fireflies seemed a burden, even the wild rose thorn an ordeal. She swelled with ripeness and hoped to find comfort in the cries of a child, but nightly she dreamed of the rumpled man. He was the gall on every oak wand, the fly in the butter, beetle in the pine. He was the dark one's cunning sergeant in the garden.

One Sabbath eve near her time, while her husband was at sheep auction and she was sobbing as she worked the churn, the mule boy Fess came up from the forty with harness to mend. Now when he heard the sounds of woe, he asked the wrong that had spurred his mistress so, and when she told him her sorrow, Fess promised to scour the county, to ferret and seek, to pioneer off the paths into swamp islands and the arrowhead woods. To scout and blaze until he found the hive of the come-sudden wildish man.

"Please," she whispered, "rush back and tell me all the doings. I would give every breath I have to hear his name."

### Collection

Boughs shivered with wind, rain hissed in the leaves. The woodkern caught her by the wellhouse.

"Soon now, miss lady, right soon, unless you know my secret."

His laugh was the sound of a tin roof ripping.

Desperate, she tried: "Is it Woodjack? General Pickett? Is it Cash or Gilman Oakheart, Dizzy-me-frenzy, Creasy Greenman, Zachariah, Chickasaw Reddle, Howard, Sourpuss, Yocona, Big Grady, Crake, Ishmak of Siam?"

The tin of his laughter sheared. Overflow in the drain ditch slurred and rippled. He howled and grinned. He vanished behind a wave of his hand.

Three days later he ambled back, and she guessed Longshanks, Dabney, Blondell, Mutt, Seamus, Sweet William, Possum Pete, Burrash, Osric Bone and a hundred others her desperate tongue struck on, but he just swiveled his head back and forth so quick his yarny hair bounced and swirled.

Filled with jubilee, he strutted through deep woods squiring his june bug on a string.

## Hide and Seek

Fess hacked through bramble and climbed the red royal oak to sweep the vale. Across knobs and down creekbeds, through slicks and lightning burns. He would lizard out on the ground to sniff and listen. Squirrels skittered and grouse drummed, crows chattered and oared their own darkness hard into the night. The stars glided. He believed he could hear them snarl.

But no trace, not a snapped twig or break in the spider's snare on the crests, across the meadow, in the gumbo slough, over goat peaks. Twice he looped back to the farm to tell her.

"But the pains come closer. Any day now," and she placed her cold palm on her melon belly. "I would give you all I have."

Fess slipped again into the thicket, working the circles of his heart's compass, his senses tuned like a fine fiddle, while a witchy mist ascended, and then as he was about to despair and surrender, sparks appeared from a clearing down in Drowsy Bottom, which he had neglected from natural fear. It was the Monacan boneyard, where the eyesore elf slept with the ancient dead. The sparks might have been fireflies or sparkles of Wisp Will, but a bird with an ember on his wing told Fess "campfire," so he dropped to his knees and crawled. On the scald bluff, spying down through the wild grape and sparrow shrub, he saw the cookfire of unscrolling poplar logs and locust, and the ragged man wrinkled as a pickle and dancing about the stewpot. He did the shuffle-ball and the wagon wheel. He cross kicked and scuffled, heel-toe, toe-heel. He squatted and jumped like a Russian. He spun like a savage, and as he moved, he rolled his red eyes and sang, "Riddle me a river, gamble me a game. Spit over the shoulder and shear the blackface ram. Kiss my rump and give me your get still damp of birth. Weep like a willow and take the blame, for you will never in a gillion summers guess that Rampskin is my name."

For a nit's minute, Fess thought to save Miss Lily himself. Swelled with a valor, he looked about for a clobber stone to smash the creature still, but then he remembered the fiend's spooky craft and powers and thought the better of it. Careful as an eft he slithered and skipped, silent, down the slope, back into the mist, and he ran like a buck deer back to the farm.

### Riddance

She kissed and wept, wept and kissed him, then sent the hero back to the barn, as the child in her belly kicked and tumbled like a little man.

By the grist mill's spillway, under the gnarly boughs and the midnight sickle of moon, she met the woodjack, and he strutted, he preened and cockcrowed and teased. "This is your end-all, your come-down, your sweepstakes occasion. Tell me, Lily Dilly the second sight, tell me diviner, you sister sooth: What do gut buzzards and buzztails call me in the trees in the foxfire in the rusty creek?"

She was unsure, she was vexed and all a-fidgit. She looked at the woodpile and the bronze bell to clang dinner, she stared at her feet and decided to risk it.

"Is it Redstick? Is it Cedar? Goat Step? Could it be Gristle or Mistletoe or Joe Sneak?"

He laughed till his eyes leaked. He jerked on the dangling june bug and popped out his watch. "You waste my time, moonshine girl, mistress butcher, needle queen the unsullied. The owl hour is on us, and you have one guess left before your own name writes itself in blood on the bottom line," and with that he produced the contract inked on chewed calfhide, the conditions sounding stern as a bailiff's knock.

Seeing it, she caught the gooseflesh. She shivered and winced. "I can't figure or seer it out, sir, unless—and this is just my pillow angel guessing in my ear—but could your name by the powers that lurk above and watch over us be some sound akin to Rampskin?"

His breath came like a freight train and he shook his head like a great hornet had stung his lip. She could hear a pileated's thrattle behind his eyes. His feet began to framble. He cut a wild buck and wing till the ground under his stomp softened and burned. He yawked and slobbered in his rut snort voice. He roiled and steamed, and down he sank, down, under ash dirt and leaf litter and smoke, into the root world, into the worm country, and all he left was a stink like hellebore in rain at Easter and on the closed earth a single stunned junebug glowing chard green.

That night she sloshed the jug's corn silver down her gullet till she cackled, touching the promise-swell of her belly with an owl feather for sharp eyes, and when her husband came in two days later she put the pig knife to new use, emptied the windpipe, showed hard blood how to be free. He was aghast, twitching to stillness, not so smart after all.

Next, Lily rolled her lawful wedded torment in the coverlet without his voice, then touched her red handprint above the front lintel and dragged him to the crib with shucks and cobs. She touched fire to the remnant corn with her companion candle and walked off like a waltz. The blaze was a ladder of gold no mortal could climb.

"I will call him Ready," she said, and when she had pushed the baby out with her rushy breath in the byre, she cut cord and made the tether knot. "Ready." Off she traipsed, calling the mule boy's name, which she had been told by the wind was Festival Quickly.

### In the Wake

They were happy briefly, the best any fugitive can hope for. A knife, a poke of hog meat, a clay face jug of homebrew, a coverlet too elegant for troubled sleep: They made their way in the world but suffered. Rumor is that the child Ready lived to be an outlaw fiddler in the Smokies, and if this tune he saws is written in blood-script, all the more reason to heed. The world is not a wet nipple. There are worms in the bacon, there is smut in the tassel. Even a lily withers, even a rapt listener yields to troubled sleep. Moonlight glows lonely on the corn.

# SUGAR

THEY HAD HEARD the hounds bell out, striking scent just at the twilight hour, and after a hundred minutes of hot pursuit, the black bear had led them back to their own campsite where the coffee had burned down to a scorch, the applewood fire was smoking and the lantern still hissed from its hickory limb. When they emerged from the thicket, the bear had already lit into the surplus tent and ripped it, then smashed the grub box, which they had not hoisted in their haste to overtake the song of dogs hot and spoiling for blood.

It was not a bear they knew much about, but already they had christened him "Sugar" because he had mauled Jim Braxton's Molly for the sack of peppermint candy she was eating from when she crossed over Lick Log Creek. Though the creature was new to the region, probably on a scout for spring forage and a sow, the hounds behaved as if some feud of longstanding were now escalating from a dull smolder to full flame.

Soul and Scar, the Karelian twins, were the first to hit him, then Big Jimmy, Pearl Girl and Whip, short for Whippersnapper. Sugar reared on his hinders and roared like a dragon, his stench like a witch cave. There was no bluff or teeth-clacking fear to him, but the bear fought with a strange, lazy rhythm, as if tranced, though the dogs were a whirlwind about him—Grendel and Salvo now, One-Eye the redbone who had been Sabre when he had two good eyes in him, Cherokee and the black-and-tans Pulley and Clink heel-snapping, counting coup with their old dart-and-dash method. Despite their ferocity, the dogs, one by one, were flung free of the melee, yelping, as every swatted paw seemed to connect with flesh—Salvo back-pedaling with half an ear left underfoot in the fray, Clink air-borne and smashing into the fire ring, Cherokee wobbling off, dazed, the claw rakings across his flank more even than the furrows of any field. The rest of the dogs came on again, fearsome, wild as their prey. They did not resemble the previous week's yard-dozing fawners, and they were now beautiful in their lathered fury.

Having downed a dozen bears together, not to mention possum, hightailing whitetails, numerous coons and bobcats, Hank and Rymen were not astounded, and when Hank offered, "This must be what's meant by tarnation," Rymen blew his hollow bull horn and the dogs all leaped back like they'd hit an electric wire. When the two guns went off as one, the slug-loaded ten gauge and the bolt Enfield, the bear bucked, shuddered and went momentarily still, stunned and frustrated but still savage of eye and posture.

Then the dogs were on him again as he lumbered toward the laurel hell he would never reach. Grendel was on the beast's back, usually a killing move, and the black-and-tans had him staggering and nearly tripped up. Soul locked onto the bear's groin, and Scar hurled himself at a leg. Big Jimmy dodged and feinted, her cry an eerie warble, bewildering, occupying the bear's attention.

Still, Sugar wrought his damage. Thrust and parry. He snarled, an infernal creature, a fallen angel still outraged and deadly. Swinging a foreleg upward as he reared again, he caught Salvo along the brisket and throat, and the spray fanning out was discernible in the moonlight as scarlet. There was vile beauty in the scene, and the men paused, as if to appreciate it, but Cherokee had fallen, too, and would not rise. Pearl Girl was no longer game, nursing her leg where pointed bone shone out in the lantern light. Even seeing the dogs so beset, other men would have made other choices, but this pair, driven by the secret reasons knotting their spirits, were sworn to the hard hunt and drew their blades.

Earlier in the evening they'd squatted over the lighterwood, split poplar and the remnants of a wind-struck apple tree trying to shake off May chill with dog talk and a flask of whiskey, the private anger suspended in mid-air between them, simmering, never mentioned but ready to spark. They were from two separate generations, Hank almost old enough to be Rymen's sire, but the pair had been hunt buddies for years. Now Donnette had come between them, sowing lies to smooth-faced Rymen about bullying and abusements, telling untruths to Hank about how Rymen was just suffering puppy love and no more than harmless. She made her schedules and deceptions. She strutted her charms, plotted her plans and rubbed skins with the both of them, sometimes in the same house, maybe even the same day. And some would swear both had a claim—Hank on the basis of first fling and village approval, Rymen on account of being closer to her age by a decade. For two days after the clues clicked together Hank had stalked his barn and garden, breathing like a demon, righteous, possessed and possessive, and it would have come to a storm soon, had not the child Molly nearly lost her head in the woods, and even now it was sure she would be a lame child, and with a scarred face Doc Dillard had re-attached with much labor. So they joined forces this last time, avoiding the open wound, walking thin ice, and they were in foolish accord that knives were called for when the bear reared up again and flung the panting pack off.

Grendel and Pully were taking the brunt, the former love-locked in the bruin's arms like a knee baby as Sugar roared and reared up for a moment, tried to shake off the lead dose like a dog with creek water. When the bear stood to full height and spun around, the men yelled *Johnamo* and dashed in, Hank's Bowie on a mission for the snout or an eye, the pig knife in Rymen's hand hoping for throat or the runnel between two ribs.

The havoc of creatures rolled and tussled, an unearthly desperation of limbs and noises. Then a voice called out of the melee, "I've struck nose," and the response came back, barely audible, "This here is a Tennessee tornado." The bear's answer began in baritone and rose to tenor, an eerie, wailing howl.

It was four hundred pounds if it was an ounce, all shaggy and indiscriminant, reminiscent of the bear clan's whole history—comb robber, disrespecter of fences, corn poacher, pet gobbler, border jumper, trap snapper, scavenger, climber, digger and trash bandit. He bucked, and the dogs clung, their sensitive nostrils assaulted by shit and carrion, musk and skunk reek, the composite of decay that spelled out glutton and survivor. The vigor of his rage would seem to proclaim the day of bear pork was over forever, the era of man-dominance at an end as the incisors ripped and claws swept the air. Rymen rolled off to get a better run in, while Hank's effort to save Whip almost cost him a human arm, the one wielding the red Bowie by its antler handle.

But they were gaining ground, despite the air full of dust, sweat and kicked ashes. Blood was on everything, the smell of scalded iron. Bear, dog and man, but the bear was heaving and damaged. Who would come through it? Would anyone live on to prowl this ridge, the green valley? Who would survive to savor spring water and paw-paws, to show the scars and shape the story? This was no French dance, and when the bear rose to shake them all off like ruined garments, it was a signal for the finale to commence. You could hear the owl, who omened it, and the moonlight pale on a twin birch seemed to call the mountain's ghosts in to witness. There was nothing left but surrender to shock and motion, the low limbs swishing or snapping, no last move but the forlorn hope assault, and the bear knew it as well but had not reckoned on the snapping turtle death-lock of Grendel. Nor had anyone informed him there would be a pistol. At close range, Hank's little Colt tapped Sugar's neck twice with soft lead before it was slapped off into the darkness, and the brain flickered, though its mouth now opened for noises like a distressed whale, and the tongue licked out black, the eyes shone with lethal redness, the teeth were a wonder to behold. All grips were surrendered, and Sugar backed off, surveying the host arrayed before him. He seemed somehow ready to charge.

And they were braced to receive it, seven dogs still game and two men nearly kin through the dark unwritten rule of co-husbands. This could be a strike to end all, a juggernaut trample, so the fiddler Hank and his rival Rymen whom some call Smiley both paused for the death brawl, knowing the devil would take who he most favored for company, but after two steps, menacing but off-kilter, the brute thing heaved, spat a gout of blood and collapsed, leaving the men panting and primed in the sudden stillness and moonlight, then simultaneously struck with the crazed option to lock together. The surviving dogs must have thought it was the he-bear's fate still at issue, but it was clear as pistol-whip moonshine to each man that the tangle now centered on the matter of sweet treacherous Donnette. Luckily, knives fell by the wayside, but it was wring and gouge, slap, kick, jab, twist and bite, an awful howling conflagration between two front-row tenors from the Riverside Baptist, and they would have it out, mortal combat, the settling of ultimate questions, now that the fierce mission to avenge Molly Braxton was achieved.

It might have been a half hour deeper into the owl's hunting that they rolled and scrapped and raved, laying their tongues to names that make "whoremaster," "Judas" and "Slut snuffer" come tame to the ear. They spat and slashed with elbows. They yanked for scalps. It was awful. They tripped over the bear's carcass and smashed against the bright sycamores. Ashes got thrown, cudgels taken up and busted, clothing ripped to savage disarray, and in the end the human camp stenched more of ghoul-like enmity than bear spore, while neither had given in.

On the trail that morning, both men had examined the shedding posts where hibernal hair had been scraped, and they bent their heads together like confederates to study nutshells, berries and pelt-lick in the scat, but all along, the venom was rising toward a Cain-Abel clash.

The song of dogs and personal mongrel-nature had brought them to this, killing a wild raider in pieces by committee, loss of strong dog flesh, waste of their close love for their animals and long-sown respect for one another's skills and tempers—the farrier's arm, the fiddler's ear. They could have done it simple, with rifles, as if for recreation, but now the field was strewn with a carnage worthy of Bloody Lee, but no Clara Barton to come wrap and soothe them.

The lantern whispered like a snake, and the mantles popped and conflagrated, then went out to summon the darker shadows. Dog whine and hard breath, Whip already rested enough to be gnawing on the enemy's crux where the pistol had ripped. Night had fallen whole on the ridge and hollar. Dead, the bear Sugar was invincible, the freshest legend. Dead, the dog Cherokee was an angel, bred to give all and never snivel nor surrender. The living hounds were heroes soon to heal and bell and strike again. What the wind heard was the slow crawl of every living thing in that black hour to its desperate zone and the distant blackberry canes audibly forcing their blossoms.

Nobody would trophy mount that gruesome head nor grill the wild meat nor skin and cure the gashed hide for a hearthrug of rough fur. It would lie on Monkey Mountain's southwest ridge for latecomers to drag at and wrestle over, to snack on and scrimmage for. Vultures would visit it, and flies, scuttlers, squirms and no-see-ums.

The two men lay indifferent to it, mangled, winded and hell-weary, both turning their minds to the same woman as she shone in moonlit pail water splashed on her shoulders or moaned under them, speaking words viscid as honey and thorned. Or perhaps Hank pictured a red pinwheel he had as a boy, how it whirred and swirled when he ran with it. Rymen listened hard, for he believed he had heard the plunk of the year's first blackberry into the bucket. As their eyes cleared and they looked up to a sky too cold for dogwood flowers and wisteria bangles, the star bear himself was still prowling slowly, posing as if his high-and-mighty brightness depended wholly on their attention. If either of them lived to see dawn yolking the sky yellow, this moment of shock and oblivion would pass as the heart slowed and flesh mended, but the grief, in full measure, the grief would come and come.

# Fig Honey

WHITE SMOCK OPENS UP for Scowler and his clipboard questions. I'm eased back on the cot and making smoking motions, but they won't give me a real butt, deny me Nehi, mouth harp, all manner of simple pleasure. Scowler brings his own stool, leans at me. White Smock takes off the night bucket, then stands, holding up the shadow wall, big fella there to see I don't take a notion and lunge. Looking at Scowler, I wouldn't ever aim to hurt him. He's a fool, but not an enemy. He already caught on I don't care for the silver circle he wanted to listen on my chest with or his touching my wrist leaders for heartbeats. He's give up on looking around in my eyes. Now it's just the questions, White Smock with his guard stick and key dangle listening quiet like a party line sneak.

"Why figs, Raymond?" He wants to catch me off my points, but I know White Smock sneaks into my writing book when they dope me at night, and all I did was write "fig" and draw them by dozens since day before yesterday. The turkey-foot leaves, the winter sticks, ripe fruit weeping juice and mashed ones sinking in the grass. He keeps hoping I'll show him the secret, doesn't call me Runt like my Daddy. Tries *nice*, instead.

No help from me, though, cause I have never even seen the woman they are looking for, not her necklace, not her red-haired head. I had my own head and the Captain's already, so why would I crave after another one?

If I was home, I'd be seeing breezey wind knock the flowers off redbuds we called Judas trees, petals my daddy called Easter snow. I'd hear the turkey hunters down by Swale Creek calling up toms with their bird voice contraptions. Can't fool me, though. Even if the fig tree was cut back to child size for the cold months, it would be limbing out and popping leaves by now like the slow sumac, the cut-off hickory's green twigs. No matter the winter, no matter the rain, they was figs every summer, and the fig tree by the scuppernong arbor was where I saw the snake who is Fig King, all rust and ripe copper braided up thick as a girl child's hair on Sunday. He reared his fang head, and his Y tongue said the dusk hour was his own and first dawn when the dew is still on the roses. Ask Rave.

Young Mr. Ravenel they call Rave and me was selling war wood. We'd taken the forge poker white hot and scorched holes in the barn planks from the stack stripped off for rotten. They was only weather wounded, a hornet nest gray and rougher than a cob, but we said it was Minié ball leads stung the holes and put our war wood sign under TOMATOES where our Reb flag is nailed to the chinaball tree. Roadside Enterprise, Rave said. Patriotism. We're selling history. I always agree. We drink Nehi orange fast till our noses bubble.

I tell Scowler how fig leaves were all a lie in the Bible. They have a sap that will make you break out and itch, and Adam and Eveline was too smart to slap scratchy leaves over their own private particulars. That brings on his next question, "Have you ever seen anybody like Eve naked?"

Scowler's a doc and doesn't take me for stupid, but White Smock thinks I'm not trick-wise. You couldn't grow up shadow-to-shadow with old Rave and not know pranking. We have seen plenty womenfolk in birthday suits, so I say he's getting foolish in his age, White Smock, I mean. Rave has disappeared and no more older than me. He's slippery as kin. So it's back to talking turkey figs. I pretend to take a deep puff, watch the ember-tip, fill my lungs, then whisper out the blue pretend smoke, just like Rave.

I say nobody knows why the Son of God cursed that plant till it shriveled. I tell him my people don't net the trees against starlings and grackle birds but get out at dawn in ripening time, touch the sweet ones into the bucket before the birds and suck-bees get busy. The fig juice spells them better than knocked-down apples gone soft. Figs swell to a split when they're ripe and favor a woman's secret. You can see in, where things begin. Farmers call it the eye, but it's red. We think it's like the Bethlehem star, all dewy. They say eating figs will make you tattle, killing a snake will bring rain. I saw that copperhead slink in the sting weeds under the fig tree's shadow. Rave saw it with me. Its head wasn't a fig shape but more like a wild Indian's spearpoint all clayish when kicked out by the cutter plow. We could of got the hoe and murdered it for the skin—make a wallet, make a belt—but we knew better.

They say Satan was snaky, the Bible does. We've got Bible every-whichaway you look, Rave and me—the thing itself on the mantel, Darling Baptist pointing its steeple at clouds just at the head of the holler. Over in Uncle Millard's mare field, there's that sign painted red on white: AWAKE! THE SOON OF GOD IS COMING. We hope it will slow a traveler now and again so he'll mull over our TOMATOES & WAR WOOD. All the paint red as a peckerwood's head. Red as what Jesus said in the Bible. Devil talks in black just like the people, though. You know the devil, he's on the picture show package of Red Hots, goaty horns and tail like a snake arrow. White Smock once asked if the devil made me hang that dog.

It was Rave. He found it strayed in the pulpwoods, spindle-skinny and goopy at the eyes. We made a pen from chicken fence and fed him up. A hound will take to cold gravy and biscuits, hambone, pie, but not a sweet potato, not red peppers. Rave said the last meal is special, so he smuggled pig guts out of the blood house, said we couldn't keep any wild pet in the winter anyway, how he'd suffer with the frost if we tried to be soft. I knew it. We had a kangaroo court, what Rave named it, and agreed how the brown stray—we called him Spy—was guilty of creeping about to no purpose, sneaking in to know our plans, snooping out our hidden things. Clothesline, catalpa tree, a squeal and flail like you never, as the rope went tight. You know a bent nail prized out of hardwood? That.

White Smock is picking at his fingernails. He's a hard man to interest, especially with tales of beasts and country fruit. He smirks, and I see. Scowler is tuned in, though. I am going on about figs, how sweet they get, like honey on bread, how the seeds are a grist on your tongue, but you can get them between your teeth and pop. They spark. You're not careful, a fig wasp will bite you. You could swallow it. Some people could die, giving up all life's signs and wonders for fig honey. It was Mama who fretted and warned us over and over, but Daddy said she was caution-bound, and it didn't even save her.

Daddy said women make no sense anyway. "Your mama shouted at me for peeing from the porch into the yard," he'd laugh, "but when I got down and peed from the yard up onto the porch, the old woman's disposition didn't improve." He liked to sit on the co-pilot seat, one without the store-bought circle, of the new moon two-seater dump house in the back just past the crib. Reading a Perry Mason book from the Salvation Army. Hardly anybody would use that hole, it being homemade, but he favored it. Wasps nesting down in there with all the dook, they saw their light mooned out and rushed up, mad as a Methodist. Daddy rushed too, bit bad, and he went real sick. He said it's why he couldn't make me brothers, the way wasps got him in the bag. Fig bag, almost, you know. At least I had Rave.

The Captain's head is why we were honest to sell war wood. Raiders stormed through, their flank like a dark wing swept over the county, ripping up rails, stealing silver and harness, burning houses and cows. *Rapine*, they called it, and *forage*. Fancy words for a no-mercy raid. Even the Yankee lovers suffered hard. They all skirmished hard at Swale Creek, and stragglers happened on each other right where our apple stumps used to be an orchard. Full moon, they say, winter of sixty-five, club and pistol gun and bayonet, old knives and axes, neighbor on neighbor, all the noises of agony and bold pleasure. They left the woods blood-flowered, cur dogs ripping at limbs and faces under the moon. The ground gut-slick. A gaffer wrote in the paper that he was a child then and saw a Yankee blown into a tree like Christ Man, a redbird perched with a man's eye in its beak, half-hearted woodsfires here and yon. That's why Redbird, Virginia, just around the river bend.

Mama's people buried them all in a heap down in the draw where ground was soft. Family talk said one fella from Mississippi was Captain Bowers, and he fell. Ghost everybody sees lurking at the end of winter we always called Captain, and when I was digging for gold behind the barbecue chimney, we found his head bone all smutty with dirt, no teeth, a genuine bullet hole in the head. It made Rave dance to see it. They say ragged volleys hit the barn, so for years we had the cold ghost smell of Captain Bowers and Minié balls in the planks, but that barn went off stick by stick long before I was born. We had to make our own souvenirs: Poker point and fire equals bullet hole. Why not? My people earned it, like a brand.

If that missing woman stopped to buy a sack of tomatoes or figs in a wove basket and had an Eve smile, it was Rave, not me, that was watching the stand, making change, smoking Chesterfields. Rave didn't have an extra head like mine. I kept the Captain in my attic sack with harlot magazines and Daddy's straight razor, all my keepsake pretties. I liked to pick him up and play toss with myself, nobody else but the perch owl to know my game. He was a hero. I whispered to his skull like some heathen in the Bible. Rave would chase it through the rye grass. He knew how to covet, but I could make him hush. I think Rave could of been river people, too, but he just showed up with no warning, no history. He could of had a horse and a boat and a bentwood rocker with a crazy aunt chained in the basement. I was him, that's what I'd say.

This time of year, blossom time, I'd sweat the days putting in rows, stringing for beans, rive-shingling the barn, corn and corn. After dinner, I'd be out with the butterfly net catching carpenter bees that lived behind the soffet and aimed to gnaw our house to dust. It was a game dance, and better with stump-water whiskey. You have to stand still as a dead man with the hoop aimed at a place in the air, then wait for one to bumble along. They'd skeeter about and dart, you couldn't catch one, but if it got curious and hummer-hovered to study you, its black and yellow fur a bead burning, then you could sweep quick as an angel's wing and snare it, then step on the net. Crunch, like a pigeon bone. When they're out, sawing like a lumber mill, you know the fig leaves will follow directly. Fig tree's got no real flowers to signal, but when the fruits come in, they're green, hard as a knuckle. They're not supposed to thrive this far up the hills, but if you're careful, you might get lucky.

"Did your mother put up the figs with sugar, make preserves for your biscuits?" Scowler wants to know for his clipboard. "How did you feel about your mother?" I told him that was the best breakfast treat on a hoe cake or cathead biscuit, the drool of syrup with skin bits and seeds tiny as a bug's eye. It's what I miss about her, and she never raised a hand against me. I remember Daddy slapping me once in the sitting room out of the pure blue, then laughed, saying it was palm Sunday. Bray laugh, cackle laugh, snort laugh, howl. He was a whole Noah boat of critters. He stayed for her graveside with the preacher and flowers. I dog if he didn't appear to be sneaking a smile. Then he lit out, took nothing, said no farewell, and who knows where he landed? Maybe Rave. I don't say this last out loud, but just stub out the pretend butt on my pillow. Scowler is giving me the hard eye. He knows I'm just making believe tobacco, and I can see he's thinking.

Mama's skin got the sun cancer and went fig color in blotches. The town doctor said too late, said just pain pills, said she should of never worked a field with her coloring unless she could keep on sleeves and a brim hat. Gloves, too. Daddy never shed one tear, then left right after we covered her in the ground. Why did he leave the hammer tool with blood spots under the porch steps. I think Rave might know, but not me.

White Smock clears his gullet, then speaks up in his voice like a mill grinding coffee, "You know we found it, the woman's body dug into creek mud like a crawdad's business, but no head. Right near your tire swing. Wasn't any Civil War mischief," but Scowler calls at him to shush, and then he straightens his back, gives me the cold voice: Own up, Ray, or face the torture of your own guilt. I say ask Rave for the noggin. I didn't need an extra. I have Captain Ghost, Captain History. I liked to kick it across the chicken yard while the rooster on the roof like a spook, his feathers all bright-spangled. I never saw that woman and can't snitch on Rave, no matter how many figs I eat, or Nehis or smokes. White Smock says there was a blacksnake all licorice-like on the asphalt this morning and smeared from tires, says he has also heard a sour hound moaning the distance at evening. He says everybody wonders will I drown next time the Heavenly Lord makes it rain.

Scowler is writing on his yellow paper. The ink pen makes a scrapey sound. I say you can't have real bliss without real tobacco. He won't look at me now. I scratch a make-believe Bluetip on my coveralls to light up another Chesterfield filtertip and blow the smoke rings nobody else sees at the ceiling, then lay back. Now I shoot Scowler my bliss look, acting like a red-headed woman's face off in the burdock smiling painful at Rave.

In my gullet I hear a voice stirring. "Wait till they leave us," I tell it. "Keep our sweet secret dark for now, my Rave."

# LUNA

LAST NIGHT'S RAIN is cool and still in the dog bowl. I don't really have a hound anymore, almost two years, but the chipped bowl from the old Caboose Grill lets me measure rain and might give strangers the idea there's a watchdog around. Beware, it says. Also to scare trespassers I have a big ring of scarred ham bone Blitzen gnawed before he got himself lost. I don't want any stumble-bys to know I'm alone.

Fifteen years, and I haven't seen the beat of it, that storm. This morning the redbud flowers are smeared everwhichway, blown down by wind and water, the trees black-branched and just taking on spring color. A few uprooted and toppled like shot soldiers. When I go over to see how much water fell last night, there's a moth pale green as new pecan leaves floating spread out in the bowl. A luna big as a fancy dress mask. He's still flittering, but his wings are torn to rags from the wish to get out. He, she, nobody could tell. Caught in the weather, I suppose, hammered down. Finishing my Spam sandwich, I squat over and study him close. Still showing some fight, but he won't fly again. Bright lights make them go into danger. Worse than humans. People and night moths, all searching. It's interesting for a minute, but then it's time to get to the river. What am I supposed to do? If I leave him, he'll keep suffering hope and working at it. I don't know do they get pain, bugs. I'm sure they've got less idea what's going on than a person. I need to leave, though, so I scoop him out in my hand, feeling the tickle on my skin, and lay him in the grass like a lace cloth some woman would spread out to dry. Still flittering up a storm. You've got to admire all that try in such a tiny body, but what's the point? Cat will probably come along. Woods rat or bird. I need to get on.

Down at the dam the water is roaring like a train race, white as ice cream, limbs and leaves whipping around, under and up, everything a whirlpool, kind of snarling in the boil and back-wash. Other side of the bridge two big oaky-looking trees are down, sprawled right across, their roots sticking out like spider legs. You could balance out and hack some limbs for firewood, I guess, but I'm here for the black bass who circle round, the bream all stunned from the sudden rushing down the underwater steps where they get bashed. The dam is old pitty concrete with *Fuck John* and *Panthers Forever* and barb wire on top, and its curve holds those fish back and thrashes them, then slips them through the spillway in a nasty spume. They're whipped then, like the rest of the world, but they need some chow to build them up strong enough to go on. Push, leap, wiggle the fins. They get desper-ate. So I come along. In the stills behind rocks where I throw in, there's not much roil, and they'll go for most anything I slip on the hook—white bread, squish worm, cricket. I am planning to haul a mess in, poor critters, and sell them to Manny the Pirate at Todd's Goshen Grill. "Pirate" because he has an eye patch but also a big grin and a parrot tattoo on his arm. He'll always deep fry me a couple with some slivered taters, ketchup. Half a High Life in a coffee mug is about all the juice he'll give an underage like me, but Co-cola aplenty, so it's good business all around.

Lots of them don't know I'm not living at the poor farm now, and Manny won't let on. I don't mean the actual house the county used to own for hobos and beggarmen, which came to belong to old Connor by some money deal. I never lived there exactly, but I had a shack in the deer woods behind the grown-over graveyard Connor let me stay in. Cabin sort of—tin roof and wood floor, power, even—good enough, but then he up and sold the whole spread to some Florida asses who want to level off the woods and cram in stupid rich houses. Connor is a Mac like the rest of 'em, come over from Scot country long ago, I expect, most with Mac as the front door to their names. MacLendon, MacAfee, MacNulty. Bankers and skinflints, but he was the least rude, till he sold the farm and skipped off. Sneaks and snakes, every one. The new people brought in sawyers and those new grabbers, skid men, long trucks and giant lights to work after dark, so I had to relocate, but fast.

Now I'm homesteading a shed belonging to Mr. Kinsington. I've got a cook pit in the yard and two rooms, screen on the window, a little willow spring uphill, a lean-to for a privy. Not bad here in April. Us beggars can't be too particular. Since quitting the school, I reckon myself a fugitive, but so far, so good. He's in the hospital with the stomach cancer, Kensington, and don't anybody, his kids or nothing, bother to look to his land. I'm on the steeps, and when the rain comes like last night, it's an attack, hard to slip off to sleep. Tat-a-tat-a-tat. The drumming wears a body out. I reckon the whole shack could just wash down with me in it and that be the end, but you've got to squat in some temporary place while you figure where you most need to be.

It's easy to reach my lucky fish pools from here, though, and I hope this might be the day to work it, but soon as I get tackled up and wet a line, two boys no older than me are diving in upstream of the dam. Lots of noise. Splash and holler, like not a care in the world. Kids, really. Not like they have to earn their way.

I might not be an orphan yet, I don't know. I was nearly onto twelve when daddy, high as a kite with a broke twine, dropped me at that church. I was tired of his wolfy voice and his hand—palm and knuckles—but the God people have a different way to batter you down. It took me just a year to figure my escape. Another to make it happen. I'm the lawn boy now, orchard monkey who comes out of the woods and says, "Could you use a day hand?" A dish rinser at the Chinese when some illegal gets hauled off, I been batching it since.

So far the locust trees are blooming with perfume and the scabby sycamores clothing up slow, but the locusts are dying back all around here. Some kind of moth gnawing them brown, but not the luna. Redwing blackbirds are riding their reeds. It's the calm after, and I'm about to get relaxed, but I'm just thinking they ought to watch theirselves, those boys, when something goes wrong, and then of a sudden their laugh-whooping gets all torn into screams. I can see heads and arms waving about in the Milk River, and I know they're not playing now.

Well, I don't know, and then I do. I'm up the bank all a-scamper full speed, a rescuer running up stream, but the water is fast, still mad about having to swallow rain all night, and the one boy—towhead, I can make out—is whipped into the center of it. I know what has him is underneath, the suck, and not a thing you can see, but he is spinning, other one floundering, slapping the water, about making it to shore mud, if he can last.

That shouting is me now, but nobody close to hear. I'm in the Milk to the knees, the close boy grabbing my fish pole, then I have him by the wet shirt, the shoulder. I can feel the water snatching at me, too, but not so bad in the shallows. When I get him up, he's like a drowned rat and shivering, eyes like mossy rocks. I've seen him before. The tow-head one has disappeared altogether, though, and I start back the other way, following the flow, hoping it spits him out.

No soap, though. I don't see hide nor hair. Back and forth on the bank, squinting where the sun is brighting off the water. The other one is in the weeds, still spitting and heaving and starting in to weep, and now a truck has stopped down on the bridge, some black man in coveralls singing out, "Y'all need some help?" and all I can throw back is the "help."

I know I don't need this. Somebody might recall my face and know I'm missing or wanted or something, but I holler back again, "Help, help me, help."

NOW IT'S DARK, gone chilly, and the grass all tramped down by the people, all sorts. Some I know from the Grill, some from just town. You'd think it a show, the way they flock in. Can't help it, I expect, but the flashing lights and everything make their mouth water to be a part. It's sucking them down, too. Red, blue, white, over and over, like a holiday decoration. Emergency. It would dazzle most anybody, pull them in. The twilight has glimmered off and gone to dark, but the moon's slipping up past Hackle Ridge, shrinking, just two nights past round. Ornery weather wouldn't let us see it at full. Now it's just another lantern mirroring back in the water. It would be pretty some other time, but the real rescue men are out there in boats and boots with their nets and such, throwing in the grapples, which are like a hawk's claws, cruel, even if he's dead, which he is.

I don't like it turning out that I know him. Wheeler McDowell, his daddy a swell with a bank and a house big as a horse barn. A Mac, like the rest. He does have riding horses somewhere, I heard, but the boy, Wheeler, was always sharp with me in that little span I tried to scholar. He would squint at me in the class, wrinkles around his big nose kind of piggish. On the recess ground he'd call me "Wildboy" and thump the back of my head. I use to think, "Should I just whip him, because I'm able?" but he had his running mates with their ball caps, their smokeless tobacco and folding knives, and I couldn't take them all, even with them being soft or just sporty, no real grit to them, no real fire. So many house pets with a swagger. What a laugh.

Upstairs, Orion the Starman is slipping along the rim of the ridge, herding fireflies. We're about done with him till next frost. Yonder on the far bank a preacher type is reading. Bible probably. Lots of people on their knees. It's like a scene, "wailing and gnashing of teeth." The lucky boy is done spirited off to the hospital or home, siren shrieking, but that Wheeler Mac boy is down there lonely with the fish, cold as moon rock, his eyes looking at nothing, nothing to see in the wet night. Hide and seek. I can feel him turning with the currents, slow like he's thinking it over, dreaming it, us dreaming him. I hope they find him soon. I don't want to snag him some morning on my rig, all soaked and swole. No market for that, no profit, which is a hard thought, but I can't keep hold of my feelings about his meanness. He's cold in there, no game in it. Tumbling, no way to ever say another word. I don't need another ghost story in my life. The mattock just barely cut Mama and took off a little toe, but then the foot got big and smelling, Daddy too drunk to drive her to the doctor. Beginning of the end. That boy will be smelling soon, too. Flesh will rot at any chance. We all hold on by a fraying string.

Now I'm finishing up my peanut spread sandwich, and somebody in a yellow coat has handed me coffee in one of those spongy white cups. Steamy, but not a sort of drink strong enough to help.

People are flowing past like water, all murmuring. I'm in a tight squat, flinging pebbles into a drain pool, bored sort of, when a cop comes up with his big light: "Son, you can't do anything here. You best run on home."

You got to laugh. The song says "gather at the river," and here we all are, me with them, still while they fidget, everybody sad, the sadness just rising like a mist off the river's skin. Lots of people hugging each other. He wasn't a mean son of a bitch to them, Pig Face, and I can't even really picture him up clear now, it's been that long since my schooling stopped. I know which one's his mother wrapped in a deputy's jacket, and she has sobbed so much they try to draw her off, but the woman no bigger than a girl just lets her knees go, slides down limp and won't leave. I think she has on a flowery dress. Is that how they are, mothers, won't give it up?

Through all my old hate—practiced and shined up most every day, even in my dreams—I can feel the other thing almost rising. If words come easy to somebody, he can call it pity. I don't have a name for it I can trust. She is sobbing and Mr. Hunter up in the sky is moving so slow, his stars like candles, that famous belt. "O'Brien," my daddy called him. Flat-out ignorance.

That must be the boy's daddy the police keep hurrying up to right on the edge of the water. I can't read his face. He's staring into it hard, the river. The searchlights are like wands waving over the surface, but they can't push in deep.

When they find the body, it's a seeker dog that does it, and him downstream all snarled in a driftwood nest. Not a handsome sight for the family to see, and they get him wrapped up pretty quick, so the search part is finished, and even if some start easing away, going back to the dry rooms and hot chow, a bunch can't let it be over. That's the usual: Tarry and tarry, the searchlights still sweeping the water, brightening it. What do they want? To be sure it's not them? To count good fortune? Lots of boys will sleep in sweet bunks and thank Jesus tonight. Even myself will be dry in the shed.

That boy, though, Wheeler. He had good qualities, I know. We all do, down in us somewhere. I'm gathering up my gear but can't find the stringer and bait box. That's a pity. Never even saw a fish. Water at flood rise like this, I was kidding myself anyway.

The path is not easy, moon low yet, ground scabby. Dogs are barking off somewhere, a cricket fiddling. Too warm for owl sound, too early. Last night I saw lightning scars twice, west, out the window glass, but I never heard the rumble. How's that happen?

I get home, if you call it that, and fill the lantern, strike a bluetip and make the glass flower yellow.

Out in the leaves like a tea table doily I find him, super moth, still in the struggle. He's game like a chicken I had once when Mama was still casting a shadow, a Kelso with black wing feathers named Meat Hook that fought six times before his eye was popped and a red rooster's gaff gutted him. When I lift up the moth, my hand tickles again, like when it goes to sleep. Just a few stars are burning through the full trees now. That pig-faced boy might be up there now I hope, and while I'm looking, the luna quits. He won't see light again on this side, but maybe when you cross over, it's there too, but different.

WRAPPED UP IN my blanket like the mud-slicked boy that got away, I look through the window screen at the gnawed moon white as a preacher's teeth but no whiter. Right now I have a thirst for kin kindness and a hairy dog-snoring friend on the floor and a hunger to see the meaning in things that go on. If you go under and come up like that, things ought to be lit different, but I personally still need a rescue from lack of being able to grieve the grief. I feel the cold water still somewhere inside me, steep, and there is a ringing in my ears I ache to be rid of.

Toss and toss. Stare at the wood knots on my ceiling like notes in a hymn book. This is what you do when you're alone and listen to the world in its turning. Me, I can't wait for the roaring noise to stop. I can't wait to be old enough for whisky. I'll know right off to drink it deep.

3

# 'SANG

SILENT BUT LESS SUBTLE with each passing season, ginseng imparts its mysteries to Clovis Emore, who has traipsed the wooded slopes of Rockbridge and Amherst Counties enough to be a Blue Ridge Magellan, a Bartram, a Boone. Now he walks the heights and hollows as much for penance as for profit, but this was not always his way. As a veteran timber assessor, he has seen coves and caves and natural amazements like a doe and raccoon touching noses or eagle talons carrying a kit fox, acorns big as a rose—sights even old Elijah Mitchell never dreamed. Flagging trees as he estimates board feet and maps skid routes while running the payoff numbers, he has lived off the fat of the land and the lean of it, as well, in the bitter years. He has gathered cohosh and galax and blackberries, goldenseal, bloodroot, apples from orphan trees on the House Mountain saddle, pelt of fox, claw, steak, gall bladder and mounted muzzle of bear. How many cords of stovewood? How many bags of jewelweed to soothe poison ivy? How many punnets of wild cherries and gums of honey, sacks of mint, possum haw, sparkleberry, the owleye catnip and chinquapins? Despite the abundant variety, it is ginseng, sweet 'sang, that speaks to him most urgently with its bannering leaves and three blood-bright berries. From the deep woods of Yankee Horse Ridge and Elephant Mountain, the herb taunts him with promise of easy harvest and reward, but it has long ago witnessed the shame now lodged deep inside him like a scrap of shrapnel against the heart.

Clovis is aware, as he looks around at the golden season, that the chance for prosperity is always close at hand, but the old secret still gnaws at him like tree rats in the rafters, termites feasting on the foundation of a barn. The secret is always there, and then there's the other flaw in the flow, Jo Aline's waxing Born-Again fever. She had always been a cautious girl, skittish in the world's mix, most at home with her mother and her mother church—a basic immersion, mute-women Baptist—but he had talked her out of the cardboard factory in Buena Vista and said, "You could marry me and pursue your dream," which was the making and marketing of cat beds, all sorts, from the disposable to the fancy. She could always use her sharp-eyed sewing skills and her little coping saws, glue sticks and staple gun. Wedded, in a home of her own, she could specialize and supply the kittens and their owners all manner of cute gee-gaws and trim work with decoupage flowers and amusing feline stencils. And selling over the Internet could even manage her bashfulness problem; she didn't have to speak eye-to-eye with any non-believer. Free from the rasp of the unpredictable, she was safe, and he was willing to tolerate her half dozen comfort cats who prowled the margins of the house and drilled into him with their curious eyes. He had even saved an orange kitten from the shelter for her birthday once.

"I can see he loves you, Clovis, even if you got no use for him."

"Dear, dear Jo," he said, "I don't have anything against them, as long as they keep their claws sheathed and their cat talk down to a whisper."

She said she'd call him Tangerine, and they both petted the new arrival, but Clovis was certain the animal scowled every time he cut his eyes toward his benefactor. That night the two of them had played and harmonized on hymns, while seasoned apple wood crackled in the hearth. Their lovemaking had been tender and open, but not without surges of passion.

But not long after the mistake that had become his stain and his secret, cat beds and singing songs of praise in the evening ceased to be enough for Jo Aline, and they'd had words and silent friction over the TV's evangelist channel and Sunday's all-day ranting on the radio. The last straw had come when he discovered how much cat money had been flying out the mailbox in the direction of Reverend Brenau Salt of Lynchburg. The preacher's radio henchmen introduced him as "the genuine Salt of the earth," and his sermons always seemed to bring up the salt-poor existence of hard times and how farmers all across Virginia had been reduced to digging up the dirt floors of their smoke houses to boil it down for salt. The charlatan relished the punning on his name and preened like a peacock, but Jo Aline was charmed.

"And now," the preacher would say, "we know the graceful Word is our salt, and we are full blessed. Praise be, glory, the Mighty Hosts." How much she'd sent the ministry for a plastic shower cap with a red hand decal on top Colvis didn't know, but he'd surprised her kneeling by the radio, her hand on the speaker, the cap covering her russet hair. Was she praying to the radio or to the sorghum-voiced Reverend Salt? Not to God, of that much he was sure, and that night a bitter quarrel had sent him storming off to the cot in his work shed to toss and struggle against the tide of regret. When he finally slept, his dreams were filled with Bibles whose pages were twenty-dollar bills.

So she had gone persnickety, neglecting to glean the orders from her web site, saying the download was too slow. Ignoring her boxes of yarn and bolts of satin, her sketch book and glue gun. Mail order envelopes filled a basket by the door. She'd also lost any interest in their evening fireside duets as she went moony and high-strung, flinching at the sound of his voice. Full of Robertson gossip and Falwell superstitions, Jo Aline saw the world as a web of transgression, and she didn't even know the half of what her husband knew.

But perhaps, somehow, she did. The wet scarlet color of the 'sang berries whispered in his mind: Your loved ones will smell the blood on your hands.

He was sure, looking back after what seemed twenty, thirty years but was actually only eleven, that he had at least been hunting in season when it happened, legitimate, licensed. 1985: His memory could summon patches of snow on the cold pastures, Charolais with their faces wedged into the rolled hay bales, seed flocks of cardinals on the roads and starling masses flying like swirled shawls. He was certain Black John and Marshall Penwiggen had sweet-talked the hogs one by one down to the willow run that morning and put the short gun to their skulls for merciful slaughter. Sometimes he would sit in his cold cab and try to conjure up pictures of that day. Wheeling his battered Ram back toward home, frequently glancing over his shoulder like a tic, Clovis had passed Marshall and B.J. butchering as he headed back to the valley. They were laughing and spattered and gloved in blood. He had been just two years married then, and didn't know yet—nobody did—that Jo Aline couldn't foal.

Leaving his muddy boots on the stoop after sunset, he'd found her stitching away on tiny blankets and bootees, whistling as she listened to "Mountain Reunion" on the Emerson, making her plans for a healthy brood and family future. When he came in, she was rocking in tune to Mundo Earwood playing his hit "Fooled Around and Fell in Love."

"No deer?" she asked, rising to embrace him.

"No, no deer."

"What's the matter, Clovis honey? You don't look right. And it's a cut on your face. Does it pain you bad?"

He'd denied it, said he was just a little chilled, said all the luck had rushed up against him and he'd gotten only one shot, a bad downhill angle, and it went astray.

"I need to wash off and warm up, get some dope on this scratch." His voice had edges and colors she could not be expected to recognize.

"But you don't miss, Clovis. You don't never miss."

She was pretty much right. Local boys had taken to calling a turkey shoot bull's-eye "a Clovis shot," and not without reason. There was something of the legend in his woodsmanship, his economy and self-effacement while he brought in trophy after trophy. Some had called it supernatural; since he was twelve, he'd been so steady nobody imagined it was luck. The tall boy with light hair, the camera flash starring his eyes as he posed at the local game registry with monster bucks, turkeys big as armchairs, trout as long as mattock handles.

That morning—he was pretty sure now, looking back, it had

been mid-November, misty and legal hunting time—he'd been scouting a scree slope that led down to bony sycamores and a lazy creek. The leaves were lank and lifeless, no treat for weekend gawkers. He climbed free of the brush and onto a summit. A braw day with just a few clabber clouds to the west. Scanning north, he noticed a stand of crabapples and beyond them a laurel hell that tangled down the bank, leaped over the water and stretched up the opposite rise to the crest. A twill nuthatch was rattling away at the bark of a windfall oak, but everything else was still. This much was hammered deep into his memory.

"Yonder," he thought, "lies my ambush. I'll likely find scat and antler scrape. There has to be a meadow falling off further north and a-plenty of browse from the rounding oaks. There has to be deer sign and deer."

So far, the day had followed the soothing curve of routine, so he was sure, looking back, that he'd not gotten excited or too eager. He was a placid man, smooth looking, not gaunt nor nervous like many of his kinsmen, and he descended slowly, the rifle unloaded, the hook-stickers and brush clawing at him. He was too wary and deft to let any stray withe slash at his cheek, though, or alter his pace. The water had been slow and the air even colder down there, but as he prepared to twine through the laurel, his eyes had fallen on the remarkable thing.

Under a stand of squirrel hickories and black gum, in a dark patch of soft dirt upslope of the stream, the slack and flagless stalks of a hundred ginseng plants stood, the shortest a foot tall, like a skinny army all hushed and arrested in formation, surrounded by browning goldenseal. Of course, this was not the right time for digging; the under-dirt would be a trifle hard, and most of the roots less eager to come out clean, but he couldn't resist looking about for a viable 'sang stick, just to examine the real goods. Already he was imagining how much Saunders Quilby would ring up after the scales showed next year's 'sang harvest. This was the pot of gold, and no need for a rainbow. It was God's own lotto jackpot. He could take out a thousand dollars worth easy and not damage the stand. Two thousand. Did he say thanks to Jesus? He'd been that sort of man back then. No zealot, still, he knew how the world was shaped and favored.

But then he heard or maybe just sensed from experience the rustle of a moving deer, or what he reckoned to be a deer. Usually, Clovis' rough woods instincts passed for gospel. When he thought there was game nearby, it became fact. When he claimed to catch buck scent, you could get the vinegar jug ready to soak the edge from some choice venison. You could poke the fire to a simmer and hone the skinning knife. His daddy Leonard had been the same, especially after Mama Marlee died. "Woods-tuned," people called the two hunters, "buck-charmed."

A man with an unloaded rifle was a man with no weapon at all, Clovis always thought, as whitetails will sense the slightest gesture, hear even the well-oiled metal moving, flash their flag and be gone in a bound. "They'll bolt," he thought. "Why they call it a bolt-action rifle," and he smiled.

Then he pulled in his breath, eased the bolt back and ever-so-secretly pushed a cartridge forward, all the while keeping his eye hard on the spot where movement that was not wind had beckoned him.

Whenever his memory brought the story that far, he had to stop. He might wipe his brow or cover his eyes or just stare at his naked hands as they began to shake.

IT WAS THE CHINESE, he had long ago decided, that made us crazy over 'sang and maybe over money itself. For white people, the root boiled up to only one ingredient of a rowsey tonic, or you could chew it to soothe a raucous belly, but the Chinese were reputed to be sex-crazed and believed in all sorts of plant magic and various body balances. It had Chinese-colored skin, the root, the treasure part. "Rattle root" the old-timers called it, or "panseer," and they already knew uncultivated, native-growing ginseng was precious and rare. An enterprising, woods-wise man with some good scouting hours behind him and a haverpoke slung on his shoulder could go into the woods for a day and make the equal of a month's wages from a loading dock, pulpwood camp or Christmas tree farm. The Chinese were crazy for it, to help an old man make babies or spark up a young man's pleasure. 'Sang was *yang* to them, the man-tiger growl. The spooky thing, what most diggers never quite got over, was the way the root resembled a human form—the outflung sinewy limbs and body, the hairy top. Some said its name was from a Chinese word for man, and who would be surprised if, despite its lack of a head, it started speaking? From man-shape to money, it was just a breath and a step with a good batch of wild 'sang. Daniel Boone himself knew it, and some still reckoned weird Eric Rudolph had lived off 'sang money from poaching in the Honey Pot down in Carolina's Smokies Park, where he dodged the law for years before he slipped up dumpster diving. Clovis thought about that. "Slipped up." Nobody could elude natural justice. Nobody walked scot free.

THAT FOLLOWING SUNDAY so far back it seemed on another planet he'd read in the paper the man's name was Sugg Gowrie. His little stand of weekend property joined up to the Jefferson Forest where Clovis had been hunting, and Gowrie had not been wearing blaze orange or a license, so he must have been poaching himself, but there was no way, Clovis reckoned, a bullet through the chest was just punishment for trespass. And he himself was surely no duly-ordained executioner.

The shot had felt wrong from the start, though the man's brown barn jacket at seventy yards—sometimes it seemed closer—had looked for that one split moment unquestionably like buckskin. Unmistakable. Still, Clovis knew he should never have let fly at even the most deer-like motion or a flash of color without sure verification: You have to map the body, find the parts—lungs and heart. You're obliged to see it clear as a surgeon, or there's no shot at all. It was a mistake of the highest order. He could even feel the Marlin's walnut stock jump wrong against his shoulder.

Clovis quickly worked the bolt again and caught his brass, then slipped the safety forward, and he had the bad feeling like cold water down his back the whole time he trampled and stumbled through the brush after the thirty caliber echo. Snags tripped him and limbs slashed, one cutting him just at the corner of his eye. When he got to the clearing, where there *was* a scrape on a big poplar, he'd seen all the lung blood soaking the brown jacket and pooling on the frosty ground, had known right off the man was a goner. Trembling, he'd leaned in and felt the neck for a pulse, saying, "Oh, Lordy Lord. No, no, no." But done was done, and he knew it was prison for poaching and manslaughter, Jo Aline abandoned to the abyss of her zeal, or else he'd have to take quick flight and keep unbearable secrets. He couldn't help the dead man, he reasoned, and he kept thinking the words *subterfuge, fugitive, subterfuge, get your skinny butt moving.* For a trice, he couldn't do a thing, crouched staring at the lifeless form and the blood red as 'sang berries and the Winchester rifle in the leaves. But soon he found himself moving lightly, not with panic but with all the woods-canniness he could muster. He brushed his tracks from the soft earth, read his compass and followed the casual water, trudging upstream, knowing he'd have two miles or more under the ridge and through the cut corn fields, or the ditches alongside them, the hardwood stands and washouts, to reach his ride once he broke out of rough cover.

So a knot inside his heart was what he brought home to Jo Aline that night, instead of a field-dressed whitetail with a whimsical scut and a fine glaze-eyed face with elegant antlers. Instead of game hanging from the hoist and gambrel on the ash branch, something was hanging heavy inside of him, and he almost believed it would start to ripen and spoil and smell so all the world would know. She knew right off something was wrong, but not what it was.

"You don't miss." Her eyes were quizzical and a little afraid.

Later, he'd said he wasn't in the mood to tune up his guitar and play some tunes with her. He sat by the woodstove, slumped over, and kept looking at his hands.

Twice in the night she'd awakened, sensed that he was not sleeping and prodded his shoulder to say, "You don't miss," but then she cuddled up again for warmth and comfort, as if she had just been kidding, just working her way into his disappointment to make light or share whatever mystery he'd brought home from the woods.

The whole story unwound in a sequence of hard-to-bear discoveries in *The Roanoke Times*. Gowrie had a wife and teen-aged son, who was himself in detention. The wife was a waitress at The Roanoker. No affluent kin, little pension. They buried Sugg Gowrie with help from the state and church, an accomplished hunter and bus mechanic from Natural Bridge who'd lately run afoul of hard times. There was a graveside ceremony at the Methodist Church of Saint Somebody. The police and wardens were asking around, but there was no trace of a witness. Reward posters went up on power poles, and the weather slowly wore them down. It would likely go unsolved, the investigators began to say, another hunting tragedy, another argument in the Assembly for supervision and workshops, registration of firearms and close monitoring of men in the woods. Clovis was not so stupid as to attend services or send flowers, so he waited a year, mourning in a private fashion that cut through his insides like a wire brush, holding himself off from spying on the widow Gowrie, making his plan to send her a cashier's check every year at Christmas, starting that second year, at least a hundred dollars, and it turned out to be a good idea because the second winter came hard.

IT HAD TO BE money from gathered 'sang, he decided, and even the first year he heard the voices like a Chinese chorus washing about down in the 'sang box. He knew they were saying, "Clovis, Clovis Emore." They came with his dreams but were not a dream. Jo Aline slept through the voices, but the two of them began to sever. Each year he seemed more and more lost to her, woods-addicted, always on a traipse but bringing home smaller timber commissions and less meat, while her interest in rant Christianity sharpened. No issue was forthcoming from their rare and desperate trysts, and they began to divide their energies like a scissortail's trolling feathers. Clovis got more roverish and silent, trekking the ridges and valleys until sunset, sometimes to guess the lumber growing on a developable tract, but more often to no purpose, drinking his beer in the truck, now and then selling off his own daddy's old pasture land on the sly.

Jo Aline worked her fingers toward the bone on double stitch and fine knotting, crochet and quilting. The cats increased their numbers, and the smell of their boxes was sharp and disgusting. Her autoharp had become a sanctuary for dust. His guitar stood in the cedar closet as the Gibson wire strings quietly lost all tension and spark. He sent cash wrapped in sale flyers to the widow, mailed it from different post offices—Fairfield, Buchanan, Vesuvius, Troutville, even down in Martinsville or communities along the shores of the Dan.

While he strayed and wildcrafted and gnawed at his lip, wondering what had become of the Gowrie boy, his victim's son, Jo Aline read tracts and surfed the gospel net. He had no idea how wildly she would swing from crying jags to swaying in the bliss of holy writ. By the time he got home in the evenings, her eyes were dry and drilling with some question she couldn't quite grasp enough to ask. If she noticed he had little to say about the roots and leaves that had brought them a second income, she never let such concern cross her tongue.

MOST WOULD HAVE STEERED clear of that patch and thicket, that dribbling run over limestone and packed kaolin clay, but not Clovis. Maybe what they said about a crime scene was almost true, but he never strayed across the creek, never looked to see if a marker had been set in the spot where Gowrie fell. Every fall when Orion began to show and the cicadas shut down, he swung his 'sang hoe to harvest the mature roots in the dusk of a cool evening, cleaned and dried them, sending the profit to a widow who didn't know, who perhaps thought it manna rather than blood-money. But, no, he thought, that was unlikely. Still, it was the one way to assuage his pain, and after a few years, it did begin to work something of a cure. He rediscovered his laugh and went alone to the Maury River Music Bash, though he mostly stood in the audience and clapped, stamping his boots, at first refusing any offer to loan him an instrument, finally giving in only to display his patented run in "Jack Stewart" and "Come All Ye Fair." But it did make him feel better, stiff as his fingers were, rusty as his chord changes came.

Clovis rendered more and more of his spare time to the volunteer firemen over in Effinger, barbecuing chickens, boiling up cinnamon apple butter. He hunted and gardened and walked the ridges with a mission. Call it penance, call it the desperate change in an accidentally guilty man. The world's weight lightened a bit, and he gradually stopped seeing his shaving mirror fill with the face of Death and the word "manslaughter." He gradually ceased flinching every time a police car's blue light whirled by.

Then this one evening after a long trek up Jump Mountain had drained him and left him head-achy and panting, feeling dizzy with a sharp stitch in his side, he was kneeling with a forked 'sang stick in one hand and a flashlight in the other, and he scratched up a plant that somehow animated and seemed to writhe like a caught crawdad. He shut his eyes tight, then opened them, and from where the head would have been if the root had bothered to be a complete man shape, a voice clear as water from a willow spring seemed to be speaking. He could have sworn it said: "Clovis is the championship killer." "Hell," he said, and flung it into the ryegrass, but it harped on: "Clovis is the master killer, a dead shot." He was giddy with disbelief and its opposite, saying, "This can't be, but I hear it. I think I hear it. This can't happen. Can't and is." All those years of midnight choir on the edges of sleep had now given whatever haunted him the strength to go on early shift. What had been kin to dream was now loose in the forest, and the voice was unmistakable as a radio announcer working the stage whisper: "Clovis is the master killer, killer, killer."

Why now? Why after all these sorry years? "A dead shot," it said, and he stomped it with his boot like stomping on a copperhead.

Rise and fall, his leg took on a rhythm of its own, a bizarre dancing, and before long, the whole yield of ginseng was mashed and trampled to a pulp, worthless as the root of a dogwood or fraser sapling.

He was terrified to go home, and as his body dampened with cold sweat, something he only vaguely sensed induced him to steer the truck toward the Blue Ridge Parkway, where the first tint of fall was edging the leaves. "Master killer," his tires joined the chorus and hissed against the damp asphalt, "Master killer."

He knew a fellow near Coburn named Tom Hardy, whose back room was a dive open late to insiders, a place to squander money on corn whiskey and cheap conversation, and his Ram seemed to have elected that destination as he took the loop off the Parkway. The sun slipped behind the ridge, and night was starlit and noisy, the wind coming out of the trees long ago turned ghastly by acid rain, chewing beetles and the woodpeckers that fed on them. Clovis kept trying to picture the widow opening the envelope—by now she must know its nature, its purpose and inadequacy—looking at the money and clenching her face against tears. She was no longer young, might have remarried for all he knew, but the phone book still listed her on T-Bird Lane. He wanted to believe she was better off without the shade tree mechanic who had that afternoon surely been up to no good himself, but that wouldn't wash.

When he turned the radio on for distraction, a fervent voice rang out, "Bathe your hands in the favor of the Lord." He switched it back off, then tried to feature the woman shopping in a brightly lit store, turning in a fresh green dress before a bank of mirrors, getting over it, getting by. Just as he was imagining a bearable smile on her face, something—it looked like a man, but was then bigger—lumbered onto the road in front of him, and he tried too late to swerve. Then everything was a blur of trees swirling and some dark animal large as a Canada moose spinning by.

When Clovis got his bearings again, his engine was hissing and popping, and the truck was pointing downhill, its front end wedged between two huge hickory trees. He knew his head was knocked soundly, but he found no running blood, and though he was slow to move, he judged nothing broken.

The wind was still moaning, but a wilder noise was coming from the ground uphill of the wrecked car. It was a labored breath like coughing, accompanied by the sound of something large thrashing against the brittle understory. Clovis got out carefully, realizing that the truck was tilted downhill on a steep, and only a half-buried rock and a few scrub hardwoods stood between him and a dark dropoff. He could see the farm lights speckling the valley like nameless constellations, the world of men distant and lonesome in the cold night.

As he rounded the rear fender with his penlight projecting a soft, soothing beam of light, he saw a large buck on the ground snorting and shuddering through its last throes. Such a sight was nothing new to Clovis, but then he spied the complication. The deer's antlers were tangled in what he first took to be a windfall limb. Moving closer he realized that a second set of antlers and part of a skull with a swatch of hide still attached had been gnarled up with the buck's own rack.

"I've heard of this," thought Clovis. Two males competing for browse territory or a doe herd might meet and duel in a clearing, run against each other with great fury. Usually it was just young ones that put so much at risk, and they'd back off after a little futile bashing, but occasionally a couple of big bullies would square off and joust, and if they got tangled, it usually meant the demise of both, a kind of Siamese twinning to death. Old ridge runners, however, would tell of one surviving, usually in an area sparsely hunted, dragging a carcass or part of one through the woods for a season or two until he fell and starved.

"Got to put him out of his misery," he said aloud to the wind, and he clambered back to the cab for his rifle, which had rattled off the rack and wedged behind the seat. Once he was able to wrench the seatback forward, he started up the hill again, finding himself suddenly weak. He was panting hard, and the sweat ran cold down his face and back. A couple of times he slipped and skidded and fell, then lay there in the print of his own body, resting as the delayed pains from the collision began to come on in waves. Clovis pulled himself onto a log, then stood again, taking deep slow heaves of night air to get his head right. He bolted a cartridge into the chamber, but when he reached the shoulder where the deer had been, he couldn't see it. He scouted quickly up and down the road and on the berm, but the animal was gone, vanished. There was no sign of its ever having been there, no sound but the harsh wind keening. Running his flashlight beam up and down the ridge, he could see that the earth had been gouged and churned, but there was no deer wheezing on the verge of death, no tangle of antlers, no fear scent nor glazed-over eyes. What he did find amid the dry ferns just uphill of his clicking and steaming vehicle was a stand of goldenseal casting their shadows behind the flashlight beam, but their typical neighbors, the ginseng, were nowhere to be seen, and no echoes of "killer, killer."

Breathing shallow, feeling a stitch in his chest now, Clovis leaned forward into the edge of the wind's sorrowful sound, then scuffled back to where his truck was wedged. The valley lights were all aimed at him now, filling his eyes, and as he felt the first tears form, he was aware of the weight of the rifle in his hands, a Remington thirty aught six he'd had since high school. He ejected the unspent cartridge, then took the weapon by the barrel and, spinning his body in a half circle, slung it over the edge.

He didn't have any idea what Jo Aline would say, but he planned to unreel the entire story and beg her forgiveness. Then they could plan the next moves together, the way it was supposed to be, the way life was meant. They would either carry the story to the sheriff and accept the consequences or keep it between the two of them, their burden, their bridge, whichever path she decided was best. He couldn't guess which way it would go, but as he moved down the sloping road, a phrase from "Amazing Grace" came to his mind— "saved a wretch like me." Despite the steadily sharpening ache under his ribs and the pain throbbing in his temples, he took a deep, cold breath and began to sing.

# Orin

ORIN WAS SITTING on the porch reading an unremarkable magazine story, while the carpenter bees provided convenient distraction,
zinging around the cedar soffet they were excavating or studying
him as they hovered hummingbird-style at eye level. The end of
April, eve of the ancient May Day revels, he thought. May Day had
long ago suggested something amorous to him: "May I?" "You may."
Birds chirruped in the treeline. A sweet breeze swept the last buds
off the Judas tree and onto the warping boards like wet confetti.
Beyond the drive, he could see the first bangle of blossoms on the
empress tree, violet, slightly darker than the sparse wisteria on its
struggling vine. He took it all in with a glance, feeling the breeze
under his red summer robe with the small polo player stitched over
the heart. His wife had presented it as a birthday gift and said it made
him look "dapper." Orin did not much care for the word "dapper,"
which sounded like some kind of house painter's assistant. He kept
a steady rhythm with his cedar rocker and felt a current of sadness
wash through him. The ardor had long been drained from May Day,
but for the moment, it seemed the fault of the story.

In a dispassionate but soigné manner, the author was delving
into the fantasies of an upscale Manhattan barber who leered at all
the women he saw and envied all the men. It was winter in the fiction, and ice glittered from the sidewalks. Pausing with his bright
scissors over a customer's thinning hair, staring into the mirror
across the room, the barber felt neither guilt nor ambivalence, but
entitlement. He was convinced he had every right to his appetites.
This was meant to signal the temper of the times. Orin dragged his
thumb across the glossy page, smearing the ink, obscuring two lines
of the story, which made him smile. He could hear a passenger jet in
the western sky, "western heavens," he thought, mocking the story's
voice, but the tulip poplar's new leaves and dingy flowers concealed

much of the sky, the morning sun, any clouds left over from last night's rain.

The sun was high enough, however, to carve the shadows sharply—leaves and porch rail on the decking timbers, his hands poised above the magazine on his lap. Lifting his cup, he found the last coffee gone tepid and glanced through the patio's glass doors, toward the coffeepot, which would, no doubt, be equally cold. That was when he saw the movement, the dark trousers and white shirt flashing at the far edge of the living room. At first, he thought it was a trick of light, his own reflection blurred by the rocker's motion, but no, the figure was beyond the sofa, outlined against the wall Mina had insisted they paint leaf-green. "The accent wall," she called it.

This couldn't, he thought, be possible. He and Mina lived in their isolated house alone, absorbed in their books and cribbage and videos, nursing their truce. No children or pets, infrequent guests; deliveries and service people were equally rare. Mina was in Italy this month with her art class. Orvieto, a famous chapel in the cathedral, a monograph she wanted to write while her students drew, or as she said, "sketched the hell out of the place." Even her language made it clear that the torpor in their life was not her doing.

He found he was beginning to scroll mentally through the list of all the visitors who had been in the house during their years of occupancy, but now, certain he had seen a person and not an apparition, Orin rose and, with the *New Yorker* rolled into a blunt instrument, he stepped to the door and slid it open.

The man facing him held a long kitchen knife Orin recognized as part of the Sheffield set Mina's mother had left her.

"Who are you?"

"Mickey. Shut up and sit down."

As the man took a step towards him, Orin couldn't see any other options, though he quickly calculated whether he could reach the stairs and rush up for the trigger-locked handgun under the mattress. He had been swift enough when he was young, athletic even at forty, but the chemo and radiation had left him diminished and timid. Fifteen push-ups was a strain. A mile walk left him winded. The intruder was lean, raw-boned, poised.

Mickey was looking at the TV, the DVD player, the white Bose on the breakfast table.

"Cheap shit," he said. Where's the valuable stuff?"

"That Bose is about the nicest thing we own. We're teachers."

"I don't like you spying on me while I work. Turn around. Look out the window."

With his back to the intruder, Orin could tell by the squeaking plywood under the carpet where the man was stepping. The hallway. Mina's study. He was suddenly conscious of being naked under the light cotton and tightened the square knot in his sash. He listened to his own breathing. The bees outside darted by the pane, and Orin started mouthing the words of the Lord's Prayer.

"Any of this art worth much?"

"It's just prints, posters. We get them matted and framed to look more like the real thing, but they're just copies of museum pieces." Why was he saying this? It was no time for art education. He noticed he was not shaking or sweating at all.

"Spruce up the place, that the idea?"

"Yes."

"So where's all the money go?"

"We've always been state salaried. We even have to work part of the summer at Battlefield Park so we can go to Europe in August. We don't save much. I'm retired now. I've been sick." Partly true, but the trips were mostly hers, his gift to her, his penance for the one indiscretion a decade back. The old, unforgivable story—a weekend workshop, too many Glenlivets, the music smoky and then the dance floor, the elevator, the green light winking as the brunette inserted the key card. Ellen? Eileen. He knew even before he got home that he would not be able to keep it from Mina. When he blurted it out a month later, she took a breath to compose herself and then said that they would get past it, that they would not speak of it again. Before closing the dressing room door, she said she would get over it and move on. She had not.

"Got any liquor?" The board at the threshold of the open kitchen creaked. It was not quite noon, Orin noticed on the face of the Bose.

"Under the sink."

If he had the cell phone in his pocket, he could make for the woods, get a good head start, dial 911. He could get down the hill to the Tildens, the house with "In-the-woods" in glittery letters on the sign. Or the car keys. In the car, he could lock the doors and then drive off. If the man had needed to pick up a knife, he probably didn't have a gun. His voice wasn't rough. He wasn't very big, really, but Orin decided it was ten years too late for that option. Even Mina would have advised against it. "Thy will be done."

"What's your favorite?" Clink of bottles, scrape of things being pulled across a shelf.

"I like the Jack Daniels best, or sometimes the vodka. It's Czarina with citron flavor." He was lying. The single malt scotches were his personal extravagance—Aberlour, Talisker, Glenmorangie, a swash of smoky Laphroaig at the bottom of its glazed holiday bottle. Every night he drank two shots in a Belgian crystal glass over three half moons of ice. Before the surgeries, he had always taken the whiskey straight and let it linger on the tongue, inhaling through his mouth as he had seen connoisseurs do, savoring the finish, but the membrane scarring was too deep now, and he had learned to experience many of his pleasures in diluted form.

"Yeah, always trust a bourbon man." The cap scraped, and he could hear the swig and exaggerated exhalation.

"Now I've got to get something real out of all this, pop, some reward. Suppose you tell me where your billfold is and what else is important here, what might bring me some money. What do you and Mrs. Pop own that's expensive?"

Orin was beginning to get a fix on the accent. Not exactly the rich old Virginia cider with its diphthongs and hollow vowels, its murmuring trail-off of word endings, but more the lazy intonation of piedmont poverty, the furniture or textile mills from the Carolinas or Southside. Danville, maybe. He was trying to picture the man but could recall only a lean, fox-whiskered face and ball cap. Against his deep tan, the shirt was white as moonlight in the shadows of the living room. Orin was frightened but, he decided, calm. He might be able to identify the man in a line-up. He would probably recognize the voice. He took a deep breath. The worst part was having his back turned. Or having on nothing but the flimsy robe.

"My wallet's right there in the cubby on that counter. It's got about forty dollars and my VISA. The only really valuable item I own is my lap-top. You'll find that on the den desk, the room to the left. The printer is junk, but the computer is a Dell we've had just over a year."

Why that lie? It was a five-year old Dell Latitude, slow, idiosyncratic, but he wanted the man, Mickey, to think he had a bird in the hand. He thought of Mina leafing through renovation plans and scrolled documents in a high-ceilinged library with angels on the walls, or in a piazza café sampling white wine from a local vineyard. Pigeons swirled, their shadows elegant on the slate. Half a world away, she was safe.

"Yeah, this billfold's pretty slim pickings. What about jewelry. There's always jewelry. Classy woman that likes art? Always. Where is it?"

He was thinking about the gun again, and it made his pulse race, his voice crack a little.

"My wife has some things in a box in the other room. It looks like a doll house church, St. Paul's, but it's hollow. The roof comes off, and it has a few rings and necklaces from her family. Her father owned a trucking company, but he's dead now. He used to give her jewelry. She doesn't much care for anything but her watch." "And the solitaire engagement ring," he thought, but she never removed it.

"No need for you to get nervous, pop. Just keep looking out that window while I step in here and snag it." His irritation was amplified by the fact that Mickey seemed to view him as completely unthreatening.

Now he could hear the boards' tell-tale sound like a small bird's mating signal, and he could hear the wind shuffling through leaves that had not existed a month ago. Oak and hickory, of course, the two Bradford pears, wisteria twined into the deck rails, the Judas tree's perfect green hearts. The scanty Rome apple tree annually, unspectacularly, failed to render edible fruit but would not give up the ghost. Its petals were already giving way to green. He always worried about the honey locusts, too, which Mina called "trash trees." Volunteers that appeared right after they built the house, sweet-smelling locusts were the last to leaf, the first to suffer from the beetles that infested the whole Blue Ridge, summoned, the experts said, by acid rain and then the drought. He tried to keep his mind on the trees, their history, the dangers to them, but he kept seeing Mina's green eyes and the graying cascade of ash blonde hair she refused to color. At least she was safe from this. She was in Italy for two more weeks. As he stared at the waving leaves outside the window, the words filled him like a mantra—"safe, Italy, safe, Italy."

Then he heard the miniature church clunk on the table and pictured its intricate painted surface, the delicate windows and cornices, everything exactly to scale. A Christmas gift from him right before he was diagnosed. He didn't think she liked it very much, but she used it, went through the motions. Mina was an expert at the motions, the insulation of ritual.

"Hide the goodies in a church. I like that. Falwell, you know, that asshole." Mickey laughed with a surprisingly musical lilt, highly pitched, a sound milky and generous, out of keeping with the rasp of his speaking voice.

Now Orin could hear the jewelry scatter across the cherry tabletop. Delicate metal on a polished surface, something spinning, then wobbling to a halt. Before he retired, Orin had taught stories to thousands of high school students. All the good ones included details like that, and Hemingway was his favorite. The crisp sentences, the shaped silence, always contained and shadowed by the way desperate people talked, or people on the edge of desperation. The precise, understated verbs.

Now he wanted this scene to be over, to finish with a terse

sentence, a rhetorical question. He wanted to return to the neurotic barber and the irritating *New Yorker* writer's fashionable ennui. He would like to will Mickey into the ink, onto the page, into the barber's wintry world. People in their dens, in yard swings or commuter trains or the leatherette sofas in some doctor's waiting room all over the country could be reading about the man in the white shirt rifling the tabletop cathedral. Orin didn't care what they thought about it, the church or the jewelry or his betrayal and the scars it had left on the marriage. He wanted to feel safe and whole again, to look into the double-glazed sliding door and see only his own middle-aged reflection—out of condition, thoroughly gray and pale-skinned, but normal, purged of the renegade cells. A cancer patient just a year away from being promoted from "remission" to "survival," he wanted to be even safer than that. He wanted to turn the clock back to a better time.

That was when he realized he couldn't swallow. No surprise there, but he suddenly needed to. The radiation had damaged his salivary functions, and not even the doctors could grasp the discomfort. He could no longer afford to be more than ten feet from something liquid and had learned to accept the trendy ubiquity of that plastic bottle of expensive water. Evian, Breeze, Freshet. The old reliable Perrier didn't come in plastic, and besides, the carbonation didn't provide as much relief, though he'd settle for it now. He had left his glass outside, along with the NPR coffee mug, but now that he was breathing heavier, now that he was registering everything in minute detail, he needed it, and the urge to swallow began to consume him. He knew it was best not to attempt it without lubrication, for that would only amplify the urge and make his throat lining contract, dry membrane on dry membrane, guaranteed to irritate and probably to cause pain. He saw that he had squeezed the magazine in his hand until his knuckles whitened, but he could not feel it. The numbness in his extremities was still further collateral damage from the chemo.

"Mickey, I need your help."

"Tough."

"No, really. I, I've had throat cancer, and I have to moisten my throat constantly. You can tell by the way my voice is changing. I left my coffee outside, and I need some water. Could you run me some from the tap?"

Mickey laughed again. "What about a shot of this Black Jack. Put hair on your ass. Maybe even heal your throat."

"No, really, I just need water." He was breathing hard through his nose now and feeling the first stirrings of panic. If he proved trouble-some, he might get the knife, feel the shock of its force between his shoulders before he knew what was happening. Would the man be strong enough or accurate enough to make quick work of it? It might take experience or training. Or maybe Mickey would pull the blade across his throat with an assassin's ease and he'd feel the rip and the warm wetness rilling down his shirt. That would be the end, and it might be best, in some respects. But what about Mina? Would she come home and find him gnawed by animals, the carpet soaked with blood? His body could lie there for days. Their isolation was that complete. Even her return to a house festooned in yellow CRIME SCENE tape was too much to imagine. The thought of her having to sit with polite dignity through the various ceremonies of death troubled him. All the pretense that he had been an honorable and constant husband, that he had faced disease with courage and had not failed her through any fault of his own. But this was all melodrama.

Normally, he did not spend much energy on remorse; what was done was done. Now, however, he felt a surprising need for clarity, for forgiveness and release.

"You a smoker then, sport?"

Was there a taunt in that? Strangers always assumed tobacco was the culprit, and since the treatments, he'd displayed the lassitude and sallowness of someone who'd smoked longer than his constitution could bear.

"Never."

"So what happened?" The barely audible rattle said that Mickey was putting the rings and other trinkets into his pocket. The ruby flanked by glittering emeralds. The black cameo. Ten Chinese pearls, satiny as magnolia petals, which he still loved to see across Mina's throat. A handsome woman. Even young men said that. And the diamond earrings he called "The star danglers." The rest was thin white gold in braids, an onyx ring, an opal broach no one under seventy would actually wear. And these the man could have, for there was nothing that mattered he could really take from them. Everything important had been spent in carelessness and enmity. Denial, too, always the eroding denial. Distraction, with the facts still smoldering deep under the cold ash.

"Here."

He hadn't even heard Mickey open the tap or move across the carpet, but he saw the glass on the end table, the disk of wavering light the sun projected onto the dark woodgrain. Orin let the magazine drop to the floor and lifted the glass, drank deeply, like someone just in from garden work.

"Now I reckon you'll have to reach your hands behind you, pop."

In two minutes Mickey had wrapped Orin's wrists and ankles in duct tape. Orin had watched the shadow on the floor before him, the knife raised, then the wide circle of tape, like the symbolic paraphernalia of some ritual. The sound of ripping tape again.

"Shut your mouth now, tight."

He was bound and gagged on his armchair, immobile but still unharmed, his glasses gently placed on the table beside him.

"I'm going upstairs and have a look-see, then I'll come back and check on you before I call it a day. Don't mess around. Don't try to get loose. Just sit still and take it. This'll all be behind you before you know it. It'll be just like a little dream."

But the man did not go upstairs. Orin could hear the entryway floorboards, then the front doorknob twisting. He heard the suction as the gasketing released and the warped door opened, the steps on the treated boards, and that was it. The man was not upstairs but out of the house.

Orin realized that Mickey hadn't planned to search any further, once he got his hands on the jewelry. He had no interest in the computer, either. He just wanted to arrest Orin further with misinformation, to hold his victim in frightened thrall while he made his escape.

The tape over his mouth was the worst part, and it exaggerated his dryness, the Velcro–like closure of his tongue against his palate when he had no water. He hated this feeling of adhesion, of skin abrading where it was meant to touch smoothly, eased by saliva. This was the reason he seldom kissed Mina, his punishment from the treatments that had saved his life.

He would wait a few minutes, then hobble over to the kitchen, where the scissors would not be hard to reach. Then he would be free in a jiffy, but first, just in case, it was better to wait.

Outside the window, the fresh boughs were waving, and he could see the pendants of blossoms at the peak of the empress tree. Orin wondered how he would begin to tell Mina this story—the invasion and theft, his helplessness, his foxhole surge of religion— without seeming even less a man than before. However he told it, he hoped he could summon the nerve to embrace her, to caress her hair and face and say how grateful he was that she was safe, that she was back home. Such words didn't come easily, but he knew he had to manage, that he could. Then he would take a long drink of spring water from its cylinder of blue plastic, and he would tell her he loved her and had loved her from the time he saw her smiling radiantly in the college cafeteria. And he would kiss her, lingering the old way, trying to become whatever they both needed him to be, whatever was next, something vernal and remarkable, he hoped, something healed.

Carefully, he began to walk the chair toward the counter. "May Day," he thought. "Mayday."

# SINCE DOBY RAN

THE TREE CREW'S sweet work. Or was. Fresh threads, Red Wing boots, Igloo water close to hand, orange hard shell to keep your noggin safe from whatever falls or flies. Refreshed, protected, sweaty and convicted, we'd pay our debt to society, while the gun bulls leered and hovered, while the Free Folk traffic whipped by. All day on the edge where woods creep toward the blacktop we'd trim and hack and mulch. Saws buzz and the chipper chopper growls its steady riff. A man can shut his sorrow spigot off: sweet Lisa cold in the grave, her mama gone to dope, my own whiskey ways. It was on a road shoulder where my baby died, a fact I can't ever quite manage to unknow. Careless is everywhere, meanness a part of our nature, but on tree crew we found ways to sidetrack and pretend otherwise.

Mornings, Bingo will tenor out Hank ballads—his bucket's got a hole, lonesome whippoorwill, crawfish pie bidegumbo. Doby would croon about a Crescent City stripper called Praline. Fritter would shake his snake rattle bracelet. We'd slash and rip and heave in rhythm like a well-oiled machine. After all, it beats the purtee hell out of paving crew, the pea farm or laundry gang. Fry cook, either. Jesus wept! But out here where the altitude gets interesting, even summer isn't wholly Hell. On tree crew you pace yourself, catch the breeze, roll with the blows. "Ford low water, ferry deep." That was Doby's code.

After lunch old Steve and Fro sometimes hum gospel. We get our rhythm and whistle up or mimic Kenny Chesney, who is seriously cool. Then there's new hits like "I Came for the Party" we got off Rodeo's radio. That one's a hoot. With the right music, you can get used to a lot, and after a spell I wasn't even so leery of chase dogs caged in the bus and nervy. The time nearbout flies. Distance is true too, and we number our steps—arm's reach, pistol range, rifle—but what we really believe in is time. Marking time, passing time, doing time, though they won't ever give us the wristwatch time. Old sun climbs, rides across, sinks. That's all they say we need to know. That's how it was.

Six a crew, maybe seven, tough gloves and snake chaps, the bull captain swollen as a tick standing with his haunch side-jutted, his eyes hungry behind the silver shades, his pump gun butt-propped on his hip, barrel aiming at sky. Thinks he is the avenging angel. We call him that—"Angel." I don't know his Christian name. I'd like to hang a rebel flag on the barrel's blue shine. I'd love to pack the hole with gummy mud, pretend to sprint off and watch the fun. "Dream on," as Doby used to say. Time was, I would. Just a cub, just a Cajun boy with peach-down cheeks and a gruesome-looking crossed-Christ necklace, Doby knew the unwritten rules, the ruses and the scams. He was the book.

We're a gang of good Samaritans, you see, sun or rain or evil weather, out there whacking back redbuds and locust, the sumac and sweet pea that grow like green cancer up here on the Blue Ridge rim. Making the curves clean enough for John Vacation to spy runaway danger weaving cross-lane at him and the family van. Free Folks. They usually give a little wave or nod. It's from guilt. Everybody's done something wrong. Most have done crimes.

A sweet shift with good chatter out here, no matter what's go-ing down at the box. That was the rule back then. You leave your grudges behind the chain link and locks and let yourself just stare hard into the woods where the big oaks, sweetgums, white pines and tanglebrush all hold together too close for double-X buckshot to spit through. You let the sweat river down and ache in the arms and back, the whole while dreaming Jesus might turn Captain Angel just one blissful minute blind, so you could rip through there like a scatback, dart and juke, legs like hemi engine pistons, no lag, never slowing, never stop, dis-a-peer. The leaves close behind you. They take you in and make you part of the land. You're a green man now, the gray world left behind, and all the king's dogs and all his men can't get it together. They'll go crazy lost just looking. They'll never find a sign. That was what we said. It was just a dream you settled for, afraid to vision up birthday parties, weekly checks, chilled Miller, your skin on a woman's and no fences in sight. Free World.

We almost believed it—wish work, hope duty, every con's top hobby—till Doby ran. Then all bets were off. I want to blame Steam. I want to blame the Man. I wish I could turn the calendar back, but you try wishing in one hand, shitting in the other: see which fills up first. Nasties happen. You spend your energy smart; you adapt.

First light that Monday Steam woke up screaming. Some stealth fucker in the night had dabbed his dick in road stripe paint. He was reflective yellow, and it commencing to burn. Everybody heard the bellow—the kitchen, the warden's trustee, guard in his shoot shack up Hardrowtohoe Road.

Steam had played some ball himself back when and still pumped the pig iron hard. "WWF," he'd say. "Someday I'll be wrenching arms from sockets and smashing heads on your TV. Waving big money in your face. You wait." He was ripped and focused with blue ink of a screaming skull on his back. We thought he might.

"I'll kill the asshole" rang and rang through the barracks. I'd been eye-up for an hour listening to the plip-plop of a leak in the can, thinking of my little girl and tasting regret, but other cons were still nightsawing, their minds off with some Sheila or Bitsy or Keanna hard to catch as shadow women. We all went vertical quick, though, thinking murder, thinking hand count and shake-down and cavity search, our lockers tossed and shit by the gallon hitting the fan. The Smoke Camp sub-warden is a hard ass: Major Constantine. He's not our friend. We called him Abu-grab.

Steam was jumping around like a go-go. On the bunk next to mine, Doby muffled a laugh.

"Knees on the floor, hands behind your heads. I mean right fuck-ing now, scumsucks." The captain and his band of merry men were among us, ready to run amok, eager to club somebody behind the knee, pepper spray a sleepy felon in the eyes, drag some rule breaker to the iron maiden. C.O.s. They've got "Correction" on their minds alright, but rehabilitation is not part of the drill. The warden always has them pumped and ready, probably humping through the night shift on blackies, turn-arounds, any breed of speed. Storm rangers desperate not to be bored.

They had us all in prayer position in a jiffy, prodding with billies and swearing. They shoved and shouted like overseers, but you could smell their fear. "Fake alarm," said Felton, and waved two gorillas to handle Steam, who kept saying, "Fucker's gonna pay." They hustled him off for a hose-down and left the rest to settle and wonder. "Mustard Dick," somebody said, "Canary," but nobody was going to say it to Steam. We all figured some comedian was in for a blanket party when Steam and his posse got the pranker's name, but that was routine enough. Then we pulled on our caps and utilities, pissed in the trickle trough and herded off to break the fast.

Grits and biscuits, gut sausage, Eggbeater glop and bitter coffee, spoons scraping plates and the talk a dirty murmur. The feed room's a dangerous place. When Bingo leaned close to whisper something in my good ear, I hushed him quick. I didn't want to know. That's half my secret.

When Steam comes into the mess with screws gripping both elbows, he gives us all the look, daring a laugh, an eyeball, inviting a sign, but he doesn't wait for a give-away. You can hear a roach fart: that quiet. His glare lights on Doby like those laser pens hillbillies at the drive-in use to point at J Lo's crotch. The big hush was on, man, and we knew he had sussed out something that wasn't crossing his tongue. Nobody sipped his cup or spooned his grits. We knew there'd be Hell to pay. Sometimes a prank is worse than a punch. For days the Yard would be haunted ground, every bean break a valley of the shadow, tree crew tight as an E string. He kept giving Doby the hex glare, then scouring the room, and once in a while I noticed his eyes were locked on me. Birds of a feather, I guessed, peas in a pod. Sometimes it's safer to be the cheese: stand alone. I kept my shadow moving. I've got problems of my own.

Right off I'd drawn the bunk next to Doby's, and once he saw I wasn't political or humpty, he showed me the ropes in the bar house, the mess and shower parlor where any mistake can get serious. He was a thief, a handy-dandy and car snatch, two counts, in for six to ten, two down. I was assault, and it impressed him. Doby was the one who dubbed me Knucks because my knuckle cracking was noisy and so automatic I didn't notice. A nervous habit, I guess, but as a nickname, it was tolerable, and it stuck. Some night bull wanted to baptize Doby Scarecrow because of his crucifix, but it didn't last. He said his prayers every night at Lights, and he'd ask God to bring affliction on the guards, his lawyer and a certain judge. He'd close with, "Mighty is the hand of the Lord, Amen," and be asleep in a whiskey minute.

On the gang, sight lines are what our labor's bent to. A Free Folk survey crew out of Roanoke trailblazes on the shoulders and blue-flags the misbehaving branches and saplings blue. Full trees sometimes: VDOT's got something against forests or us, but those strip-of-sky ribbons just about make me smile because I love the way wind ruffs the hair behind my ears and the feel of a Poulin shaking my bones. A breeze will flutter the markers like satin in a girl's hair.

Steam is the motor man, keeps the bars tight but lubed and carries extra plugs. He drags the gas can and wears a tool belt and spends lots of little recesses in the shade of the bus adjusting and brushing and breaking engines down. He talks to little pistons, fuel lines and carbs in a whisper you have to pretend you don't overhear. It makes the hounds edgy. He's in for armed robbery and two counts of carrying concealed.

Overall, it's good work, a good rush. Who knows, I might've been born to this. It's power, you know, that chain round and round like treads on a tank but smaller, faster, sharper. I do savor the feel. And Doby was my best labor buddy. We swathed and cleared like a dynamic duo, a pair of Siamese lumberjacks. He showed me how to milk the throttle and keep my chain oiled and keen, how to swing a brush axe from my knees up and let the blade curved like a chicken hawk's beak do the work. "Just ride it," he'd say, "just ride the bird.

Leave the saws to skull man when you can." I knew there was history between him and Steam, but it didn't seem to include me. I didn't care to know.

The smell of fresh-cut wood has always been the perfect perfume to me. When I walk among Free Folks again some day, I want a woman named Laurel or Ash or Myrtle with a sweet dab back of each ear and between her tits of some special scent invented over in France and called Wild Apple, Sass Your Frass or Juniper. Juniper! It's all gin to me, and when I'm at full throttle, ears muffed and eyes behind the goggles, what I know is breath of the deep woods, root to roof, bark to heart. Angle in, let it rip. It's ache-work all right, and you crash into your bunk at Lights like a head-shot squirrel, but that perfume sap is beauty after the stink of piss and disinfectant, the shit they ladle out for chow, the quarts of sweat from "bastard malefactors" like us. Abu-grab's words. Damn his gray world. Those woods are the hideout you want to reach and settle in with the crickets and deer, spring seep, blackberries and cress and poke. It's a grocery if you know how, a Promised Land. Also a path back to those you love, if you've got some. Doby said it, too. Some could live there like a Tarzan. Maybe a place to shed your own spite and mischief, a place to get forgiveness.

The Bible says most folks live lives of desperate quiet. Not the tree crew. We make our own weather, our own steady song like old-time slaves. We swing and strut and keep the music live, and there's always and everywhere a murmur like the ocean, that low noise that says any minute a storm can rise up whirling, but out here, we drown it with the saw and chipper, gasoline, steel on steel, steel on timber, internal combustion scarring the dream way clear.

I expect our hard labor at a distance doesn't much differ from a crew of Free Folk trimming up a park or rich man's yard on contract. We keep our rhythm, and the bulls don't want hassle any more than us. Keep it easy, copacetic, sweet routine, no sign of the hopelessness, the incarceration blues, though it's always there, under the skin, under the breath, behind the lips, a cold cud we work on the sly. Still, I'd like to have seen us from the eye of a circling bird, not a buzzard but maybe some hawk more curious than hungry. I bet we looked orderly and moving to some music from a quiet choir. That's what I like to think. My daddy believed God's concert was in everything, but it didn't win him a happy life nor an easy death.

"Rake man," Angel trumpets. "Clear back, shithooks, the chipper's gonna spit."

Any halfwit could feel it, the taste of minor power, the juice, even when somebody was growling at us. That's how it was once, copacetic, the happy times, the old bliss minutes just flying by, but never again since that Wednesday when Doby ran from Steam with his rat tail file. I don't even like to remember what befell and then unfolded. I don't like looking over my shoulder and always wondering, "What next?"

It's not like I've got no private things of my own to confess or hide. At Big Lick Textiles I started as a line doffer and worked up toward foreman, but there was a Scotchman in my way, burley type with a foolish accent and eyes in the back of his head. A Christian Soldier, a Bible thumper who wouldn't let you lunch in peace. I had to work a little sabotage on his watch. I had to spread some rumor, but I was smooth so it couldn't trace to me. When the looms went wild and snarled a mile of silk wefting, the supers saw red and his ass was gone, deleted, just history with a pink slip. I only had to bide my time. It's a world of shit, and you might's well learn to swim it.

I won't say I was even close to getting over Lisa, how she was on the highway that night trying to wave down a ride. Where to? I get black headaches when I can't keep my mind off it. Stormy urges with no real purpose. The trucker dozed and rimmed the shoulder, said he never saw her, and the smokies swore his breath was sober. What was a ten-year-old girl child doing on highway eleven near midnight? That's what they asked me, the troopers in their drill sergeant hats. If I hadn't been deep into Master Jack at Elo's Catfish Cabin, I'd been at home where I ought to've, exercising responsibility, tucking her in and keeping the daddy vigil, but the law didn't have any crap to offer me. They talked neglect a while, but Milly Barnes next door had promised to look in. She spoke out and was tore up about it, so that all got dropped. Worst thing they could of done was give her back to Brenda, who's off the meth now, grapevine has it, but the child was dead, and that was it, no more custody questions to keep the lawyers sucking up my paycheck. Still, you don't necessarily let yourself off that easy. I took my deep vacation at Margueritaville, Jack-Daniels-by-the-Sea, which was everywhere I went. Whenever a hard question came up inside me, I took the fifth.

That started the pattern—binge and desist, the Wild Turkey and the cold turkey—but it wasn't working out. I couldn't find the focus, couldn't factor out why and what and wherefore. A man can't bear such setbacks, downright catastrophes, trying to forgive himself, and quick as a mink's prick I was slipping at work, fumbling, sleep-walking, fucking up royal, then demoted down to a wage weaver. You knew they'd stick me on graveyard shift, but that's when the union shop plotters can sneak off into corners—slack watch, drowsy hours, the goldbricks float and dawdle, and the shadows keep your secrets. There's all those stacked cloth bolts and broke down engines to hide your works or a short dog bottle. I hid my share, swigging on the sly. About dawn, still worn down from work, still trippy-tipsey, I'd drive up to the boat ramp on the bend of the James and weep like a colicky baby. I never did take her fishing once or in a motor boat. It beat me down for a while, but I'd been trying to get better a stitch or two at a time. Slow, though, real slow. Nights off, I'd drive over to Roanoke for some R-and-R, a little lowdown music and maybe a last beer up on Mill Mountain where the big neon star lights up different colors to report traffic disasters. I used to take her and her momma up there near Christmas to see the city sparkling like jewels. After, it got to be my reminder that I needed to heal. I was starting to show signs of mending, but I guess it couldn't hold.

Last fall when the pumpkins were turning, cobwebs stringing together the morning, leaf sugars sulling up and getting ready, I be damn if I didn't backslide whole cliché, a man with no new reason to fly off the handle, but there you have it. I was out to hustle nine-ball at Minnie's Mingle Shack outside Buchanan, but losing serious scratch to some Troutville raw bone in a Hokies cap, a cow farmer with a mean rack break and ace English on the snowball.

"Hey, Tex," the blonde in the corner called. I was wearing Western, shit-kickers to crimped Stetson, and I didn't know the woman from Julia Roberts or Reba McIntyre, but she was showing deep cleavage and giving me the come-hither eye, so I strutted over, wanting to slide my mind off the game, quit tossing good money after bad. I didn't slur out ten words before the cue cracked down over my shoulder, and that was that, down and dirty, gouge and throttle, the whole room flying around like a ride at the Devil's fair.

Somebody left a Red Rock longneck on a table just where my hand was thrashing. It was a sort of accident. Instinct, I guess. If you've got a free hand, an opposing thumb, you grab.

He recovered, just a concussion, but you'd think the way the prosecutor told it he'd been sweet Jesus and me the Roman spear sticker. He was just another agri-redneck, really, not so different from my own daddy, with trouble back at the farm. Turns out he had this new sneak girlfriend, the blondie, which must of made him touchy, and I didn't start it, but the world dizzies you, spins you off, and shit happens. You splash about till you get used to it. No bridge in sight, you swim. That's what I thought Doby was teaching me, kissing his crucifix and winking, saying "make do" and "fit in," promising "the Lord will provide. Mighty is the hand."

That's why tree work could always give me good distraction, and we were all in it together—Bingo, Steve, Trips, Steam, Skunk Trumpet and Doby, sometimes Fritter and Jude—keeping the pace easy, sharing the heavy duties, making jokes and japes, even on days when we had to sludge a shit ditch or saw knotwood, wrangle through the blackberry prickers, all that. We'd jibe each other, even Steam, about last night's dominoes or sweet-scent hurry-home letters, but keeping it light, copacetic, copacetic, steady-eddie, till the yellow dick trick and Steam made his move, and Doby ran.

They tell you when you process in some fool fresh fish will sass and get the blackjack and a lesson in shut up. Some antsy idiot on the road will rabbit, but he'll come back dog-gnawed or heavier by the weight of an aught-six slug. A quick study, I took it all to heart. They'd herd us up on a Sunday and let us watch Angel and Jackson hone their skills on our pop bottles, set them up so far off we could only guess they were still on the planet till we heard the shot and glass spattered. Dead soldiers then. I knew to keep my nose clean. I wanted to do straight time, earn my parole and get a life. I'd wised up. Anybody who dabbles in self punishment ought to try the coop. You'll learn: The world's got penalties enough without you pitching in.

Not to say I didn't weary from the get-go of shuffle lines in our Worst Western and bar forest right off, but I savvied just to take my place in line and make believe the bulls knew justice and holy truth. I didn't give eye contact in the Tunnel and tried not to think of clocks, calendars, the rattle of chain links. My own bees-wax, sole and only. That's how I got tree crew. A mild con, cold sober and not flinching from a challenge, but never drawing attention, a man on the edge and on nobody's list. "Yes sir, boss!" Even the pruno cock-tails they brewed up didn't have my number, not the Aryans nor the Jesus Brotherhood. I was a born loner thinking a private chalk line to nowhere, walking straight arrow. And I can still pull a shift. I'm able. I've pulp-wooded, picked apples and packed rigs for Thurston back when Brenda and me were still in harmony, Lisa just a smiling, shitting bundle of joy. I've always been able to shoulder my load. They saw it. The keepers. No sewing machine rehab, no laundry or machine shop or mandatory yoga and therapy shit required. I was tree crew material, and it was the wearying freedom I needed. But it's been a different planet since Doby ran.

The best part, I can testify, was always car women from the Free People. They flirt. Even the ones you scare will shoot their eyes sideways, and if you're the sign man in his hunter blaze vest, you speak into the talkie box's crackle like you're in charge and swivel the stick from STOP to SLOW. You nod and shoot her the short-timer smile. Just a second, though, no hard eyeballing, no lingering. And you can dress up a whole day on what you get back, meager and slight and shy or even sometimes the brazen "don't you wish?" in a risky one's eyes. Hell, I didn't have it much better when I was bitch-hitched to Brenda. On sign, I liked to push the talk-squawk and say, "Trips, coming your way, beaver alert. Get ready to get randy."

But it's hard to style and court and feel you're just a man in bad straits when you're in shackles and the posse is three screws to every crew, like lately, even the sleepy bus chauffeur weighed down with a Remington riot gun and sidearm. Now we cuss the work, we think of Mr. Copper Snake and can't rub on enough bug dope to unhinge the skeeters. We're walking on eggshells, trying not to hop. "Yes, Boss." "Quick as a jiffy, Boss." "That's gospel, Boss, that's scripture." And it's not always safe. A man whose sling blade whips through a yellowjacket nest ain't got a popsicle's chance in hell if he's shackled, and the old freedoms have melted like mist, the old pleasures. Or a wild driving tourist, mechanical failure, miscalculation. Even out here, shit happens. And we've been wearing heavy leg iron, all of us, since Doby bolted.

That Wednesday after the paint stunt Steam whispered to Doby as we were getting the quick frisk before trucking up, "You just slept your last night in Smoke Camp, motherfucker." I heard it and didn't want to puzzle out his meaning, but nobody would take it for a benediction. Everybody, like I say, was tight as a banjo string. We were headed back up the crooksnake road between Vesuvius and Montebello, everybody swaying as the tarmac hairpinned back and forth, our yellowjacket-striped bus rattling like a junk band. Sky overcast, a chill in the air for late spring. I was popping one knuckle after another. Through the chicken-wired windows I could see dog-woods in blossom, redbuds, once in a while a forsythia like a yellow firework in somebody's yard. I was trying not to think of Lisa, trying not to think of Steam who was slumped down in full menace in the back. He'd snarl at the dogs in their cage, and they'd snarl with him.

We were half way through the morning haul, starting the down-side toward lunch break. Skunk Trumpet was back in the sick shack with the heaves, Angel wool-gathering on the berm behind us,

Jackson taking point, walking with his pump gun across his shoulders like an ox yoke, followed by chubby Bingo hefting the bush axe for the few stout sumacs and other softwood. Mostly it was easy-breezy, no saws, just a line of men working the sling blades, the road quiet, the tools whistling as they cut through weeds. It was work that didn't need working, my favorite exercise, but it was warming up.

"Water, boss?" I hollered, but Jackson snapped back, "Not yet, shithook." My mouth had the droughty cotton feel, and I could see Steam up ahead, his shirt getting darker with sweat, a stain like some ink-blot test. He'd now and again steal a gander over his shoulder, looking past or through me, eyes lighting on Doby. A couple of times I heard him rasp, "I see you," and then maybe, "Dead meat."

We knew we'd be afternooning near Raphine, flat ground, some hard cutting through a bad laurel stand, and everybody was saving some. The bulls saw it, too.

"Quit sissying," called Angel, peering from under his pith helmet like Jungle Jim. "Put some grit into your wrists. I want to see them blades whipping. Fro, let's see you step it up. Act like you like it good as nookie."

I put a little more of my back into it. I'd been thinking about Brenda, though I try not to. Thinking about her and me at the beach just before Lisa was born. We were walking on the edge of the water, barefooted, her hair loose in the seawind, me swatting at the tide with a stick I'd picked up back in the dunes. We said we'd come back when the baby could appreciate it all. Switch-switch, switch. I picked up my pace and cut harder, thinking on how Brenda had turned weird when we moved to the highlands and put Lisa in care at the church, how I was worried she'd gone crazy before I found out it was crystal meth she was getting from another gal at the beauty shop she'd started cutting at. Switch-switch. I'd make believe I was slicing at her ankles.

We passed a stand of redbuds in full blossom, but I didn't give them a thought, I was so caught up in my mind. I could hear Bingo jabbering to Steam about contraband scams, skin art and rumors of a road gang from the women's facility working the eastern part of the state. Steam wasn't giving him so much as a nod. Then Steve drew even with the water, and I paused in all my attentions.

"Okay to take the drink, boss?"

Angel answered, "Quickly, pilgrim, quickly."

That was when I gave a three-sixty and saw how we'd made the bend and would almost double back as the road weaved uphill trying not to be steep. Given our spacing, I couldn't see the bee bus behind us, and by the time Doby reached the curve and then Jude, I wouldn't be able to see Angel at all, which would be a nice minute or so. The woods looked cool, too, dark green already, the first dogwoods showing white, which reminded me I'd have to bum some skins for roll-ups at lunch, but that would be later, after noon.

Snick, snick, the sharp blade turned the tall weeds short, made the wild shoulder look tame, and I took my strides, rounded the bend, moved on, Jackson the only bull in sight, and him a fair space ahead and unmindful, probably happy to be in the doze zone.

Just when Doby arced the curve behind me, blocked from Angel's view by an outcrop of poplars somebody'd have to level someday, Steam dropped his weeder and sprinted back, making a shout like an alarm, pulling the rattail file from his belt, passing Jude and Steve, then me before I could adjust to believing his violating intervals, breaking rank and charging. I was frozen still, like somebody in shock.

As he shot by me, Steam slung out with the file, and I tried to step back, but the pointy end cut my shirt and scratched my shoulder. Over I went, flat on my ass, and I turned my head in time to see Doby drop his blade and launch over the ditch, then rush into the trees like a man afire. Not a word, not a cry, just hotfooting like nobody's business.

Jackson was yelling, "Hey, you mother...," getting his big bulk in motion, pausing to point his gun at who-knows-what. Then he fired into the sky, and the penned dogs in the bus went nuts. I thought Steam wouldn't catch him, even if he cut the butter, but Steam just stopped sudden-like and grinning, wiped the file on his jeans and stuck it back into his belt, like nothing had happened, except he was pointing at the woods where Doby was thrashing fast.

That was when Angel's rifle rang out. I felt like the noise knocked a crack in the sky, but he didn't have a lane to aim. The bullet snicked through leaves and twigs, the dogwood petals shaking with the passage, but Doby was working serpentine. Angel jacked another round into the chamber, but there wasn't anything he could do. He turned to us with those silvery shades, something out of the "X Files."

Everybody else stood there, not wanting to seem a part of the whole scene, and then I heard Steam holler out to Angel, "I seen he was taking to run. I tried to get him to stop. Want me to get the dogs?"

It took too long, of course, to get us all back on the bus and uncage the hounds, Jackson now jabbering on the cell phone, Angel trying to hold Pluto and Goofy slow as they sniffed deeper into the woods, leashes taut as fence wire, till we couldn't see them. They had me on the front seat, Fritter splashing my cut with propyl, then giving me the compress to hold. They had cuffed Steam to the ring already, despite him arguing that he was just trying to stop an escape that would land us all in deep shit. Cutting me? He said it was an accident, that I jigged when he tried to jag by, but they weren't of a mind to make close distinctions.

"Rash," Jude was saying, "Rash rash rash," but Jackson said to shut up; he didn't want another peep. He was uncoiling the galley chain with its shackles, and as we passed them back, he said, "Clap these on an ankle, pissbrains." His gun went into its clamp, and he had the blackjack in his hand, ready to show who was boss.

For two days there was no road work, just shit chores around Smoke Camp, a lot of strange cars and badge-toters coming and going, everybody carrying ordnance like the Al Quaedas had landed. We kept our chatter down to a hush, but everybody had a theory. Ghost man, who was a pea farm hoer, said he believed Doby and Steam were in cahoots, but Steam lost his nerve. Fro allowed that Doby would make it, jump a freight heading for the Big Easy, where his connections could disappear him. Everybody tried to guess the terrain he'd headed into and what his prize would be when they grabbed him, if the slack-jaw dogs were much help, what they'd tack to his sentence, this-and-that. I tried to keep out of it, but the questions kept coming back to me.

"You his compadre, Knucks," said Steve. "You had to know he was going bushman. He'd of told you sure."

I said I was in the dark with them, but it looked to me like Steam was planning to waste Doby, and when Doby saw it, he did what comes natural. Abu-grab wasn't so easy convinced. They brought me into the wringer room with the two-way mirror, even into the visitor corral on Friday night with about fifty mounties and bulls and suits. They gave me up and down, but I played dumb and was pretty convincing. Every time they brought me back, Steam would pass my space on his way to the pisser and whisper, "Don't tell what you don't know, second string. There's more surprises yet coming." I could feel my neck tensing. I didn't like his smile.

Saturday was a stiff version of the usual—smokers and runners, swapshop, some shooting hoops, others building cabins and bi-planes and churches out of matches. Somebody reading a book on the press bench, two Soul Bros flexing and swaying their curls, the six Aryans planning to make a plan. I held my distance, kept staring at a funny book, cracking my joints, hoping not to be named some kind of accomplice. Then it commenced to rain. I spent the weekend in my rack, reading movie magazines and wondering if they'd snag him and if I'd ever know. I got offers of smokes and pop, books and stamps, pruno and even a little radio if I'd cough up, but I swore it just looked to me like Steam scared him, and he saw no hope but turning pioneer. I'd lie there and listen to the water rat-a-tap the roof and try to decide if Steam was smart as I reckoned.

My theory was simple. He never meant to touch Doby, never planned to step into the deep shit himself, but he knew he'd gotten under Doby's skin, into his heart. His threats were making an

impression, and if he could make a man scamper out of plain nightmare, that man would be truly fucked the minute he stepped out of
line. And he was counting on the Man and his dogs and his tools.
Like Fritter said, "You can't outrun no radio waves. Cellphone will
catch you sure as a lasso. Cell, you know." So if Steam was that
smart, if he was that toxic, what was next?

After a week passed and the parade of strangers fell off to a
trickle, and still no word, we commenced to handing fantasies
back and forth. Doby is nearly there, already got a cache-and-cash
from his brother in Bayou Teche. Or he's detoured to Memphis,
where the trains come and go regular as an assembly line. What's he
drinking now, Jack Daniels? Is he getting cheese grits with jumbo
shrimp? He's got a girl, somebody'd say. Not the wife he writes to,
but a secret second who sends coded things through his pals on
Pontchartrain.

Steam would walk by laughing. "They gone get that jackal. He
never get past Carolina. Keep a prayer they don't de-head him,
chop his feet or something." His posse was always following, taking
in the joke, saying we were stupid to dream. It seems like anytime
you get a good hope going, it's in the nature of the beast for people
to stamp it out.

Another week, almost summer. We'd see flag lilies blooming,
catalpas dropping their popcorn. Tree crew was working a stretch
near Steele's Tavern, doing some serious deforesting so the state's
Free Men could cut a ditch. It was cloudy. It was a Tuesday. Fro was
cussing under his breath about some letter, we were all hobbling
and sweating, the shackles still rubbing raw what was supposed to
get tough, all of us feeling in the chains like so many mongrel dogs.
It had grown normal for Steam to give me the eyeball in a way
that used to mean "let's mix, no mercy," but now he knew every
swinging dick was wary. He'd have a hard time pulling any kind of
stunt on the sly, and he'd already lost visiting privileges and phone
time over the "accident" of nicking me. The bulls watched him like
gut hawks, supposing he might have been in some deep conspiracy
with Doby or might have some other revenges in the works. They

shook him down regular and read his mail. Still no clue, but you can't stop basic meanness.

Most of the cons had their little pilot light burning: He made it, he beat it, he's Free. That was the word: They don't catch you in two-three weeks, you're rescued, you're at liberty. Common belief. I wanted to join in the quiet chorus, but I was too occupied not letting Steam see my back, not sleeping too sound, not showing an opening. Even Fro and Steve gave me a wide berth, Fritter and Bingo kept distance. Jude slipped me notes—"Keep moving," "All shit must pass"—but he did not cross my shadow in the yard. The isolation gave me chances to think how I should've done things different: with Lisa, maybe Brenda, my whole sorry story.

Angel sang out, "Water run. You, Knuckles, hop to." And when I dragged my shackles to the truck for the pitcher, he fished out his watch, silver as the lenses over his eyes, and popped its lid. That's when I saw the chain dangling, swinging back and forth like a pendulum, and at the end, catching sun so it glittered, was an agony crucifix I'd maybe seen before, the Christ writhing in miniature, his nails showing and the thorns big enough that you wouldn't want the thing pressed against you. It looked mighty close to Doby's luck charm.

So I thought I knew, and they weren't aiming to tell us, even give us a hint. Did they just catch him and shift him off to a steeper lock-up? He'd of made a big case out of the missing cross, if some-body just filched it. Did they dragnet him in the Quarter, find him through a snitch? He was gone, I was sure, probably under dirt somewhere, and when Angel saw me seeing, he grinned.

"What you looking at, Mr. Knucklebutt?"

"Not a thing, Boss. Spare the time?"

"Not in this life. Get your spit bucket moving." He knew I saw it, and the understanding was boring in me deeper. "Innocence" is pretty near a useless word.

So I rattled off and knew this was their new game: keep us guessing and almost knowing, keep us back on our heels and on our toes at once.

Soon it'll be a year for me, halfway to the cake, but I can forget good behavior. I can forget the old peace of doing my penance in a line of blades swinging easy and jokes and slack bulls while we stare into the green and think there's a path inviting, a gate that would swing open for a good man who'd made some mistakes but was coming around to righteous ways. It's come to a more savage time, and I don't understand it, but I have to forget the wind and bird music and the rhythm that used help me mend, and I have to be always on my toes, ready to jump, ready to duck and shuffle and evade anytime I can't see where Steam is lurking. I'm a man standing on the bullseye of a target. Just like everybody else; it's what they mean by "the human situation." I've got to swing my blade and put hope behind me since Doby ran into the shadows and brought the bitter change, but I've got hope, to believe in relief and trust in luck. Mighty is the hand of the Lord.

# WISHING

YOU WERE NOT SAFE anywhere: Della Moxley Medlock knew it to be so. The weather channel said it was ninety degrees up in New York City that minute, a quarter past midnight. Old folks were in danger of heat stroke, infants fevered in their cribs. Japan had floods and typhoons, while in Colorado, record-breaking wildfires raged. Locally, the corn silk was all a nasty brown and the cobs were ugly nubbins. The yard flowers leaned over, thirsty, even with the gleety dishwater splashed across them daily, and neither the leftover drips and dribbles of Coke nor the beer dregs thrown out on the brittle lawn perked it up. Above the air conditioner's straining breath, the cicadas jittered like sleigh bells, and the half moon beyond the double-glazed pane was red as a tomato.

Trying to ignore the throbbing ache in her face and the wooziness from the pain pill, Della let her eyes scan the luxurious mess of the bedroom, until they fell upon the snake tattooed across Cleve's arm, neck and shoulder. Flinching away, she noticed the Bride Starter Kit strewn across the dresser top around the clay face jug Dill Silver had presented to Cleve.

That afternoon Della had been to Tiffany's wedding to Ed Sleen—if a ten-minute civil ceremony qualified as a wedding—at the Justice of the Peace, and when the receptionist had presented the Courtesy Gift Package to the new bride, Della had blurted out before she even thought the words, "Hey, I didn't get one of those." Then she was blushing and explaining how she had said her vows in that same shabby office the year before and received nothing feminine on the spot but the bouquet of pitiful Dutch irises Cleve had bought at the Kroger. Her memories of the faux oriental carpet with peacocks, a perpetual motion desk toy and the autographed photo of a grinning Mark Warner on the wall had lingered more vividly than the gap-toothed magistrate or the ceremony's bland words. They'd had to recruit witnesses from traffic court, but the bailiff and reckless driver had applauded the symbolic kiss and beamed "Congratulations!" just like real guests, and that quiet approach had saved her from any misbehavior on her family's part.

Now she surveyed the meager contents of her belated gift pack: a sample box of Cheer, some off-brand toothpaste, powdered salad dressing, green Prell, Tampax and a whole sheaf of coupons. Why it should matter was a mystery, considering that Cleve, who had become a famous outsider artist, had already given her a closet full of expensive clothes and a violet six-cylinder Stanza with a wide white ribbon and bow on the hood.

Still, the sight of such piddling gifts wouldn't let her alone. Not even the recurring pain prevented her mind from wandering. Since her own wedding, every change in the world had been for the worse, and she felt she might have wasted her only chance for happiness when she turned down that Harrelson boy before he went off to seminary. Now she was seeing her future shrivel and topple as bleak as the parched garden.

Cleve was wasted again, sprawled on his back across the bed, the TV providing the only light in the room. It was just bright enough to gleam off the glaze of the face jug and the Budweiser bottles on the floor. All summer he'd said he was doing his conservation part by pissing off the porch instead of flushing, just running the beer through him. "The two-legged irrigation wonder" he styled himself. Only sixteen months since she married him, and already he was a disaster. Her daddy Autrey had said she was a ruination to everything she'd ever touched—party dresses, a five-speed bicycle, the pearl button Soprani accordion he'd given her, the used Toyota she had briefly driven to the college. Now the famous Cleve. But she knew for a fact he was just changing into himself, a bullying creature she could never even have imagined, much less created. Tonight, he had proved it.

When they first actually met, he was something else, just starting to taste celebrity. He had always been one to draw, his people said, and he'd kept it going even while selling footwear at Sears. He'd quick-sketched customers and spent his lunch hour inking in piney landscapes or sagging abandoned houses. It was when he got the squamus cancer and had to take chemo that he stopped rendering his portraits and deep country landscapes clean, started making big gauzy wings across every picture. Pretty soon he was lacing the wings like a wasp's or dragonfly's, or maybe adding intricate bird feathers as his own weight dropped and he began to resemble a shadow.

Della was relieved when he rolled over and she could no longer see the inked serpent, and she remembered how the paper had done a feature story where he claimed he saw everything with angels just whooshing by. "He's got courage," they said. "The strong will to live," and "touched by the spirit above." And as the artist had shrunk, the canvases expanded and took on the eerie amberish light that became his signature. Then came the letters, before there were even words, just little bursts of the alphabet worked into a princess tree's limbs or the woodgrain of a barn door. His mouth and radiated throat tissues were too sensitive for anything but dull food like cream soups, and while his appetite dropped and dropped, he kept working. That's what the story had said.

Then the local station's gal-everything interviewed him on "Down-Home Folks" and did a tour of his humongous studio that had once been a Woolworths. He was smiling and walked with a cane, "a man with a mission," the cheery reporter said, and the famous face jug potter Dill Silver from down in Rabun, Georgia was quoted: "Cleve Medlock is the most original, God-shocked artist in the south today." But if Mr. Silver was so set on God, Della wondered, why had he given Cleve that red demon-faced jug with the Satan stare? It sat there before the mirror, snaggled white teeth jutting from its snarl, goggle eyes, big yokel ears and two little spike buck horns. Its red glaze was the exact color of evil, of monstrous sin, and every time Cleve saw her shutter at it, he'd say, "It's a magic jug, Della. You just blow across the mouth hole real gentle and whisper your wish. You know the devil has the power to grant favors. Try it, even if you don't trust him. Make a wish. What can it hurt? Go on."

Then he'd laughed that broken laugh. Maybe Mr. Silver had seen something terrible behind the glowing talent.

Della had known of Cleve long before the media barrage, of course, had seen him playing baseball when they were at the high school. "Go Rattlers!" she'd holler from the stands. He was a star shortstop back then, reckless on the bases, sassy to runners, a golden glove. And the time she passed close by him at a church ice cream supper, he winked and said, "Hey, Sweet Cheeks." She'd blushed, while he kept walking, but she couldn't resist sneaking a look as the back of his tousled head merged with the crowd. He had a magnetism, an aura that made her heart rush in an unfamiliar fashion.

The next year she was in college over in Radford, dropping things, as usual, losing her keys, forgetting her clothes in the dryer, a loner but doing well enough in classes, reading up on Charlemagne and economics, that crazy Edgar Allan Poe. When she made the Dean's List, her father set down his Mexican beer long enough to say to her mother, "Olive, it's about time a Moxley showed them how smart we can be. Boy Howdy, our girl has found her niche." An instant later he spun around and snapped at Della about the outlet cover she'd cracked that morning. "I didn't see it," she said, meaning the strung-out vacuum cord, and ran back to her room crying, aware that not even the Dean's List could save her from being Bumbling Della, the big girl with sparkling red hair, good intentions and precious little grace. The object of everybody's scorn. The next winter she left school with just the associate degree and became a teacher's aide.

She winced when a wave of pain crossed her brow, and she squinted again at the TV.

As the light-colored black woman with the stormy hairdo swept her hand in a swirl around southside Virginia, Della recalled how elementary education had seemed to scoop her up. "It looks as if this low pressure center to the south is going to bring us little relief," the woman announced with no traceable accent. "We're still at zero for rain this month, and the governor is calling for disaster aid to help the beleaguered farmers."

The climate cam revealed a fogged-up satellite shot, then zoomed in on a parched field of soybeans—measling, wrinkled things. "I wouldn't say we need a miracle"—she was pinching up her face in a grin—"but these folks around Dixie could use some wet intervention in the worst way. We're keeping an eye on developing tropical storm Gustav, keeping our fingers crossed hard." She held up a hand with two long fingers twined.

"Goosed off?" Della wondered. Cleve adored this cable forecaster, whose name was Lanelle and who was a certified meteorologist. She looked tall, but you could never tell in front of that shiny map, because they never showed her standing around other people. Della chuckled, because an earlier report had said it was a good night to go out and watch the Persiads in the northeast sky. That, she believed, was what a meteorologist ought to be doing, studying up on meteors. Then Della snickered, recalling what she'd heard about there being no real geographical picture behind the weather people. They had to memorize where the maps would show up on the screen, because all the signs and symbols of the climate were virtual, projected for the home audience. That Lanelle woman in the foolishly short skirt and brassy earrings the size of fruit jar lids was actually standing in front of a screen as blank as a movie theater at high noon. If that didn't beat all.

The weather situation was not quite distracting Della from the pulsing current of pain. Rolling over to retrieve her ginger ale and bourbon, she felt a sharp pang where she knew the old bruise glowed under her T-shirt, right over the ribs. It was pretty typical: He'd pushed her into the side of the chiffarobe on Wednesday. Now the spot was a big island of colors darkening toward the center like an oil spill, painfully beautiful, but nobody else would see that one. It was as if the man had a sixth sense, even when he lost his temper, about what way to shove her, how to create those little accidents that fit in with her clumsy history and didn't signal abuse. Tonight, however, he'd gone whole hog. She uncapped the plastic bottle and downed another caplet. Two.

Hearing the sawmill of his snore rise a pitch, she looked over at his face, which was not in focus tonight and seemed to have changed into somebody else over the months as he drank the weight back on. The changes had been good at first, adding up to a gallows cheeriness. He'd gotten soft-spoken, too, and a little funny. When she'd seen him at the gallery opening just a year and a half ago, he'd made jokes about how his hair was coming back with the feel of crab grass and how his feet were so numb he couldn't remember whether or not he'd put on his fairy slippers. His toes, he joked, felt the green way they'd looked years ago in the Sears shoe department's x-ray machine. He'd shown some spunk in his light-hearted approach, and she had taken a shine to him. After all, why not? The papers said that collectors from all over the country were hungry to buy his paintings "Survivor Art," they called it—and the pictures had titles like "Pecan Tree No Seraph Now" and "Filly with Angelosis Mane," "Major Bovine Hosanna," "Halo Bullock."

He no longer looked like the Gitmo camp inmate from the TV news, but he smiled and said no thanks to the wine she offered at the gala reception: "My throat can't take it still. Those chemicals leave their mark. Good wine and cheap salad dressing feel like uncut home squeezings going down. I mean BURRRN!" He laughed and said he remembered her from that time at Adoration Baptist. "Home-made tutti-frutti," he'd said, "peaches and cream." Cameras flashed, and she smiled.

When Della was honest with herself, she knew she'd started hoping right then he might somehow be her ticket out of a sorry existence, a chance to see Richmond and D.C. and maybe New York. Hello to elegance and respectability, goodbye to raggy collards and her daddy's sour rebuke wearing away her heart like a tireless sandpaper. But that wasn't why she'd said "yes" in the end. In the midst of a whole county mired in what she called "hillbilly blandness," Cleve had personality and natural zip. He could make you believe the world wasn't standing still, but spinning in fascinating ways. She had never guessed what direction the spin might take, that it might become a tornado swirling her to destruction.

Now here he was, a famous loafer with satiny sweat suits, wrap-around sunglasses and a cell phone, assuring his Atlanta dealer every day that he had a new series of canvases stretched and blocked out with a dozen sketch pads ready to contribute the details. He'd spend hours diddling the Internet, working up his home page with tidbits of inspiring language and scanning in photographs of his early art. Then he'd drive his Montero down to the Hollow Log Lounge and buy beer for the other shiftless loungers. When he'd had almost enough, he'd come home and snatch the remote from her, click on the Weather Channel and say something like, "What's the forecast, sugarpie? Anything. I can handle it. I'm a fucking survivor."

The snake was the worst part. Fond memories of the baseball uniforms had recommended the idea to him, she was sure. Because the tumor had been in his neck, all that tissue along the jaw and under the chin around the surgery scar was nerve-dead to him. He'd had to switch to an electric razor because he couldn't feel sensations enough to know how much blade pressure he was applying. He'd drawn blood a couple of times, just a trickle seeping through the lather, when he figured he needed to give up the plastic Bics before he murdered himself. The buzzing Remington with its twisted cord must have let the inspiration break through, because he came up with the diamondback idea on his way out of the twin-sink master bath.

All that morning he'd danced around the house imitating Grandpa Jones' song "Here, Rattler, Here." Now the tattoo was coiled around his left arm, then over his shoulder with the arrow-point-looking head across the area of the incision. He'd been sure the needles wouldn't hurt him in the tender parts because he'd scarcely felt anything there since the surgery. He'd been wrong on that one, but OxyContin, he'd said, could work wonders. The way he was sprawled at the moment, Della couldn't really see it, but she knew it was over there, fangs bared, tongue forking out like a scarlet Y, gold eyes with a sparkle that looked alive. He'd drawn it up himself and persuaded another layabout—"Visionary Artists" they called themselves now—to work from his stencil. Snakes had filled his sketchbooks for weeks. Coiling snakes, s-shapes on rocks, tangles of them in deep viper nests. She had seen enough threatening reptiles to last a lifetime.

But that wasn't what got him famous. As he worked late into the night at his jumbo easel, the letters that appeared in fencerails and rhododendron blossoms had begun to arrange themselves in snaky cursive words, bits of scripture at first, then improvisations on the holy verses. The pinions and breast feathers of those crossing angels were made of word-scribble which could be read with a magnifying glass. They were like some radio preacher's raving, full of warnings and Hebrew names—Tophet and Shem and so on—but interrupted with stranger American words like "honeymilkswill," "petalshine," "serpent-frail bruise" and "Cherokeet commandments" repeated three or four times sideways, topsy-turvy, kittycorner, trilled out with extra letters and cryptic emblems. And the colors he swirled were just brilliant. He had stolen the sheeny look a crow's colors take on in slanting autumn sunlight. He had a theory that every swatch of black in the world was made of all colors. He believed that evil was made up of every sort of goodness, just overdosed till it couldn't sustain the good anymore. Museums in New York had started buying his work, and some oncologist organization he'd given a slide show for now planned to purchase enough of his paintings to hang in every waiting room their outfit had a hand in. If they only knew.

"Requiem of the moral spectrum." "The composition of sinful light." "Glory of Sheol's impasto." "Resurrection of the pastel." That was how he had talked when they began spending time together, and he'd get excited and show her huge art books, pointing out how the famous masters of history all agreed with him. She had found it all so hypnotic that she was willing to ignore the times he'd lost his temper over small things—tacky texture in a new tube of acrylics, the lawnmower cord that snapped, a waitress who was not peppy enough to suit him, brushes that shed their expensive hair into his eerie moonsets. She believed he might be a genius, so little things, minor maladjustments, were understandable. He had gazed

Death in the face, and he was still just starting to mend. She saw the same high-strung touchiness in the third graders she worked with, and she knew that artists had to cling to some of the child in themselves to keep away from the spoiling effect of society and business and the like, but it wasn't a pretty process. "Shut your pie hole," he'd say when a temper fit came over him. "Woman should only be seen." Sometimes he'd take a butcher knife to a finished picture, and Della had to leave the room.

Lanelle Weather was talking about a forest fire near the Parkway. It was ravaging parts of the Appalachian Trail, and the wilderness animals were scurrying like crazy, though many of the poor things could not outrace the blaze. Firefighters, she said with a sorrowful look on her face, kept running across whole patches of assorted bones where the many species had gathered, cornered by the common peril of encroaching flames. Smoke jumpers and men on the backfire line were in constant danger from poisonous snakes.

Della knew that look on the woman's face, though, and it was fake. She was sure it was taught at broadcast school, and most of the weather women had a version of it. Not so much the men, who tended to look puzzled when their scripts called for either a smile or a turn toward the serious. Della was worried the whole planet might combust.

She also knew that Cleve would be onto this bone thing quick as a terrier. He'd start planning to paint animal remains with apocalypse warnings in the shadowy streaks. He was all elaborate plans now, beer and schemes and a mean streak smoldering but always ready to blaze. She hated him. When she said it out loud, the syllables slurred and hovered: "I hate him." The pain in her cheek surged to confirm the three words hanging in the stale air.

This had not started as one of the worst nights, but his bringing home the life-size cardboard effigy of Dale Earnhardt Junior from the bar was a new low in childish mischief. The cut-out was outfitted in that red Budweiser jumpsuit and grinning like a possum out on bail.

"Here's the man, E-Two," Cleve had said, waltzing the cut-out around the livingroom. "I'm going to get them to commission me to paint his car. That will make my paintings the fastest things on mortal wheels."

Then he leaned his hero against the china cabinet and threw himself into the recliner. "Sweet Cheeks, it doesn't get much better. I should start putting the Winston Cup in my farmscapes, race fans in the tree bark, hubcap for the sun. Crack me another beer."

She knew he'd had this thing, this itch for the Earnhardt family's fame, when he started growing the little goat beard he called his "NASCAR extension." As far as she could tell, the car races were as monotonous as the weather channel or the O. J. chase from a few years back, but he'd get excited talking about all the art opportunities at racetracks—Danville, Talladega, Atlanta—and when he got in a heat, his blood would pump and his neck swell up, lending the snake emerging from under his collar an even more menacing profile. She'd seen a TV movie a spell back called "Slither." It was all about snakes that were not one whit afraid of people, and Cleve's pulsing neck reminded her of the special effects. She'd had nightmares.

"Get me a goddamned beer."

That was when she'd made her mistake. "That snake on you is a waste," she'd said, turning away, only half wanting him to hear, "because you're a snake your own self, a Satan snake." She'd been whispering, but then she whirled to face him and nearly spat it: "You've betrayed your whole art inspiration and become a greed machine fuelled on bottle beer. You're just faking it now, Cleve Medlock, you and your Junior Dale. You're pitiful."

What she remembered—lying still now with her ginger ale and vibrating pangs, while Lanelle explained how ancient people had seen drought as a punishment from the gods—was coming to on the floor of the dark, blurred living room. "The phrase "talk back to me!" still echoed in her head, and now above the courting insects she could hear a mockingbird outside like a self-starting juke box, and the "Local Weather on the Eights" theme was coming from the other room. All those mixed musics made her lie back down and think, "I'll get up directly, and everything will be fine."

It was only when she had tried to move that she realized how much her cheek bone just to the side of the left eye ached. Raising her fingers to test it for blood, she found there was a tender knot there the size of a Muskogee pecan. Making it to the kitchen, she'd put ice in a glass first, along with a dash of ginger ale and a glug of bourbon. His pain pills were sitting on the table, and she twisted the cap off and tossed one down, swallowing hard, feeling the tablet push through her throat. She could taste the mediciny dust, so she took another long swig, then pocketed the bottle and, wrapping a double handful of ice cubes in a dishcloth, held it to her swollen face as she sipped from the glass. Her lips and tongue could feel the dried lipstick on the rim, and she knew there were tears sliding down her cheeks, but she wasn't exactly angry yet, just bewildered at what made her blurt out such a face-on, asking-for-it thing when she knew full-well how dangerous he had become. Standing up, she felt the room begin to shift and shimmer in a way she didn't altogether dislike. "No," she thought, "no. I am angry."

When she reached the bedroom and found him asleep, Della had to work hard not to see herself in the mirror. She didn't think she could stand the sight of her damaged image, and then a wave of alarm shot through her, because there would be no way to hide this mark the next day. She couldn't let the children see it, nor Edna Doone, the teacher she worked with. Edna loose in the world was a pitiful thing, a bone-lean spinster with a face pitted as driftwood, but in the schoolroom, Miss Edna was the empress, and she bullied Della as much as she did the children. More than once she'd already remarked about Cleve's downslide, how he'd begun to lose respect from everybody but the loonies who thought art was just a sarcastic riddle. Cleve had snorted about old Edna and said, "Quit the place, Della. Suffer the little children. Walk away from the bitch. We surely don't need the money," but she needed something regular and useful to hold still in her mind. The children were her lifeline to the world.

Right now her greatest fear was that he'd stir from his stupor and get randy again. She had not minded the sex part at the beginning, as he had been tender and a little pitiful in the weakness brought on by all the medicinal shocks to his system, but as he had gained strength, his lovemaking had become more robust and, eventually, rough. Mostly, he'd been too soused to rouse lately, but the three or four times—no: It was four; she could remember—since the rattler had been hued in were horrible to her. She had to close her eyes not to see the snake throbbing above her, its eyes and fangs eager to penetrate something. This was not very different from the life of fear she had tried so hard to avoid, always hearing her father's voice in the background saying, "She ought to marry some tobacco farmer whose life can't be spoilt by clumsiness. If she ain't going to pay closer attention to this world, she might's well sweep a yard and milk a crippled cow."

She had to brush that voice away from her mind like a spider web. Tiffany Beale would have said to dial the police. She could almost hear it: "Get that blue-light special working for you, woman. Run that redneck paint man out of your life." But looking at the cheap samples and their purple plastic bag on the dresser, Della began to sob. A dizziness rose up through her, starting in the stomach and climbing to her head, as she lay back on the edge of the bed. Lanelle was chirping about fronts and pressure patterns behind her, and the TV light made the room want to swim.

That was when he rolled over, came back to earth, but she could hardly believe what she saw. Cleve still looked asleep, dead to the world, but what had rolled him over was his arm, or really, the thing on his arm. She was sure the snake was actually writhing and hissing on his bicep, its rattles down by his elbow making a shiver noise. "Hush," they said, "hush." When its tongue flicked across Cleve's neck and the eye gleam from its sockets intensified to pure fire, Della dropped her drink and brought her hand to her mouth to stop the scream. It couldn't be, but it was.

The room was foggy, but she was sure the pattern on the snake began to move and glow, to pulse like a winter star, and she could see in the gold and rust chriss-cross, letters were forming in a tiny cursive. And it made sense: Finally, the monster had taken him over. Cleve might already be filled with the poison; He might be dead and already swelling, for all she knew, but the snake itself was live, winding, its head shaped like the design on the ace of spades, its split tongue darting in and out. She knew it was trying to trance her, as its one word over and over was "whisper, whisper, whisper," merging with the dim choiring of cicadas outside, and she was afraid of swooning, of falling over in a spell till the snake crawled across the green sheets, slithered upon her and went for her jugular vein. She backed away, her hands behind her fumbling for something to wield.

It was the red face jug her fingers found close by, its rounded handle accepting her grasp, its weight in her hand something perfectly calculated, its surface gleaming in the flickery TV light. High above her head she raised it, while she finally looked the shimmering worm directly in the eye. Then she brought the demon face down with all the force she could render, and as the vessel struck the snake with a clonk, the sound that came out of her mouth was, "Whisper this!" Her arm rose and fell four times before the jug shattered, each stroke accompanied by her battle cry—"whisper! whisper!"—and when she regained her breath and her balance amid the shards of scarlet clay, the snake was limp and ripped open. Cleve himself was covered in blood, mangled and without life. It was as if he too had been glazed, and the words on the snake scales had returned to the body artist's needled inks, now meaningless and without menace.

Turning to the mirror, seeing herself bruised and bedraggled and out of focus, Della slowly lifted the complimentary comb from the skelter of items on the dresser. Her hand shook, and her whole body felt a chill like electricity.

"Oh, God, oh, God," she sobbed, but slowly her voice changed and took on force. "I have to fix myself so nobody will know," she said to her reflection, as the room went dark and tilted, but her voice was cracked like a broken windshield. The weather woman, meanwhile, was promising people in southeast Texas an overnight gully washer.

"I have been a bride, after all" thought Della. "I have to make myself presentable. Isn't that right, Cleve? Isn't it so?" Opening her make-up case, she looked back and forth from the mirror to Lanelle on the TV screen. If she could only get that stormy look into her own hair and hide the bruises with pancake, maybe no one would notice, and perhaps, while she was at work with the children, all the snakes of the past year would slink back to their caves and crannies, and everything would be better, clean and changed. What she would do with the body, she wasn't sure, but a capped well on her daddy's back acres had always seemed like her to be the entrance to Hell, but that…or something…could wait till morning.

Her hands were too unsteady to apply the eye liner evenly, and she gave that up. "Tomorrow," she said. "I wish tomorrow was already long gone."

Leaning closer into the mirror, she smiled and mimicked Lanelle's hand motion for a rapidly developing low pressure system. It was like old Vanna White's gesture toward a vowel on "Wheel." Maybe this was the perfect moment for another lovely pill.

"Later in the week," the weather woman said, "you ladies and gents better hunt down your umbrellas and galoshes. Once the Big Easy gets its drenching, the Greater South right on across the mountains can expect our prayers to be answered by what the Gulf is sending—just in the nick of time—buckets of precious rain."

# FLURRIES

As Kingsley Fishpaw rocked his chair on the edge of the forest, the creak of bent hickory on the platform's barnwood planks spurred the ostriches to pace their pen. Nearly seventy, a half-breed with thousands of miles on his engine, he was not ready to be old or weary, but he did want to be safe. The wicker seat beneath him, however, was rotting with weather, the boards of his raised sentry platform frayed and splintery. The sun paused briefly on the horizon, the pine spikes on Whidbey's Ridge an opal-blue with weather and distance. A few early dogwoods waved their petals in the wind. Thank goodness, he thought, no one comes to gawk at the birds. Someday, maybe, boys will come to spook them, or older peckerwoods to point and laugh, the world being full of mischief as it is, but not so far. Not this evening.

He sipped instant coffee from his thermos and ran his hand along a bristly cheek and jaw. Soon the deer would be moving, foraging for the early shoots and remnant mast, leaving their sharp marks in the mud. The moon would come up, and he could go home to supper and Big Dipper's "Easy Grass" program on the radio, but for the moment, the aroma of Sanka was pleasure enough.

Since spring he'd followed this trade savoring all the solitude he could wolf down in the open air while screened from the sun and wind by three full cedars. He liked having freedom to move about with nobody watching over. Weekly pay envelope, steady shelter, no intrusions. The easiest job, his poor mother had said, would be the last one, and he wondered if that stage had finally arrived.

Afternoons he fed the creatures, watching them beak up the greens and dog food, their heads like war clubs with a jutting pike point like he had seen in the *Geographic*. Iroquois carried those. The black males with rude plumage, the females colored like cowbirds.

They tended to drink funny, staring at the sky while the water runs down that long neck. Bald-looking. They could run fast as foxes, and their kind do not actually bury their noggins in the sand. O'Donnell tried to fill him in: African origin, kin to emu, omnivorous and so on. He didn't care. When did you feed them? How much water? What if one gets out? O'Donnell claimed they were the largest living birds, and King asked if that meant there were other species that got larger when they died. Bloat, maybe. He chuckled. These were already about seven feet, he reckoned. Almost two dozen. The weak wings were like some creation joke, or just obsolete. Either way, just embellishment now. He'd grown tolerant of their squabbles and haughtiness, but he bore them no affection.

What he savored was the quiet. Birdcall, a farm dog in the distance, cows lowing back in the pasture, pleading "moon, moon." At night there were wild canines in the hills, but his own shift ended around dusk. Part-time. The main responsibility was to keep them fed and watered and contained. Not wrangling, just keeping watch. At night, it seemed, they turned calmer, more content to nest, and the Stevens boy keeping the sheep safe from canine raiders of all sorts would patrol them steadily when he finished up his other chores.

Backward and forward in the ladderback rocker, like a small boat moored against a slow tide. Pulse-rate, lulled. He remembered the old jobs, ran through them daily, calling up the pictures and smells. Just this afternoon, thoughts of Lisel, a blue-eyed German girl, would not leave him alone.

He had been a pin boy in khaki coveralls where the lumbermen came to bowl duckpins and unwind. "Kingbird," they finally called him, but at first it had been "King Breed." He shared the work with Elvin, and they would alternate smoke breaks on a busted mattress behind the alley. You had to be nimble. Those woodjacks would roll the muskmelon-sized balls at you when they got a snoot full. He was shaving then, not a small boy, and he knew how to glare at a man dangerously. The fishhook scar on his brow and the dark skin made him look like a fighter, and his nickname sounded like it was won in a ring. Nobody grabbed or swatted him like they did Elvin. They poked some rude fun and moved on.

In the Ty-D Laundromat Lisel could stuff all the front loading machines, switch them on and slip out to stroll in the moonlight. First time, they talked about the timber company and the Peavey Grill. The second time she passed him smoking in the dark, his cigarette like a firefly beside the bricks. She twirled about and approached him, then said, "Fishpaw, you know you like me, do your duty." Then she was kissing him, and he was helping. Before long her pale breasts were visible, the olivewood cross swinging back and forth as the two of them swayed together. He could hear the rumble of bowls down the waxed wood, the clamor of pins scrambling. In the corner of his eye, white suds gurgled from the Ty-D's drains like some mechanical variation on snow.

Maybe that was what brought her back now, the rhythm of his rocker like sex after the suddenness passed. She was the dangerous one, and when he left the next summer to sell hardware in Silva, she swore to kill him. For a year she sent letters, general delivery, but after the first one, he never opened another. It had said, "King, there will always be women and women, but they can't all bury you. Just one. Lisel." She was one of the world's complications he was glad to have behind him.

The cock ostrich brayed and stamped. He had an old Winchester lever-action, and he had the power to free the world of this odd thing that made gargoyle noises and looked like a Martian. "Click-and-clack," it said like the rocker, like cranking a shell in. Who would eat such flesh? But tourists did at the Southern Grill, paid plenty. He figured it would be string meat, a bark taste. The feathers went in women's hats once, but now they were to decorate your guest room. He could shoot it and stop the racket, but then he'd have to find another job, slip off by night. He'd done that enough times already, and what other boss would let him whittle, his shavings like pale fiddlehead ferns spilling on the ground? Who else would let him cup a grass blade and call out to crows and sparrows across the green evening, all on the clock, the pleasure all twined up with making a wage?

The worst job had been chopping cotton, fifty years back. He'd tried peanuts, but the crop went bad early from a slack farmer's fertilizer misstep, too much nitrogen, so there he was, middle Georgia, a world of dust and the local cotton coming up. He hoed till his back nearly broke and blisters covered his hands. When he rode the wagon to the gin, he saw white men wave pistols at each other over money. The Thirties, hard times. Because crackers down there believed he was a Negro, he settled into Darktown, just an orphan boy himself by then, or so he reckoned. In the workers' shacks he tried his first frail at the banjo and saw he had a knack for it. Walking the pastures, he liked most of all to watch the egrets picking bugs off the backs of cattle. Sunlight sparked on the Chattahoochee River. Seeing no other prospects, he stayed for winter, helping mend things, learning to drive a nail straight without bending it or scaring it silly with near misses while he bashed and damaged the wood. He had gloves and a swollen thumb, but before long he was able to take pride in the unbent steel and nickel. The morning it snowed down there—people said first time in ten years—the children hid under the bed, afraid it was some new brand of winter cotton they'd have to pick.

When he went back to the highlands near Rabun Gap, his brother Spatch took him to the alley. "Duckpins," Spatch said. "You just set 'em up and set 'em up and set 'em up. Roll them balls back down the runnel. Keep moving. This here's Elvin. You watch what he does."

When a bluebird from nowhere darted in and perched in the service tree, King shook free of the reverie and wondered what the bird had to be shy about. He had plenty of reasons himself. At the Bristow furniture plant up in Carolina he'd first met Taddy O'Donnell. King had been thirty, "unskilled," as the foreman and bosses in string ties called him. It was a loud, brash place, bad with shellac fumes, and it eventually took two of his fingers. That was where he had his first dance with John Law after a fight at the

Fiddling Fool Club. Trouble will follow a half-breed, but Taddy had bailed him out.

Working wood. Skill saws and band saws, the blades always singing their war song. Men from the spraying room came out with their breather masks and goggles on, splattered and coughing, worse than the picture show's space monsters. He learned the draw knife and stain mixing, saw the wood dust spray out like snow in the wake of a roadplow. From across the room it was a flurry, a sweet scent, but up close, just so much grit-shot. It could choke you. It could blind you. One day at a time, it could make your death.

Even now he despised the grind and whine of a triple drum sander, its pitch a fierce yearning like a sequence of harrier hawks. He also hated the boring machine and the glue made of fish-meat and horses. It was a prison camp for misfits who lived in shabby bungalows and rusting trailers. The routine of running the template and jigsaw, template and jigsaw, working the kiln-dried wood down to lazy curls, had been enough to drive any man crazy. It had snatched at him, a bent saw blade wobbling off center, and taken two fingers at the joint, like a tax it was owed. When he got back to work, his stubs stiff and tender, they put him on the lathe, no place for a cripple, but he'd managed well enough, learning how to turn a sweet spindle before they side-moted him to security guard, adjusting his banjo picking until it was a weird hammer-claw, comfortable, simple and strange.

It pleased him now to scan about and know O'Donnell had no plans for these trees around the pen other than to stovewood the blowdowns. No Early American dinettes or Great Northwest bedposts. Maybe another shelter in summer when the eggs came, just a lean-to requiring no major felling. The leaves could just keep budding and curling open, blazing and browning and floating down to the understory according to the natural scheme of things.

Thinking back on those years interfered with his peace. He would have rolled a smoke to calm himself, if he hadn't taken to wheezing a few years back. The doctor said tobacco would kill him. Now he reached down into the pocket of his denim coat for comfort and rubbed the porcelain door knob, feeling the hairline crack like tiny lightning. It wasn't a habit to start with, but more practical, the only way to keep his cabin private. He just twirled out the side screw and plugged the knob in when he came home, dropped it into his coat pocket when he ventured out. Sometimes he'd think he had forgotten to remove it and had to push his mangled hand in to make sure the knob was there. His palm found relief in the cool, polished thing, and he often imagined the shallow crack that ran across it was similar to the lifeline in his palm. Just touching it made the calm of his new life seem more real.

Somewhere behind him, a limb snapped, but when he turned, nothing was visible. Jumpy, he thought. Just another hour. Just the wind.

The only trouble at this place had set in with O'Donnell's other hired man, Victor. Raising the pens, the foreman had caught him hiding some wire snips, and in his cabin behind the milk barn they'd found other tools and some silver knickknacks Taddy's wife thought she'd misplaced. King wasn't in the picture then, had settled, he thought, in the back of the community shelter. A broom closet, really, and what he did was sweep up, clean the toilets and lock the doors every evening. It was a good place, but not free from disturbance. He had a bunk and a radio playing old time tunes, a library card and his Silvertone with a splint on the cracked neck. He could still strum up a few.

He washed his teeth in the big sink and bathed in the basketball showers. If it was like living in a cell, it was a welcome one, almost a sanctuary. Not easy street for a man in his sixties, but better than death or "managed care," he figured. Vigor still ran in him, and he liked to stroll about, get into things with his hands, carve a bird or cow out of softwood.

Of course, it wasn't that simple. Victor was an old rival from Bristow, somebody Taddy and King had known before Taddy's daddy left him the farm. King had pilgrimed about for two decades, had a wife and lost her. No offspring, which was lucky, considering his uncertain economics. Then he was back, stumbling onto Taddy at the Food Lion just after Victor's stealing episode.

"Come on out," his old friend had said. "We've got the renovated blacksmith cabin and need a man for some daylight hours. The birds are my great experiment."

And why not? Taddy was the cheery red-headed sort with a kind streak, and King could always get to his funny bone. "What about the talking gander?" he'd still ask, just to re-hear the story, just to have the laugh. "And the salesman and the Swiss farmer's daughter...andyouroladytoo." They both took a drink, but nothing to excess, and they were matched for working together, though the Irishman was ten years younger. Or had been matched. Now Taddy's boy did the real work, and the boss had his hobbies—wine grapes, the CB station, flat-picking an old Gibson, and now the ostrich scheme. Most days Kingsley didn't even see him.

The real trouble at Bristow, King reasoned, had started with pranking. Victor used to like yanking on his chain and whispering "redskin" just barely in hearing range, just to get his goat. "Breed. Hey, breed." A bunch of them would take their sack lunches to the canteen—Hawk (shipping), Preach from the rub room, Cleatus Moonrobin, a full-blood Chippawa who hailed from up north and was a finisher; Tayshan in spray. Victor had the sharp tongue, the smart mouth from the sanding room. The wood flour had worked into his skin so intimate he was oaky.

"Didn't you do some chiefin, wear feathers up in Cherokee and pose for the gawkers? Didn't you play one of the bare-ass savage avengers in that 'Unto These Hills?' I believe I saw you once when I was up on vacation."

"Never been to that one," King would answer. He didn't even know for sure what tribe he was. His father's side, and he'd not known the man.

"Wadn't the Kingfisher some darkie in a TV mystic knights club?" asked Preach.

"You mean Boston Blackie?"

"Naw. Some smoothie city Knee-grow." And some of them would laugh uncomfortably as King finished his pineapple and peanut butter sandwich. Then he'd open that hawkbill knife and concentrate on whittling a remnant. Looking back, he no longer wondered if they saw it as a threat: He knew they believed he was brandishing, a warning to navigate the conversation in some other direction. That was just fine. The banter swirled and dipped, repetitious, tireless, with Victor the engine of its predictable rhythms.

Once the sander asked if his name was a secret clan or society, "Fishpaw, agile, like a raccoon using his paws to corral trout?" King didn't know.

"I'm a loner. I'm not a raccoon, not so much nocturnal by nature. I like to see what I'm catching." Then the knife again, whicking a chair scrap to a point, harmless but emphatic, the ominous sound of sharp steel moving. Usually Victor's voice would back off and Preach would presto his mouthharp from nowhere to treat them to a golliwog song or "Oh, Shenandoah."

Friday nights they took the whole act to Stroud's fish camp where Ester Jean was the target of jibes. She gave back as good as she got, usually carrying a pot of scorching coffee, just in case. She sort of liked Cleatus, though King walked her once to the fire tower when the rhodies were in blossom and filled with bees. A hot day, and she shucked off her shirt, the braids tapping on her shoulders. King had to walk behind, but he saw enough, knew by the time they pried that lock on the ranger hut that he was going to get the high ride people whispered about. Unlike the others, he never told, but Victor eventually sensed it, saw the lack of teasing when she brought more hushpuppies, crispy and hot with cane sugar taming the cornmeal and onions.

They'd been enemies since Victor caught on. The man didn't say it, but King knew. When the company moved him to night watchman, he suspected Victor of some of the petty vandalism—spray paint, missing drink crates, a jimmied outbuilding. No real evidence though, and since King wasn't around for lunch, they passed from each other's sphere.

Evidently hunting season pretty much occupied Victor's thoughts and spare time. He was caught up in his archery feats and the tail end of a rookie cashier at Biner's. He had a new audience, new victims. Within a year, King had gotten restless and moved on.

Now he was thinking of his cabin at dinnertime, door bolted, the glow around the stove door, hen eggs splattered on the griddle, the briney ham hissing in the skillet like a varnish sprayer. He liked the sharp smell from marrow in the center ring of bone. The biscuits would rise golden, the ham fat crisp out. It was a deluxe daydream, but no ostrich eggs. He'd heard they were strong and gamey, likely to show a thread or two of blood. No, let the birds raise their kind and eat their salad and gruel. When he got home, he'd pitch in kindling and fry himself a treat he could savor with nobody to meddle in his pleasure.

Suddenly, as much as he wanted to be wrong, he realized something was really moving behind the stand of laurels. The wind was riffling the new blossoms of dogwoods. This was his favorite part of spring—the redbuds signaling Easter, the forsythia bushes around O'Donnell's house gone hysterical with yellow. But something was lurking, creeping, holding close to cover. Then he heard, as if his memory had called up a ghost, Victor's voice with its unmistakable edge.

"Fishpaw! Redskin! It's over for you. I've got you surrounded."

Nothing he knew about the ex-marine was promising. He was pretty much your standard-issue bully who used words like throwing stones but could not always be depended upon to back down when openly defied or thwarted. And now, evidently, a thief, caught and expelled several months ago, replaced by an old enemy. Victor was a man who might feel he had to avenge himself against somebody, and Taddy, who had fired him, was probably too settled, too prominent and respected to be the target. Maybe this was no more than a braggart's ruse. But King knew he was himself no more than just a half-breed, a transient who had sort of stayed. He was not protected, would not be much missed in the event of trouble, and there had been a few stints—brief ones, misunderstandings—in custody when he'd been young. He couldn't bear too much scrutiny.

Last year's dry leaves rustled again. Just barely, but he knew that Victor's claim to manly reputation was outdooring. He'd brought trophies and snapshots to work and told how many other men coveted his accomplishments. Canoes, 'sang and galax gathering were his specialties, bass fishing, hunting. The bow was his boasted weapon, and he had liked, years back, to describe the way the razored broadheads went in, breaking bone and chewing up the vitals, dooming the target animal.

"You can kiss them stupid birds goodbye, Fishpaw. I'll show you all who's the king."

An arrow zipped past him and stood trembling in the nearest cedar. It was aluminum, and it caught the light. King leaned over for the rifle and swept it up, moving at a pace he thought was pretty fast toward the shed with tools, water jugs and Purina sacks filling its shadows.

"Victor, you don't want to do this." Holding the weapon, he let his right arm swivel in the socket, his stiffened wrist like a cam shaft, then back. The bullet eased into the chamber with a sweet click, the whole lethal machinery in sync. The hammer had cocked, showing its bantam profile, and he was ready, but he had never before fired this rifle.

When Victor called out, "You ain't safe," King could hear the spirits in his voice, probably blended whiskey, some cheap stuff you could get by the jug. Even on beer, the man could be a belligerent drunk, but this was beyond guessing. "What next?" King wondered, but just then another arrow passed overhead, whispering through the evergreens, lodging nowhere. The words that formed in his mind were, "What is he planning?"

But that wasn't quite it, either.

"I don't know that I want you dead, breed, but I want you gone, and I mean to barbecue me some of that dodo meat before I light out. We got to figure a way to work this, you and me." The hyena laugh that followed was no guarantee that Victor was to be trusted about anything, and King felt his recent promises under fire: He had told Taddy he'd look after the birds, he had said he was up to it. He had not said he was fearful. He had not said he'd abandon them if things got stormy.

"Not joking you, breed, not pranking you. I can pick off them goofies with my eyes closed."

But his eyes probably weren't closed, as the next arrow thwacked into the huge body of a hen, which voiced an ungodly squawk and fell dead in a spray of its own blood. The shaft appeared to have kept going, perhaps in search of another easy victim, and King could imagine a scene of complete carnage, depending on how many arrows Victor had brought. He thought six or eight was normal for a bow quiver, but there was no way to guess it, and he knew he would have to act, would have to use the rifle. He swiped sweat off his forehead, and he knew his shirt was wet. Would a warning shot solve anything? Maybe with a sober man, but this was different. Warning was not what he needed to do.

When King pivoted around the corner to get a look, he shouted, "Victor Westy, how many arrows you got there?"

The responding "Nuff" gave him an idea where the voice was located, right at the north edge of the stinkbush stand, just under a cloud of dogwood flowers, some of the petals ready to flurry down. What King meant to do was to shoot close, use the whole element of surprise, since his attacker didn't seem to know about the rifle. If he got close, showed any hint of proficiency, even a fool like Victor was likely to turn tail. That was why he aimed high, but he had not counted on the drunk rising to run for another vantage, had not intended to even approach hitting the man. Neither had he expected the birds to stampede.

Everything went fast, like a whirlwind. The bow made a spanging noise as Victor flung it outward to grab his head. The arrow went off toward the meadow as the archer howled like a sledged calf. The noise the birds made as the herd broke through the rails was ghastly, so many angry ghosts, and they caught King stepping free of his shelter, terrified that he had killed Victor.

He took a minute to understand he'd been trampled, that the bushy bodies of his livestock had rushed out in full panic, pumping their tinker toy legs, leaving him mouth-down in the dust, feathers all over him, their footprints on his jacket, and of course, they had shat as they ran. The air was putrid with the smell of it. His good hand was grasping a glop. It was on his cords and jacket and gumming his tied-back hair. But the worst part, as he stood up and inventoried his bones and functions, was knowing he'd just killed another human being. Memories of lock-step marching and shake-downs, the cells and shackles and clammy grime of animal despair shook him. He breathed hard and trembled as he ran.

Maybe, he thought later, he had been lucky, but he couldn't say for certain if it was good or bad. Thrashing through the bramble, he heard the moaning, and as he stood on the small bluff above where Victor had fallen, there was blood everywhere. Victor's windbreaker had been a spruce green but now it was slick with red. Blood was all over his jeans and brogans, but he was lashing and kicking out with too much energy to be mortally hit.

When King got his tormenter still enough to examine, he was astonished to see the snaggle of flesh where the ear had been, but under the blood, which was now covering King's neckerchief, it looked like somebody had just snatched it off, cauterizing the remnant shreds. Victor's face was contorted like a face jug.

"Oh, God, I'm killed, goddamit. Damn it, damn it, you black Indian." That was pretty much his wail, and Kingsley could hear the riddled muffler of the Stevens boy's Chevy truck as it bounced over the pasture terraces. Maybe the shot had actually brought Jimmy, who was due to relieve Fishpaw soon. The most astonishing sight before King's eyes was the clutch of ostriches, now calm and looking merely puzzled, clustering in the field and allowing themselves to be truck-herded back toward the pen, as if the muffler noise were the day's only distressing feature.

By the time the pick-up rolled to a stop where King was sitting back in his chair with the Winchester across his knees, Victor had disappeared over the ridge, and a frosty wind riffled the leaves behind him.

"What the hell was all that noise? I thought I heard gunshots and people screaming."

"Rustlers, podner." His breathing was almost even again.

"What?"

"Ostrich rustlers. Redskins. A whole war party of them with bows and paint and shit."

"I reckon shit is right, seeing what's all over you. How many birds did they take?"

"Looks like you've rescued most. One's dead with an arrow in it. When you get the others rounded into the corral, we'll drag the casualty into the truckbed to show Taddy. I guess it's time that bird came to dinner." He was pointing to the single downed animal, which made the boy blink in confusion.

Wheeling back to the round-up work at hand, Jimmy said, "Looks like a little snow tonight, maybe the last of the year," then under his breath, "But rustlers?"

The bluebird lit again at the heart of the service tree, his azure chest flickering in the sunlight's last rays as he preened, a blue pilot light keeping the faith, keeping life steady. King ran his palm across a whiskery jaw, poured the last of the instant and rocked on, breathing the savory steam.

"Savage avenger," he thought and smiled as his hand slipped into the denim pocket where it found the doorknob's soothing contours and cool seam.

4

# CORRESPONDENCES

"NEVER KILLED NOBODY, never raped, never molested a child—everything else, I done." When I read that sentence, I should have torn up Dink's first letter and filed it in the woodstove, but I was more curious than cautious, so I kept reading. Much of the text that followed was, I figured, intended to flatter me. In the prison library Dink had read a small article about my trip to Mobile to lecture on the camp life of Civil War enlisted men—from cush to banjos, busthaid whiskey to prayer meetings. The article mentioned that I had written books and that I taught American history at Auburn. The little professional information included was all he needed to seek me out.

According to his letter, Dink was impressed with my interests and credentials and wanted both advice and assistance, the latter consisting of a roll of stamps and "any old used books you don't keep reading." He was desperate to become a writer, to account for his life and times on paper, and deep in the maze of Breedlove Correctional Center, he had plenty of time to devote to the project.

His life story, he said, was pretty simple. When his daddy died in a construction accident, he'd fallen in with a bad crowd in Columbus, Georgia near where he was reared. Youthful indiscretion had given way to criminal intent, followed by detention and its predictable inconveniences. "I learned the way of life in stir," he wrote, "and it made my path thornier. Reform always seemed a dream just out of reach."

Fraud was his specialty—bad checks, improvisational swindles, grab-and-go, obituary Bibles, all the time-honored scams. Because either his skill or his luck didn't quite equal his ambitions, he developed an unfortunate reputation among the Peach State authorities, so he drifted west a few miles, across the Chattahochee and into Alabama, where the Central Time Zone offered the promise of a new life, which differed from his old life primarily in the matter of penal facilities. Two years before, after a brief spell constructing oyster poorboys, groping a night shift waitress with the unlikely name of Morva and siphoning cash steadily from the till, Dink had landed in Breedlove with a sentence of ten straight Ace Hardware calendars bearing HARD TIME stamped across every square. It was, evidently, enough to turn him literary.

And I was easily drawn in. Tired of Auburn fraternity boys destined to ease into their fathers' cattle or equipment or soybean businesses through the accounting department and no more intrigued by the Forget-Hell unreconstructed rebels in my Civil War courses, I thought it an altogether good and lovely thing to correspond with someone who was actually thirsty to learn but whose wildness was not channeled into the safe and forgivable exercises of naughty privilege.

It took me a while to realize that I had bitten into some carefully constructed bait, but even then, the cost seemed small. Every month I'd pack up a box of paperback novels and history books I would never open again and books of travel and adventure gleaned from Yearout's Used Book Arcade. I'd package the precious stamps separately, post them from the History Department and await the next chapter of Dink's epistolary meander, which was not exactly a triumph of style.

What it lacked in polish, however, the narrative made up for in surprise and urgency. One episode chronicled sleepless nights listening to the cold rasp of metal on stone as his cellmate Neville fashioned a shiv, while another recalled the summer he worked on a poultry farm. That engagement ended when he took exception to an unappealing edge in his employer's voice and began pelting the man—all tricked out in a crisp seersucker suit and panama hat—with the bloody heads of Rhode Island Reds he'd dispatched that morning.

Dink had indulged in one wife, now lap-dancing in Anniston, had sired no offspring he was aware of, had picked both cotton and peanuts for wages by day and everything from corn and watermelons to suckling Yorkshires and yard gnomes by moonlight. He had driven a pulpwood truck for pay but "borrowed" it for a beer run, had carded in a textile mill where he ran a football pool, had tended, snipped, dried and sold a patch of marijuana planted by someone whose agricultural ambitions had been abandoned or interrupted. He had been a framer and a memory book salesman, a cobbler's assistant and for one gloriously lucrative fall a train brakeman who looked the other way when the still operators slipped their cases of stumpwater into the caboose under the conductor's supervising eye. Anybody could see from his unfolding vita how all his attempts at legitimate enterprise led to backsliding into crime. Unable to imagine that any of his honest jobs provided much reward, relaxation or amusement, I sympathized.

Unfortunately for him, Dink believed he was particularly good with words, especially what he called "sweet talk," which meant casting sentences over women like nets, all with intent to swindle. Waitresses, shop girls, seamers and doffers, phone operators, desk clerks and dedicated vodka drinkers were among the sort who seemed easy prey for him. "Seemed like I was a magnet," he said, and they all wanted to give him something, though he often wound up taking something they had not offered. In one case it was a newish ("plum-colored," he said) Plymouth station wagon. The victim's name was Ruth, and she had a purse pistol, which Dink learned about only from its alarming report as he sped away without headlights in a spattering rain. "Not smart to fuck with Annie Oakley," he wrote.

But what right did I have to scoff at his way with words? I was concerned about Dink, afraid that the hardships of prison might prove too arduous for his uneven vision of the world as a place where sport and pleasure routinely outweighed any threat of punishment. I encouraged him to keep getting his history down, to accumulate pages, rough as they were, and plan to worry about refining the details and structure only after he had accumulated a hefty draft. I would help him, I promised. I would be his mentor, donate my time, edit and correct and suggest. In short, I consented to collaborate, but what drew me into this frequently tedious and not altogether rewarding or respectable labor? What was the bait I snapped at? His words.

I'd grown up with boys in LaGrange who had followed the path of least resistance that lured Dink, boys who shared his appetites and deficiencies, his need for immediate gratification coupled with a belief in the Big Score that would justify all the petty failures. Boys like Jeff Cude and Ricky Rabbitt who had taught me to smoke and swear and fight, while showing me how much better at these things they'd always be. There was even Dynamite Lafferty, a reckless halfback who won a scholarship to UGA just to be nabbed for housebreaking on Christmas night of his sophomore year.

I won't say I was doing penance or evening up some theoretical tab by corresponding with Dink Giles, but I did keep saying to myself, "That could be me. Two wrong left turns and a spell of bad luck, and I could be serving up scorched beans and cornbread while looking over my shoulder or exhausted from laundry work and too terrified to sleep nights in some altogether disagreeable state facility. It doesn't take too much imagination to see how easily one life—a respectable, soft and satisfying one, especially—could veer downhill and tumble into disaster. After all, entropy thrives, gravity pulls us. All fall down.

Dink's correspondence gradually took on a more familiar tone. I went from "Professor Lail" to "Jared" and then to "Buddy," each set of revelations earning him a little more intimacy, each month's pages more thorough about his needs in prison and what sorts of items he was allowed to receive. I found myself buying cigarettes by the carton for the first time in my life. I sent instant coffee, magazines, cassette tapes of country western music and pouches of soup mix. In return, I received the envelopes with a long number and ALABAMA CORRECTIONAL in lieu of a return address.

In addition to his scrawled history, I accumulated recipes for kitchen brew, a glued matchstick coaster, drawings of tattoos Dink had seen or given or wore himself (the angel with a pig's head was his favorite), not to mention explanations of how Farragut should have attacked Mobile Bay or what course would have allowed Stonewall to turn the tide at Sharpsburg. Dink grew especially fond of ridiculing the follies of Burnside, Hooker, Bragg and Johnston, and it slowly became apparent to me, as I filed the penciled letters on institutional stationery in my equally institutional metal cabinet, that he must be somehow following my scholarly work. I wasn't sending it to him, but he was finding it. That was when the cartoon lightbulb first snapped on and I realized I had no way of knowing how many exchanges were bringing the outside world into Dink's cell, allowing him to stockpile the currency of information and offering him the opportunity to both vent and explore. Perhaps even to exploit.

But such realizations didn't deter me. I was too convinced of the essential value and harmlessness of my charitable "hobby." And I felt completely safe. I marked my papers, counseled my students, pursued my research, courted an adjunct English instructor, played a little softball and regaled my friends with critiques of films I'd seen, exaggerations of fish I'd hauled in and occasionally, at the tail-end of a party or after a slow Sunday bull session with Guinness and onion rings, I would segue into one of Dink's more vivid escapades. I'd say, "Let me tell you a story. This happened to a friend of mine. He's in jail."

The one I savored most was a hunting story. Poaching, really, and it held a mysterious allure for me, like watching a winter sunset that lingers and shimmers, though it's too cold for any sane person to be outside soaking it in. Maybe "savored" isn't exactly accurate.

It was autumn. Dink had ridden a Greyhound to Marion, North Carolina, where Sutter Boggs had said he'd find easy work at a plant making and assembling surgical tubing and IV drip bags for hospitals. Dink had been eking out a living cleaning two private drinking clubs after hours in Chesnee, and nothing native to the drab South Carolina shins of the Appalachians was urging him to stay. He wanted to see the leaves gild up and burn and squander themselves in the high mountain woods. He wanted to feel the sharp air and witness some of the famous highlands splendor, so he went.

The job in question wasn't the worst he'd had, and the production line was so laid back, they virtually sleepwalked through the night shift. He quickly acquired the knack of fitting the leads into the pouches and affixing the clips and drip nozzles, checking for kinks in the tubing and mis-matched seams. He liked the soothing music over the intercom, and for once, he didn't meet anybody he hated right away.

One of the real benefits was living with Sut in a trailer located outside of town, down a winding road flanked by rhododendrons and lady slippers, which were still blooming orange as the maple leaves charged their sugars and a light frost rimmed them. He thought he might settle for such a life. Access to a car, weekends off, much of daylight available for a sparse sleeper like himself to wander about. No temptations in plain sight. He just might behave and settle.

One morning, ambling about on the Shortout Mountain Trail just above the Linville River, alert but still a little hazy-eyed from work, Dink peered down into the gorge where the current was breaking white around the river rocks, and there he saw a big buck, antlers like a hat rack bowing down as it drank from a backwash pool. "I could kill that bastard and eat it," thought Dink. "I haven't shot a deer since I was a boy running bitch redbones with my daddy." He was sure Sutter would let him hang the head in the trailer, and they could freeze what they didn't consume right off or throw a party. He could invite Wilda, the Cherokee girl with a yellow dress under her work smock. He had never rubbed his necessities against an Indian, but he had always meant to.

What he needed was a weapon, and he wasn't to be thwarted by parole regulations. Maybe it was this optimistic resourcefulness that induced me to identify with Dink. I wanted to believe that I, too, could muster my aptitudes toward my ambitions and get what I wanted, though I was far more committed to the basic social conventions than my shadowy proxy. I felt my chances of making a success in life were, in fact, increased if people with disrespect for rules were locked up, but in this case, I thought I had found an exception. I was glad Dink's frustration was only temporary. I would launch into the story with renewed animation.

Sutter didn't own a gun himself. He was just six months off parole, carefully sustaining the habits he'd developed under supervision, and he didn't want a firearm around. But at Meditek, Arnold Doppler said he owned a decrepit Parker two-hole, a .20 gauge his father had given him decades back. When Dink quickly invented a farmer who, he claimed, had offered him the right to hunt his land and then had just as quickly alluded to a current N.C. game license, Arnold offered use of the piece, as well as a few shells, in exchange for Dink helping him tear down and haul off an old muscadine arbor that was producing nothing anymore but discontented wasps. So Dink swapped a Saturday's work for loan of the Parker and began scouting the lower Linville for scat and rub marks.

Work nights were tedious but easy, and Dink's thoughts continued to circle back to a noble-looking trophy head, laughter and comfort as solid friends shared plates of smoked venison. The maples flared and rusted, the oak leaves showed a mustardy color, and the mercury dropped far enough that Dink had to buy a patched jacket at the Goodwill shop.

Then his morning came. Official hunting season was still two weeks off, though some bow shooters were in the woods, but Dink in camo green and blaze orange was ranging about in a national forest where the whitetails were permitted to roam about unmolested, as yet unalerted to their peril by kill-happy Nimrods. This was back before deer became the infestation and hazard they are today, yet telling me the story, Dink swore he already knew they would outnumber their food sources before long. He claimed to be a conservation pioneer. In my role as raconteur, I took his stance.

The fog wraiths were still creeping out of the river that morning, floating up and conferring upon the Linville a mystic, postcard quality, as Dink moved slowly, awkwardly through deadfall and difficult underbrush. The sweet stench of early leaf rot clung to the air, and he had already scratched up his hands fending off prickers and sticks. Under the spell of my embellishments, I could almost believe I'd been there.

After a frustrating hour, he stopped to smoke a damp Marlboro, then continued through the woods, breathing hard. Emerging from a deadfall tangle of old larches and new growth redbuds, Dink looked upriver, then down, and flipped his cigarette into a pool. The rushing water was loud enough to override his stumbling climb over the logs and his labored breath, so the downstream, downwind buck nibbling a sparkling green moss didn't register the man whose features were probably obscured by the dandelioned sun behind him.

The river there was rocky and treacherous. Patches of fog rose and drifted. In the peeling and leafless sycamores no birds sang. Then Dink saw his dream beast and, winded as he was, swung his barrels up, but the deer, instead of bolting, swiveled his neck toward Dink and blinked its eyes, seeming merely curious.

More startled than his target, Dink shot the deer in the face. Then panic cut in, and the buck turned, flagged his scut, stumbled, then scrambled along the bank, headed downstream where the shores flared out and the silvery surface no longer revealed rocks. It was aiming to cross, but before it could enter the water, the deer tripped, with Dink clumsily in avid pursuit, screaming to the animal to "get his deer ass self back here." When the deer fell, Dink fired his other shell, this time hitting a hind leg where it hinged. The deer rose slowly, limped two steps and collided with the massive root ball of a fallen hickory the river had rubbed smooth. That was when Dink realized that his first shot had blinded the animal. He began to laugh, but when he reached into his jacket pocket for his two other shells, they were gone, jostled out in the chase.

Going by smell no doubt—the familiarity of the river's odor, the sound of the water's voice, the threatening scent closing in from behind—the deer plunged in. Dink could hear it snorting that eerie, angry sound they make and was sure he smelled the creature's fear.

When the whitetail leaped for the current, it didn't jump high or far enough but succeeded only in reaching the snarled limbs hanging over the water. The original, skeletal branches had snagged driftwood from the river, forming an intricate snare. And while Dink stood on shore, stomping his foot and damning everything he could lay his tongue to over the lost ammunition, he slowly realized that his prize was tangled by its antlers, caught, thrashing madly and bellowing, desperate to break free and enter the current's rush.

Mouthing something like, "I be damn if you'll get shed of me that easy," the would-be hunter ran to the downed tree and teetered out to the end, where the tiring buck still flailed in the natural snare. At first the man tried swinging down the shotgun like a ballbat onto the deer's bloody skull, but he lost his balance and tipped into the cold water. With the waves slapping at their faces, the deer and man hung there, one trying to break free, the man holding a snag with one hand while swinging his awkward bludgeon with the other. The antlers fended the gun stock off, and a couple of times a point would gouge at Dink's hand or arm. The water was shallow enough for both man and deer to gain momentary purchase with paddling legs, but then the current and their own thrashing would throw them off balance and submerge them again.

They formed a desperate tableau with the water's roar nearly choking, drowning out the animal's bleating deathsong and the man's angry shouts, and just as the weary deer forced a final bellowing thrash with its muzzle and gave up, inhaling the water till its muscles went slack, Dink managed to break one of the brittle boughs, so they floated free, the bloody and disfigured face of the deer and its seven-pronged antlers shining above the surface now, the man straining to hold one of the animal's ears but feeling his down jacket grow steadily heavier. He sputtered as he paddled toward shore, but he could hear the water speeding up, could barely make out the narrows they were headed for. Even though he knew he might not make it, might go under, and with angry tears streaming down his face, he refused to release his prize, even as the current ducked and stung him. He damned the sky once more as the waves renewed their force and jerked the ear free of his grip. Then he gave all his energy to survival, stroked with all his might and reached the bank just as the cold water pitched the dead animal into the rapids, twisting and breaking its limbs.

"Laying there," he wrote, "I couldn't hardly get the air in me. I was crouched up, fetal-like like an unborn and sucking at wind. Then I just let my whole self crumble up and roll, sprawled-like on my back. I shut my eyes hard, but I wasn't shivering, just clenched with spite, drooling cold muddy water. The sun was behind some pines, splintery, when a flock of weird birds come swirling down in a big wing-rush. I watched them settle on black limbs where leaves used to be. They was squawking, but their noise kind of blended into one voice. I thought they might be grackle birds, cause there was a lot of shiny colors in their black feathers, and I felt like I had for just a spell stepped away from the earth and could see things clearly for once.

"The giant bird voice was telling me to let the deer alone, let it all go, to try to make my way in this world without doing so much damn harm. Then they all flapped up and whirled away like a dark plan.

"I laid there a minute and got hold of my breath. I thought about what they'd advised me and the wonder that I was able to understand them at all. I hadn't ever had no experience like that, and the leaves in the trees and blue air said that what the birds said was true, but when I could get up, I scrabbled my way down along the bank, around the rapids and a dogleg of smoother flow, looking for where the Linville River had put my trophy deer. I wanted whatever I could get of it because it was mine by right of the hunt and because I just wanted it, birds or no birds. Who cares about birds? I didn't find it, though, and the lost Parker, that was the start of another passel of trouble. It wasn't long before I was back in deep shit, but for just a minute, still heaving breath, I was happy enough to be living and looking into that river bright as a silver knife."

That was the story I told people. It was the knot all the strands of Dink were snarled up in, and I couldn't let it go, as the enigma of his moment of clarity coupled with a stubborn desire to have the deer in spite of nature's admonishment seemed like the key to why I was so compelled toward him. The deer episode, every time I told it, drew me to the threshold of the numinous and something I wanted to understand about myself, but I could never cross over, no matter how sympathetically or carefully I rendered the story's details. The whole time I corresponded with Dink, I never successfully articulated why this one episode retained its hypnotic hold on me.

I executed all the duties of a history professor, kept my social life nourished enough so it wouldn't quite die, but kept thinking I needed a new venue, a chance to exchange ideas with some more accomplished or dedicated students. I needed, as we say in academe, a lateral move before I was tenured and promoted into comfort, which almost always leads to inertia and discontent. I burned the midnight oil, exercised my interlibrary loan privileges and cranked out two articles, one about Horseshoe Bend, the other on Confederate policies at Andersonville. I polished my vita and monitored the job market as closely as a broker.

After almost a year, the dispatches from lock-down had tapered off, became less disclosing, less like exercises toward an autobiography. I remember one letter in which Dink bemoaned the rumor that he was to be moved to a work camp. Up in the governor's mansion, His Majesty Fob the First had decided that the sight of chaingangs sweating at roadside would provide the final ingredient in the state's recipe for crime prevention. Dink feared the blistering sun and the demands of the sling blade, but most of all, he mourned the loss of Mobile and the smell of the nearby ocean. "You never can understand," he wrote, "how beautiful and amazing a gull can be till you catch it just for an instant gliding across the little bitty patch of sky you can see every day through your window bars. It gets to be everything you hope for." He was often capable of that shock, that beauty-struck moment of awe, and the unpredictability of it was part of his allure.

That appeal, however, shrank suddenly when, after nearly five months of silence, Dink wrote to say the parole board had consented to interview him, and he needed someone to write a high-sounding official letter saying how much progress he'd made toward rehabilitation, someone to sit in a white room with what he called "the council of free world assholes" and say all the necessary things. Would I be that person? His pen-pal girlfriends had both refused outright, and a Pentecostal preacher who usually kept in touch was dealing excuses from the bottom of the deck. This request, which seemed to blaze up from the cheap stationery, was the first letter from Breedlove that had been delivered to my home address.

Suddenly, the mystic bond unwound. I knew I was involved in a con, but I didn't even know who the mark was—me for allowing the seedy attractions of a scoundrel to hypnotize me, or him for believing I was off balance enough to actually risk something for a stranger I had every earthly reason to believe was essentially destructive. One thing was certain, I wasn't operating from any invisible sanctuary, as I had previously believed. I had to get more distance from this, resist the suddenly-inconvenient attractions of the correspondence, or things might change for me more dramatically than I had ever been willing to imagine.

I replied that I was getting interviewed myself, looking for another job, one that would rescue me from the numbing frontier of Alababa, as I often called the state. "As you'll remember," I wrote, "I've been trying to get out of here for a couple of years." Of course, he couldn't remember what I'd never confided, but I was hoping this claim of discontentment would lay the foundation for my evasion strategy: I couldn't be a sponsor; I was escaping myself.

If we didn't live in the era of answering machine buffers and routine filtering by those devices to protect us from people we yearn to avoid, I don't know what would have happened when he called. Sitting there on a Wednesday evening, drinking a Sam Adams as I ceased attending to Letitia Warren's hagiography of Jeff Davis to listen to Dink's matter-of-fact reminder of who he was, I felt ashamed. The man was incarcerated, denied access to all the things that make life wonderful and satisfying, even bearable, and I might be the one person who could turn the key. A college professor and solid citizen, an effective speaker and writer, a man who knew the twisted history of Dink's unfortunate slide away from the straight and narrow, I could be his rescuer. I knew how much bad luck, an unsavory environment and simple miscalculation had deepened his crimes. I could argue for mercy under the circumstances. I could make the case.

But I did not pick up the phone. I leaned my recliner away from the pool of lamp light and listened to his plea. It was understated, calm and careful. He guaranteed that we wouldn't have to tell a soul that I would be leaving the state soon; it wouldn't matter, old Buddy; nobody would ask. "Just stick around long enough to spring me. You owe me that."

I had expected his voice to be coarse and raspy, strained from smoking and harsh homebrew, twangy with central Georgia, but it wasn't. It was soft and hypnotic, like fingers caressing silk, but not without a thread of malice. I did not pick up the phone.

By coincidence, I developed another telephone irritation about that time. Hearing from friends that my occasional companion Joan was "seeing" one of her colleagues, I had announced an abrupt end to our long-term, low-octane affair, and in a fit of pique I could only see as exaggerated, she launched out at me with a storm of unforgettable language. Since she was the one who had violated all our half-whispered, half-earnest vows, I was bewildered that she would claim the moral high ground and begin flinging hard words. After I left her apartment, refusing to subject myself to further insults and threats, Joan began calling my house and office, each time leaving either a charged silence or a furious and obscene message. Any ring of the telephone became an alarm.

Unsure of my rights in such a situation, I consulted a lawyer, who wrote Joan a letter suggesting that the phone company would be very interested in the tapes from my answering machine and that on my behalf he would, however regretfully, pursue all legal avenues to insure my peace and privacy. The abusive calls ended, but the hang-ups continued, interspersed with a few messages from Dink:

"Let me hear from you, Jared" or "Here's a number where you can leave a message for me" or the more effective "I know you can help me out," always cajoling and controlled.

Whenever my phone rang, I flinched. When I came home to find the red light blinking, I'd take a deep, weary breath. Even when the tape was blank, I couldn't be sure if the non-message was from a telemarketer, a scorned woman or an inmate whose rap sheet was long as an adult copperhead and whose patience was growing thin. An inmate with a history of holding onto grudges until he could even the score.

By spring, however, the anonymous calls had pretty much ceased, and I was busy with pre-interview jitters. I was desperate for a change. One women's college in Virginia and an even more prestigious private school in North Carolina had invited me to visit the campuses to consider my fitness for their history departments and their appropriateness for my own half-focused aspirations and needs. I was moving ahead, concentrating on both my professional future and the thought of escape from a socio-political Sargasso that had kept me bored or depressed or both for half a decade. I was even able to view my apprehensions over Dink's and Joan's calls with a self-admonishing laugh. It all looked from my new and optimistic perspective like small change, really, the coincidence of two brief, unstable shadows crossing my life. I admitted to myself that maybe I had toyed with both my telephone antagonists, that I was guilty of dabbling and thoughtlessness. I promised myself I'd be less reckless, mind my own business, not meddle with those whose lives I was not committed to. And I forgave my sins and miscalculations. I had erred, but I was capable of better.

A couple of weeks after I accepted the job at Hollins and began to attend to the details of moving, as well as proofs for my new book on Confederate medicine and prosthetics, I found a letter in my office mail with the red ALABAMA CORRECTIONAL stamp in its northwest corner smeared almost beyond legibility. I didn't have to distinguish the words to know what it was.

Walking the hall back to my office, I felt chilled and sweaty at once. I remember looking out the window at the dogwoods on the quad as a gust of wind shook down a flurry of petals. But the deep breath I took seemed, almost immediately, unnecessary. Dink's letter was as chipper and unthreatening as anybody could want. He was working in the commissary and taking a pottery class. There would be a poetry writing workshop in the summer, and he might sign up. He had a reefer buddy who kept him supplied, and he had been in no trouble for months. Dink was especially enthusiastic about joining an "anti-gang" started up by the "strong hearts" who didn't want to be in a gang, so there was, he said, none of the "brother-hood bullshit." They just looked after each other. No reference to parole or the chronicle of his life, no griping about the facilities or the treacherous nature of the screws. Not one mention of the phone calls. The whole missive was as inoffensive and matter-of-fact as a letter home from camp. He seemed exceptionally proud that he had learned to shape elegant pinch pots for bowls and ashtrays, and he'd devised his own special glaze and was eager to learn the kick wheel, which he would attempt that very evening. My relief was palpable, and I felt a warm breeze from the window as it rustled the student essays and university exit papers heaped up on my desk. Convicted, I had been granted clemency.

Perhaps those purgatorial years in Alabama were not so harmful after all. I find my colleagues at Hollins welcoming and generous, the facilities here and at UVA more than adequate to my research, the girls majoring in history quicker, more industrious, less cartoonish than the average Teke. The autumn here has been splendid, and I've fallen in with a witty trio of new liberal arts profs, each of us quirky in his or her own way, all of us fond of a good story artfully told. I've even ventured, a couple of times, to wind down the evening with my old "let me tell you something that happened to a friend of mine." It seems harmless enough, free of the queasy baggage the stories had accrued that last year in the state whose motto is "We dare defend our rights."

This morning, however, everything changed. We're having a sweet, late Indian summer right here before Thanksgiving, and since the students have the week off, I decided to stay home from the office and read McPherson's new book on the war. I was on the deck savoring my morning coffee and a moving account of Pelham's last artillery action when the phone rang. Through the glass door it was just a purr, a little alluring in its unobtrusiveness, but I wasn't expecting anyone to call, so I let the new digital machine pick it up. I couldn't really distinguish the words of my own message, though they were stamped in me as precisely as on the microchip: "This is seven oh four, three double nine oh nine four seven. I can't answer the phone just this minute, but leave a message and your number and I'll contact you soon as I can. Thank you now." Business-like. As anonymous as can be. I couldn't make out the caller's voice, either, but the message was brief, and I resumed my reading. Poor gallant Pelham, bright star, untimely end.

When I went in for a refill, I laid the book face down, wing-wise on the cherry table, which was stained only a little darker than the deep wine of the lingering dogwood leaves outside my window. That excellent tree, sturdy for its kind, old already but showing no signs of breakage, was one of the house's prime selling points. It forked into two major trunks, and I could just now begin to discern that the separate leafless crowns would stab skyward like antlers in the coming season.

I pressed the switch and walked my cup over to the Mr. Coffee. "You have one new message," the electronic voice droned, "received at ten seventeen, Monday, November the twenty-fourth." A longer-than-usual silence, and then the silky, razory voice: "You're not the easiest man to keep up with, Jared, but I'm glad you found a new nest. I hope you like it better than Alababa. It's still hot down here on the Gulf Coast, old buddy. Still sweaty at night with the big survivor skeeters. Boeing jobs. And everybody in Breedlove is highly pissed because it's been lock-down for a week on account of some bastard with business that wouldn't wait bolted from a road gang. That don't make nobody's choir sing. Now you, you're close enough to the big mountains to start doing some hunting yourself in a couple of days. Isn't that right? Good luck then, Jared, and be careful of the dangers. You know what sort of surprises can happen out there in the woods, Buddy. I'll be seeing you." And then the low-pitched, taunting dial tone.

# RED JAR

MEADOW'S WIFE WAS with child, and it had given his mind no end of trouble. That Saturday in April he was out at the family's country property, running the noisy tiller along the flat bank just above the Maury River. Since the newcomer wasn't due till early August and he had heard what a misery it was to carry a baby through dog days, he figured Sandralee would find some relief lounging in a wicker chaise under the willow limbs and gazing at a broad bed of Red Mammoth sunflowers and beyond them the silhouette of Jump Mountain. The view would be especially soothing here alongside the cascade where the little river rounded the bend and headed west, the stretch his father still called "Indian territory."

It wasn't the muggy discomfort of the coming summer that troubled him, though. It was the mystery of Sandralee's moodiness back in the fall, the strained times they'd been through as he attempted to decipher the cause and then the final numbing answer itself, which was that she'd been sharing vodka tonics and a Buena Vista motel room with Josh Riles, a night dispatcher from the Sheriff's Department. And though she'd wept and begged, prayed with him and sworn *Terrible mistake* and *Never again* and *Please forgive*, anybody who knew the facts and could count to nine would guess that the child might not be endowed with Meadow's green eyes and rusty hair, and that was only the superficial wound.

So it was not exactly affection that brought him down Route 39 and onto the graveled spur he had called Arrowhead Way since childhood. It was a kind of revenge he was both ashamed of and addicted to. He had forgiven her, a part of him reasoned, and acted out of exaggerated considerateness only in order to remind them both what domestic harmony was like, to set a good example, to open a new path. He would make her a sanctuary out here and in the process perhaps find some remedy for his own torment.

As the ten horsepower Mantis bucked and sputtered and threatened to stall in the rich loam, Meadow realized he'd snarled into some roots, so he tightened his grip on the throttle until the tendrils were worked through and the curved handles reverted to their usual low-key trembling. The contraption always amazed him with the way it easily churned silt and clay to a powder lit with chips of chert and mica. He knew from experience that he was also leaving bits of history in his wake, as he had found shards, birdpoints and antler tools since he was old enough to be enchanted by the fact that native people had once lived and farmed this stretch where his family fished and picnicked and pitched horseshoes. And just across the stream, where the bank had severely eroded in the past two decades, he'd been the one to discover a rare and haunting funerary jar. But that was back before he'd even begun to shave. Now, the whole span of river seemed occupied only by the engine's hungry roar and the anger nagging his mind, and it was hard to believe this place had been the site of long-ago ceremonies and his own encounter with the face of the dead.

He also knew that his current benevolence wasn't fuelled exclusively by forgiveness. A darker part of him, which he wasn't proud of but could not dispel, wanted to rub her nose in his goodness, his victimhood. That was the outraged Meadow, the uncharitable part. The part that savaged his good intentions and Christian virtues the way the teeth of the whirling blades gouged through the dirt.

During the first six years of their marriage, Sandralee had seemed for the most part a caring and engaged partner, tolerant of his quirks and shortcomings. She was the older, settled version of the saucy and clever art major she'd been when they met. He had mellowed in similar fashion, and they had become quiet complements, a widely admired functioning couple.

Most mornings she dropped him at school with a kiss and a smile and drove off humming some Lucinda Williams tune. She then spent several hours dealing with customers and other co-op members at

Good Hands Gallery, which displayed and sold the silver jewelry she fashioned. He would call her during his planning period, often using a playful Swedish accent, and they would chat and flirt. At home they shared the chores and a taste for BBC movies, badminton and Mexican food. They occasionally attended First Methodist in Lexington and made time for many of the string quartet concerts at the college. They enjoyed vacations in national parks and summer weekends at the river, usually with boisterous family members. Babies would come, they always agreed, but they hadn't been ready yet, despite noisy encouragement from Sandralee's mother Maxine. For the time being, they laughed a lot, and neither seemed to have much cause for complaint. So Meadow had believed.

Because he loved and was attentive to his wife, the fact that she had become more lulled than excited by their marriage was not entirely lost on him. Meadow was a sober man who spent much of his time marking Civics papers, reading books on European history and running the ticket office at ball games, while Sandralee made change at the gallery or sketched and molded her Celtic silver out in the renovated workshed. Occasionally he would uncover the cases of his boyhood artifact collection in the den and improve a label or rearrange some scraps and stones. Sometimes she would go out to a fern bar for daiquiris with her friend Margot. And though he knew their hobbies—"Light Classics" on the satellite radio and *The Mayor of Casterbridge*—were not exactly exciting pastimes, their routine was reliable and as mildly satisfying as their weekly love-making. He tried to spice things up with weekend trips, flowers—streaked irises or stargazers—and cards, other surprise gifts, and he believed that helped some, but he was given to understatement and had little of what his father had always called "ambition" and "drive." Ever since they'd graduated from JMU, he'd been teaching at his old high school, and she'd been "devoting her time to her art" and planning a gallery of her own. It seemed a viable existence.

One evening last summer, as they'd been lazily gliding on the porch swing and watching the sparking fireflies, Sandralee had set aside her vodka tonic, taken his chin in her palm, stroked his cheek and kissed him, very lightly, almost like a secret.

"It's good to feel safe," she whispered.

He listened to the clink of ice chips against his lemonade glass for a moment, feeling the steady sway of the swing.

"You make me happy, Sandy," he said.

"Safe is a kind of happy."

"A kind of." Perhaps he should have wondered more about that phrase, but in the dusk her face appeared placid, and though it was early, they soon went upstairs to bed.

Turning the tiller at the end of the plot and starting to break up a new row, he looked across the water to the crumbling bank where he'd once found the remains of two people from the distant past in one red clay container. While he was reeling his mind back to that day, a wasp hovered before him, and as he swatted at it, his memory shifted to the first time they'd met Josh Riles. It was right after a baseball game, and Riles had been there to watch his brother Buddy play. The boy was good, a peppy shortstop with a clean swing, a whip arm and an overdose of hustle. He was also a military history buff and wanted his teacher to meet the famous older brother, who was a Colonial re-enactor and had once hit four home runs in a high school game down in Norfolk.

"Mighty pleased," said Riles, as he wrapped his fingers around Meadow's smaller hand. "I just moved here from Richmond. Not much Revolution re-enactment up this way. Looks to be all Civil War hoopla around here, but I hear the trout are fine."

"Do you fish?" Meadow was himself a dedicated spin caster who had never quite gotten the hang of fly fishing.

"I can't stop myself." As the tall man smiled, Meadow registered that he had the *Field and Stream* outdoor look about him—deep tan, crow-black hair, a taut but slender body, strong veins on his wrists and hands.

"I'm Sandralee." He had neglected to introduce her, and Riles was now taking her extended hand.

"You teach too?"

"No. I'm an artist, jeweler mostly. I make things from silver."
She was wearing her proud smile as she tilted her head to display a
dangling, fern-shaped earring.

"Maybe you could make me some lures."

They all laughed, and by then Buddy was shifting about, eager
to get back to his teammates. There was a victory party for the boys
at somebody's house, so they all said goodnight and the encounter
was over. On the way home, Meadow had tested his wife's response:
"That Riles seems like a nice fellow."

"I suppose." Her silhouette in the dark of the Toyota revealed
nothing, but when headlights of approaching cars washed across
them, he noticed how her dark hair seemed to sparkle momentarily,
and he looked forward to getting her home.

"Buddy's got promise as a student, and you can see the athletic
streak runs in the family. Maybe he'll become a first-generation
collegian."

She didn't respond, so he let it drop. That was the only time he
had observed them together, and later, uncovering the details and
logistics of the affair didn't appeal to him. He'd seen her agitated at
the end of summer and through the first chill of fall but hadn't even
registered that she was avoiding functions at the school and working more at the gallery than in her workshop. Perhaps he would
never have known if Steve Magee hadn't mentioned seeing Sandralee and someone in a police uniform having coffee at Burdette's
Trucker Haven.

It was a warm spell around Thanksgiving, and the geese were
flying low, arrowing north. Watching them through the windshield,
he felt a tinge of envy. He'd had a frustrating day at school due to
a student's borderline plagiarism, and then he and Sandralee had
begun sparring about where he hung his barn jacket, what he'd
forgotten at the Quickmart and an unpaid State Farm bill—tedium,
really. Just in passing, he mentioned what Magee had said. She'd
dropped the pork chops onto the floor, but Meadow hardly noticed, as he was across the room searching for the remote to get the
TV on before ABC moved from real news to human interest fluff.

She was still apologizing for the chops as they ate their ice cream, and suddenly she covered her face with her hands and started to cry.

"I don't understand it myself," she had said later, following him as he paced the edges of the dining room. "It was crazy, a cheap thrill. When we went from coffee to drinks…I don't know how… I'm the most ashamed I've…You know, it's over. Completely. It wasn't anything but stupidity."

Then she sat down on the carpet and sobbed, rocking back and forth, until he'd kneeled beside her and put his arms around her shoulders, almost like a mother protecting a child. He knew this was what he should do, what she needed him to do, but it seemed unfair for him to have to. After she went to bed with a large glass of wine, he would spend the night sitting on the sofa, examining bird points from an old denim sack his mother had made when he was in Scouts. He'd hold them up to the lamp one by one, as if he had never seen them before, and try to register their slightest nocks and imperfections. Eventually he got around to the frog fetish he'd kept from the burial jar. After all these years, it still had a mysterious hold on him, still seemed a personal message concerning mortality, a message he lacked the power to understand. He kept sipping orange juice from the quart bottle and fighting to control his anger until, near dawn, he slumped over and slept.

There was no way short of DNA testing to be sure of the father, and abortion was out of the question for Meadow. Since Sandralee's coloring wasn't too different from Riles, they just might keep the secret, if he could find a way to stand it. "We still love each other, Sandy, so we'll have to make the best of it," he'd said after things calmed down, and he was trying to sound convinced, working to believe it. Maybe the child would bear his features after all. Maybe that relief was in the cards. Still, the other voice from back in his primitive brain said "betrayed" and wondered if trust could or even ought to be restored between them.

The subsequent evenings were often chilled by mutually acceptable silences, but occasionally he would snap at her over nothing, then apologize as she stared away. Their sex life was meager and wordless, a distracted and selfish fumbling in the dark. Sometimes she would sulk about mornings and couldn't go to work, but they kept up appearances, made the announcement and learned to deal with Maxine's excitement. He spent more time idling over his collection, almost but never quite keeping at bay the image of the crouching frog and the ancient deaths he had discovered on that day long ago after the Maury went wild and jumped its bed.

Riles' name was never mentioned again, and Meadow figured that exactly how Sandralee had broken it off was another thing best left in the dark. Though he often pondered the word "safe," turned it over in his mind like a stone polisher, it was a syllable he kept out of his conversation.

When they got home from Meadow's awkward birthday celebration in February—his parents' living room, along with Maxine and Margot and Bob Wilson, a carrot cake with sparkling candles, a cashmere sweater and comic cards—they discussed a counselor but finally decided against it: small town, extensive grapevine. If it weren't already widely known, better for a teacher to keep such a thing as quiet as possible. If students found out about an affair and had even an inkling of problematic paternity, it would make him an object of both pity and contempt. It was hard enough for a bookish thirty-year-old ignorant of iPods and reality TV to maintain the students' attention and respect without the complication of snickering gossip, and Meadow did not relish the thoughts of either Manny Sams and Kristen Harpaugh winking behind him in the teachers' lounge or of relocating altogether.

Shifting his weight onto the handles for leverage, he lifted the locked blades out of the earth and used the share as a pivot to turn the shuddering machine around. His father had taught him this maneuver, but it required all his strength and weight to execute, as the old motor raced and the struts and loose bolts rattled. This was a lot of effort to build a sunflower bed for reasons he couldn't quite sort out. When the teeth were again spinning and ripping, he began to rehearse some of the revenge fantasies he returned to like the tongue drawn back to a chipped molar. He couldn't go to Riles' supervisor and accuse the man of bothering his wife, because that might lead to wider disclosure. But he could write Riles anonymous letters suggesting he go back to the coast, if he didn't want trouble. But what trouble could a man like Meadow stir up? He could insinuate and make veiled threats. Puny, at best. Other scenarios in his mind ranged from raking his keys along the side of Riles' Jeep to making bogus midnight emergency calls to the sheriff's office and even to spilling kerosene around the man's garage and burning his house while he was at work. Once, when he'd seen it in a TNN movie, he thought about splashing acid in the dispatcher's face, but it was just fantasy and less satisfying than alarming to consider.

The tortures his mind provided for Sandralee were more subtle. He could leave crime novels where she would see them or mention Buddy Riles' school work. He could use the phrase "joshing around" now and then. Or he could employ her jewelry vise and magnifier to start tying trout flies. He could propose dinner at Burdette's. It was stupid. Why did he want to even think about all this? And he had now developed a new and subtle gaze that she quickly recognized as hostile, which didn't make their truce any easier. His mind was saying "safe," while his eyes were at once sad and accusing. Meadow wasn't a cruel man, he knew, but he wasn't a saint, either, and though the light in his mind made it clear that even feigned forgetfulness would be better, a voice at the edges—feral and almost completely foreign to his nature—kept whispering, "That bitch, that bitch. What has she done?"

When he had heard her singing in the shower that Saturday morning, the knowledge that she and Maxine were planning to go shopping for a basinet and crib in Roanoke brought the random thoughts in his mind together in a wicked chord, and he needed to get away, ride out to the river and sweat some of the malice out of his system. He clenched his fists hard, as if squeezing the life from something, and he knew from experience that nothing but a few hours of work would calm him.

When she stepped from the shower, pink and shining, her belly and breasts flushed and clearly swollen, he couldn't help thinking that the cliché was true: Despite the circumstances, she had a radiance he found beautiful, which just amplified his sadness.

"I'm going out to do some work at the river."

"Okay. Be careful with those mowers and things. Take your cell phone, okay? Anything you want from the Star City?"

"Not today."

As he turned, she'd said to his back, "Tuna casserole for dinner? Take care, Meadow."

Suddenly, the whirling tiller blades clanged against something, and the machine bucked hard, snatched at his arms, then tilted right, almost far enough to topple. Meadow released the accelerator grip and dragged the Mantis backward until it was clear of the patch where he'd struck something under the surface. If it was a big rock, he'd have to retrieve the pry bar and spade to remove it, as he'd had to do several times already. They didn't call it Rockbridge County for nothing.

But that thought was quickly brushed away. It was impossible not to remember that long ago July, and a shiver went up Meadow's spine. He'd been squirrel hunting with his new .22 pump, and when he knelt at the river to splash water in his face, he'd noticed all manner of objects protruding from the opposite bank where the fast water had ripped away tons of dirt. He already knew the place was rich in small reminders that Indians had camped here, but the newly-cut soil was revealing its secrets by the dozens. Wading across, he found a lance head jutting out and several palm-sized bowls, some pestles, literally hundreds of chips and bits in black sockets of earth that must have once been firepots. Then he'd seen the lip of a large red vessel jutting out at the crest of the bank.

He knew he shouldn't disturb anything. Though he had not yet become a student of finding and saving, he was sure experts would go about securing the items by making string grids and working with spoons and brushes. And this was different from just an arrowhead or shard. Even on his family's land, he thought he might get into trouble. But how could anybody stand it, when there was something begging to be seen, beckoning to him, maybe something amazing? When he reached down and pulled on the edge of the jar, a huge piece snapped off, and he fell onto his backside with the momentum.

What Meadow had seen that afternoon, as he crawled forward with two dead squirrels in his pouch and his tailbone still smarting from his fall, had lingered in his dreams for almost twenty years, sometimes as radiant and satisfying as seeing an angel, but more often a frightening reminder. Had he even once made it a whole year without waking up in a cold sweat, breathing hard, even crying out at the image? Probably not. The bone face peering upwards at him was indelible.

An archeologist or even a serious amateur staring into the grave would have been more delighted than startled, but Meadow had seen in the dark, dead gaze of the skull something private and final, a premature reminder of the end of the road. Still, he reached down and pried off another chunk of the jar and was able to see dust, scraps of clothing, ornaments all mingled with the bones. On his hands and knees, looking down, he saw that the shadowy sockets peering back at him were not all the container held. Though the jaw was missing, strands of hair still clung to the pate, and the nose was a hole shaped like an arrowhead.

Seeing the remainder of the skeleton, the entire body folded like a jackknife, he realized that, amid the debris, there was a second occupant, a coil of kitten-sized bones caged within the ribs of the larger skeleton. Even now he could remember the river whispering over its path of stones, some kind of bird—had it been a jay?—scolding in the distance. He was sure of what he'd found. The jar had served as tomb for a woman and her child. That was horrible to him, a tiny child dead, and a mother, but he could not be certain whether the figure with a skull no larger than a plum had been in the belly of the woman when she died, or if it had already been born and was buried with her, the bones slipping into the larger ribcage after the bodies had decayed and the ligaments gone to dust.

He didn't have a name for the current that jolted through his body, but he had begun to shake, and tears ran down his dusty face as he examined the heaped-up debris under the bones. The pale green soapstone frog seemed to offer itself, and when he pulled it into the light, he knew he would keep this small token and report the rest.

This time, he was much more informed. The people from the college back then had worked furiously to grid and scan the far bank, to read it before the rains resumed and washed the valuable evidence away. They'd found, amid the dust that had been these two people, scraps of deer hide, scattered molars, a turtle shell and some stone-hard kernels of corn that resembled human teeth. A cup-sized gourd with a crude bird scratched into its bowl was one prize disclosure, and in the midst of the remnants, they'd been delighted to discover a dozen small saltwater shells, which seemed to reinforce a recent theory about trade patterns.

As he kneeled now to brush aside the loose soil, he remembered how kind Professor Siefert had been, explaining that stumbling on a grave was not like disrespecting one, though Meadow had never really been convinced. He kept pitying the people, even as he said, "I don't know anything about them." And he had stolen the frog. He kept waking—nightly for weeks, then less frequently—with faint echoes of some curse the dead people's kin might have chanted still whirling in his mind. It was all a riddle that cried out for solution but allowed none. Several years passed before he would go to the museum to look at the display where the sign announced the place and date and credited him with the discovery.

Now, moving carefully, he found a red slab of freshly broken pottery smaller than his hand and shaped somewhat like South Carolina. It was evidently part of some larger object. The more dirt he moved—first just scooping, then breaking off chunks—the more smoothed curvature of russet clay he revealed, and soon he understood that he was uncovering another large jar of some sort, more substantial than any artifact he or anybody he knew had ever stumbled on, what archeologists would surely call "a find."

Probably, he should stop. The experts, Siefert, would still know far more about how to excavate a fragile object with minimal damage. It might be another museum piece, an important clue to the past, but he scrambled around and found a green stick, then began to probe the immediate area anyway, to determine the dimensions. It was his land, he thought, and up to now, his secret, solely his possession. He wanted to see what it was that his family had walked and played over for decades without guessing, and something inside him wanted to break the rules for once, to follow his own desires, no matter what.

As he carefully trenched around the spot with his mattock, Meadow rehearsed what he knew about the local Indians. Probably not Saponis or Tutelos. Monacans, he'd read, up from the James, would occasionally venture this far for summer hunting camps. Sometimes they'd stay long enough to put in crops, the "three sisters"—beans, corn and squash. They lived in bark domes, avoided other tribes early on and usually buried in mounds. It was probably a Monacan interment that Jefferson had excavated near Monticello right after his wife's death. The Founder's habit of documenting everything had earned him the title "Father of American Archeology," but even the new high school textbooks mentioned that Native Americans thought of him as just another grave robber with a tendency to advertise himself.

As he worked, rested, then threw himself back into the labor, he lost track of time and let his mind meander.

Since he had shown her his collection (the frog excluded), Sandralee had developed an interest in the trinkets and adornments of the woodlands terminal tribes in the area, and he recalled one trip down to a big flea market near Asheville. They had met an unforgettable character named Paul Price, who had collected all manner of charms and jewelry from other rogue relic hunters, and he could knap Clovis points like an arrowmaker.

Sandralee had found the carved fetishes and shell jewelry fascinating and considered up-dating some of the designs to a new line, but she quickly abandoned the notion because, as she said, "We've pirated enough from them already."

The more he dug, cut and yanked roots and scraped around the vessel, the clearer it became that he had again chanced onto something unusual. It was much larger than a jug, larger even than a butter churn. Bits of sandy earth cascaded into the hole he'd made, but he scrambled around his little crater, shoveling and pitching, more excited by the emerging curvature of the container than by any thought of contents. Neither tuna casserole nor re-enacting deputies so much as crossed his mind.

Severn Rameau, a local antique dealer and collector, had told Meadow that there wasn't much native material left to find in the area. After all, Monacans had been transients in this neck of the woods, though a developer up near Steele's Tavern had uncovered some middens and a cache of trade goods. It made the papers because everyone was amused that the site contained over two dozen Jew's harps, common items any blacksmith could make, but which the Indians seemed to prize and present as wedding gifts. "Incidental" Severn had said, "complete serendipity. You could grid this valley and scan it systematically and still not nose out more than one or two comparable troves."

The sun was edging toward the piney rim of Jump Mountain by the time Meadow had entrenched enough to see how he might move it. He wiped the sweat from his brow and eyes, not noticing that the clay and silt from his site was so ground into his jeans and cotton shirt that he had begun to resemble something that had been excavated. What he was thinking about instead was secrecy. If he could raise it, would he keep it to himself this time? How long? Where? And how much pleasure would that yield? If it wasn't his by right of location of salvage, did it belong to the state or the county or the Monacans whose descendents lived down by Natural Bridge? Could you trespass on your own land? What could you really own, after all? What were the laws?

As soon as the notion of justice entered the equation, he blinked hard, and a red flash almost like a cardinal darting through his mind turned his thoughts in a different direction: the dispatcher with a silver star over his heart, almost something Sandralee might have designed. "Authentic?" "Safe?" "Trespass?" He imagined the sky-blue Jeep outside a room at the Days Inn, a scratched door with tin numerals fastened to it, but he wouldn't let his mind turn the handle.

She didn't deserve to know about this incredible jar, he thought, and he felt a little pleased he'd never shown her the frog. Maybe she'd just forfeited her right to beauty. He could hear his breath coming fast through his nose. He felt his pulse running faster. What had he done to make her so unhappy, so desperate and foolish? "I didn't do a damn thing," he said aloud, "she was safe," but it took only a minute for him to feel ashamed of his spite, and he tried to shake it off as he returned to the task at hand.

Although he had cleared away the surrounding soil, he couldn't get a clear view of the contents. He worked carefully in the clay, as precise as a sculptor freeing a figure from its natural habitat. The vessel itself was as large as the circle he could make with his arms, and the top was stoppered snugly with a wooden disk which showed scant signs of rot. He didn't have a flashlight, but he was now desperate to know what the jar concealed. He paused in his efforts to listen for a car crackling the pebbling around the bend, but he heard only the whisper of the river, some wind in the leaves and a pair of quarreling crows in the distance, downstream. The water, fast from last week's rain, glittered with sun silver.

Since the jar seemed not to have any other fissures and was probably more cumbersome than heavy, he fashioned a ramp to roll it up. This was the most delicate step, he thought. If the clay around the hole his tiller vanes had chipped open took the stress wrong, cracks could spread, and he might find himself with more jigsaw than jar. He wiped sweat from his face with a sleeve and inhaled deeply.

Then the relic was nearly free and he was in the trench, cradling it with his chest and arms as he eased it along the crude ramp and toward the lip of his excavation, and though he felt the strain in his back and shoulders, it was working, the jar moving, his boots gaining traction as they inched forward.

Slowly, slowly, alert for any insinuation of something wrong, a change in the feel of the surface, a shift. Soon, on his knees, just as he was ready to give the red jar the last nudge, he felt something, or perhaps imagined it. He paused and hoped he'd been wrong, but then he clearly saw a fissure spreading like slow, dark lightning just inches from his eyes. He could feel the change in his own muscles adjusting and tried to ease his treasure back down, to control the cracking, but he wasn't in the right position for that—too little leverage—and as he relaxed, it stalled, teetered, then rolled back, pushed him over and broke into a dozen large slabs.

This one was empty. No charms or bones or fetishes. No vessels or shells. Nothing but a ferric-looking dust, and as the understanding that he had been spared washed over him, he sighed deeply and said, "Thank God."

The sun was nearly gone behind Jump, and the current turned a dull pewter, shadows connecting to one another all around him like a too-vivid dream. A chill rippled up his neck and flared out to his face, spread to his arms, and he felt it in his groin, in his knees. He knew that digging up these people's graveyard was a sacrilege. He could almost hear their kin chanting that curse again, calling down vengeance. Why in heaven's name had he meddled here so long ago, and now done it again? These were the remnants of a people who had never made war or stolen land or been spiteful and cruel... but he couldn't sustain the speculation, and suddenly didn't feel he knew anything, except that the job of the living was to help one another heal, to create trust and safety and keep things whole, to sustain them against all threats of storm.

Staring at the wind-swayed leafage in the crowns of the river-side hardwoods, he didn't know exactly how he would say it all, but he would start by calling Siefert and reporting his discovery. The fragments of the jar could be gathered and re-assembled, mended, and perhaps some restoration expert could return it to the strength and beauty it had before. Even empty, it was important, and as he felt the tears begin to come again and his body shake with the effort of holding back, he knew he was meant to welcome the child and care for it, too, no matter what color eyes it had, no matter whose blood.

When he reached home, he would ask Sandy to sit with him at the dining table, where he would take her hands in his and, for a change, look straight into her eyes and speak quietly. He would try to convince her that what the future held was everything, the past just a series of lessons. He was over it, all of it, and what they now needed to do was build a life based on a larger view of the world, and of themselves. He would get past his reserve, tell her about both burial vessels and the frog and the dreams. As the light failed and peepers started their lullaby in the understory, he looked at his clay-stained palms ready to lead his wife and their child to whatever safety anyone could hope for. For the first time since the previous autumn, his hands looked clean.

# Ruminants

THE DEER WOULD NOT be moving much tonight, for the wind muddled their sense of smell, and they could not travel safely. On a still evening they could hear smoke or see an eye blink; they could smell the silver of a ring. When the air was gusty, they nibbled leaves and lingered close to their beds. That was the common wisdom, but Swofford knew they were insatiable once the first passing bird pecked a few pears open or early windfalls broke in the orchard grass. The bolder ones would always venture out, the hungry ones in whom the drought memory was still sharp. This late in September, there was never a night free of their pillage.

The fruit farmers all along the Blue Ridge struggled for solutions, but nothing else was hit as hard as the Asian pears. Swofford and Su had tried hair bundles, rattle lines and chicken wire fencing, then electric current, and just last year a posse of restless young redbones who would interrupt their border patrol to gnaw any fawn that went down. Swofford shot bucks and dragged their bleeding carcasses around the perimeter behind the Allis Chalmers, but 3000 mature trees were a lot to protect, and still they came in pairs and threes and droves. Su was troubled by the casualties. One morning he had found her in the orchard still dressed in her terry robe, moist-eyed and stroking the neck of a doe he'd shot the night before, and though she didn't speak, her eyes said, "How can we?"

Perched on the rusting tractor's seat with a six pack and his Silvertone tuned an octave above music, he questioned the worth of it all. In early spring they'd installed motion-sensor floodlights and alarms, but that technology just disturbed their sleep and didn't seem to phase the whitetails. He and Su could hardly make love without being alerted that their profit margin was under assault, and some nights in full fury he'd run out wearing only boxers and swinging a shovel to whack the scavengers on the flank as they stretched their muzzles into the laden limbs and devoured anything they could reach.

And in a way, the musician in him understood. He knew what it was like to be delirious with some undersong larger than any creature's will. By late summer the sugars were twirling wildly inside the Shinsui, and by the time the pollinated fruitlets of Kosui and Shinseiki had begun to blush, even the bee skeps had to be moved, for the workers who had savored the flowers in April would swirl around, desperate for a different harvest they couldn't define. Everything was intoxicated by the crispness and texture, the sweet flesh and pineapply aftertaste of Hosui or the insinuation of apricot in the pith of Arriang. *Gourmet* had written up Cavalier Orchard's Asian fruit as the best on the East Coast, and people drove to Charlottesville all the way from Maryland and Pennsylvania just to buy them fresh-picked, to stroll amid the orderly rows and point out the soothing blue sawtoothed rim of the surrounding mountains as they sampled the available assortment and complimented the proud growers.

The market was there, but so was the wildlife problem, and since he and Su had begun to argue over how badly the deer forage might cost them, he had started to see the Albemarle County herds as a threat to his security. Not that weather and insects didn't exact their own toll, not that the calendar and refrigeration problems and the national economy didn't get in their own licks. Everything had local consequences, personal ties. In his life with Su, the time was ripe for a child, he knew, and she was tired of experimenting with greenhouse hybrids and devoting her whole existence to the orchard. Her dark eyes would glow whenever she spoke of the need for family, and he knew she meant both her own people back in Korea and an urge stirring within her.

Marriage was the knot in the wood. He'd been a migrant strummer for so long, pushing farther and farther from his history, stretching the road, seeking the next stroke of luck. To embrace the present, he now thought, you had to stand still and admit to your past mistakes, to say you have a real life, not just a snag where the stream paused before rushing on.

That was why he sat in the lee of a swashing autumn wind just after dark twanging out "Danville Girl" and "Wild Bill Jones" on his dissonant banjo, reflecting on his life and hoping to frighten a few trespassing yearlings off with the metallic notes. He remembered the first night he was picking with Fringe Wisdom at the Pink Cadillac out on highway eleven. Su came in with a blonde girl, and his first glimpse of the deep lacquer of her Asian eyes made him fumble at the strings. He'd had enough beer to loosen his tongue, but not enough to play the fool, and when he spoke to her at the break, he could see her face changing to take in the words like a soft wind in the corn tassels. She reminded him of Cherokee girls he'd known, but she was more focused and delicate, more secure and aware. It didn't take them many days to drift into sweet words and the pleasures of touch.

Su's father had been a farmer, and she'd been the one who received all the secrets. Her first husband Kim had fallen from a rafter as they raised the sorting and packing barn, and after two years she was no longer wearing white mourning, no longer blind to the world of need. Even now, Swofford was astonished that she had taken to him, had made him promise to shave his stage whiskers and cut back on the mugs and pitchers of froth-crowned brew.

If this fragile situation began to collapse, he didn't know whether he could go back to minstrel travels on the Old Time circuit. A hard life of earning his bread and keep amid the beery bright lights with his quick fingers bent to claws had made him grateful for these four years of palming the exotic pears, savoring whatever he touched, and he had taken a shine to the softer person Su had made him in the aftermath of those raw edges. And yet, just walking the wind swales between rows, he could not deny the rise of the old iron anger as he looked down at the cleft hearts of deer hoofprints stamped in the mud like the taunting signatures of foes.

As he was frailing on "Sugar Blues" in the favored wild style of Dogbite Butch, a god-awful noise in the north rows made him exchange the instrument for his shovel haft. Venus was a sparkle to the east just beyond the sliver moon, and even as he ran uphill toward the commotion, he felt there was something dangerous and damning in his effort to fence out the famished deer.

Swofford was aware that the does would graze among his neighbor's charolais herd while the sun was up, keeping to the edge of the woods, blending in but flinching at every unfamiliar scent. Grass didn't satisfy them, though, in spite of the way their four-roomed stomachs were built. Like cows, they would swallow the vegetation, and in the rumen it would ferment and be returned to the mouth as cud. It was as if their own systems brewed a kind of small beer they could relish over and over, and he had sometimes felt this inflicted a special kinship upon him.

So many roadhouses, dives and VFWs, so many hundreds of cases of Bud, but his own beer hobby had not been in the service of rumination. In the deep past beyond range of his active memory loomed a night of sheet lightning and sudden violence, the Tennessee cove where his own cold road had begun with the hard words that had exiled him. The way of the scavenger, the path of regret, a thousand jam sessions and motel nights, but now this lucky refuge threatened only by his own indecision and the intrusion of ravenous deer.

When he reached the source of the sound, he was shocked by the drama he discovered. In the mid-high boughs of a spidery windbreak apple tree he'd transplanted and allowed to thrive just as a whim, like a custodian over the manicured pear trees, a magnificent buck was thrashing amid desperate bellows. His great rack of antlers was tangled in the limbs, and the deer had exhausted himself in the attempt to wrench free. Moonstruck to frenzy, the creature had eaten everything on the ground and low branches and had clambered up just enough to get snarled in a fork. The hunger it could not quell was killing it, and Swofford's first thought was, "Good. I hope your last meal was worth it," but when he clicked on his flashlight, in the beam he could see the life passing from the animal's obsidian eyes.

Swofford stood there in a trance and listened to the wind. It

seemed to be saying something in a code just outside his compre-
hension, but then he felt something give way inside him, like an old
A string that had been tightened once too often. He could almost
hear the plaintive twang as it snapped.

It would be easy, even wise, to stand back and let nature take
its course, but the low limbs had been trimmed off with snags still
protruding, and Swofford knew he could pull himself up to get
hold of the antlers. He'd be shielded from any desperate hooves,
and he just might be able to set the thing free. Looking back at
the steeply pitched house, he could see the bedroom light was on,
like a beacon calling him back to safety. Listening hard, though, to
the sound of the evening air in the leaves, he could decipher at last
the wind's message, and he understood it was not just the deer's
life at issue. For Su's sake and for his own, he dropped the shovel
and began to climb.

# THE PIG IS COMMITTED

ALL MORNING THE PEAFOWL had been at the deputy's body until it appeared to have been felled by a shotgun, at close range. The buzzards had settled into the thermals overhead to survey the situation, and now nearly a dozen circled, forming the outline of a grim rose in the sky. The sun, Gar thought, was the color of newly brushed blonde hair, and it made their strange flower yellowish as the scavengers coasted. Gar knew he needed to make the 911 call, but seeing the body's bird-pecked condition, he grew less and less convinced that anyone would believe in his innocence.

Still, he had to try. One more load of marijuana stalks and a garbage bag of unsorted leaves waited to be hauled and dumped into the green eye of water at the bottom of the quarry before all the evidence of illegal agriculture just beyond his property was erased. Rusty would have conniption fits over the lost profit, but deep sixing the bales he had already disposed of was clearly his best hope. He chased the hens back to their dusting holes, where they lay down and brayed at him like so many jackasses.

THE OTHER DEPUTIES had always been accommodating—Laine and Robert and Joe Steve. They received their packets of cash and baggies of carefully sorted product on schedule, and they looked the other way, drove the other way, thought the other way with the sharpness of professional survivors. After all, wasn't old Ben Stewart operating a poorly-concealed stilling operation just south of Brushy Fork? Weren't the Bishop sisters running a stable of quick-trick tarts out of the Cedar Court Motel? Didn't the NASCAR rookies still gun their street cars like demons down the back roads of Floyd County? And the murdered Sallins family, nobody had ever solved that. The local constabulary, thought Gar, had more than enough to occupy them without rocking the boat over a small-time pot garden thirty miles from nowhere. Besides, he thought, the local officers had never seemed interested in driving all the way out there to squeeze the Thaxton brothers over an acre of scraggly plants. They were all practical men and not greedy, good employees for the county.

Maybe that was where the new man came in. Maybe this Moyle was some kind of rogue looking to sweeten his deal. As Gar pulled the choke and turned the tractor's ignition switch, he wondered if this stranger now lying face-down ten feet from his porch hadn't been behind the arrest of Ollie Strawbridge, who operated a floating gamecock pit from the back of a flatbed truck. For years nobody had bothered to even shake old Ollie down. Then, two weeks ago, bang: He and his whole clientele were arrested while setting up behind Eddins' lumber mill. The chickens had been confiscated in their crates, the gaffs bagged and tagged and all the men handcuffed in a line to a planing saw frame while they waited for a school bus to collect them. Gar used such thoughts to shield him from the image of the deputy lying cold on the ground, his life over but his family and friends and the rest of the world not yet knowing they had cause to mourn. Then the heavy smell of honeysuckle led Gar to picture a funeral, wreaths and bundles of flowers, a stone marker shaped like a stump: Woodmen of the World. A raw plot circled with children in black. A wife being supported by two men in uniform. No, a widow, maybe blonde, maybe green-eyed behind her dark veil. He closed his eyes tight and felt the salt sting, then shook his head. He couldn't think about that now.

GAR HAD HEARD the peacock's announcement of an intruder—*help! help!*—and met the deputy beside the catalpa tree where morning light was softened in the speckled blossoms. He walked carefully in his bare feet with a cup of coffee in one hand and a sticky bun in the other. The cop's brick-rough face was new, though the uniform was familiar—the khaki with brown epaulettes and piping, the tight-brimmed Smoky hat. A girthy man with a face redder than barn paint. The name tag said *Moyle*, which didn't ring a bell, and Gar noticed that the leather of his elaborate pistol belt was intricately tooled with *Hoyt*. He wore a scowl and had his thumbs hooked into the belt like he had studied law enforcement on the nostalgia channel. His squinted eyes were menacing. "Pig's eyes," Gar thought. "Trough boss."

Then he spoke: "Hoyt Moyle from the sheriff's office. I'm over this way to inquire into reports of some unfamiliar vehicles moving through your neck of the woods. Nocturnal, around midnight. You'd be Garner Thaxton."

The nearest neighbor was a mile off, so who in heaven's name could have noticed that Rusty had brought in a van to load up the better part of the harvest and haul it over to Pulaski County by dark? They had already separated and bricked the dried leaves of most of what they "exported," as Rusty called it. "We sell smiles," he said. "We're the happy merchants." It had taken just under an hour to load up and replace the false bed, then send Rusty on his merry way north, and the van itself was inconspicuous and quiet.

Just as Gar had said, "Ha-haven-haven't really noticed anything. H-how recent?" he saw the deputy's eyes grow still, his upper body flinch and shudder. The man's breathing was labored as he went fire-faced and suddenly stiffened, shocked-looking, as if hornet-stung. He groaned and sank to his knees, eyes bulging, hands grabbing for his collar, as if his black uniform tie were strangling him.

Gar looked around for a shooter, but he had heard no shot.

"Wha-what is it, officer? What's wr-wrong?"

The deputy made no answer beyond a gagging noise and, clutching his chest, rolled his eyes and seemed to collapse, to cave in all over. Gar dropped his breakfast and scrambled over to undo Moyle's tie, but the fellow had fallen into the gravel and after one big exhaling gasp and spasm didn't seem to be breathing anymore. Gar wasn't absolutely sure where to look for a pulse in the neck, but he felt about his own throat and found the place easily, as his heart was racing. He remembered touching Lynda on that spot in different circumstances, but the image dissolved as quickly as it had formed.

There was no corresponding throb in the deputy's neck, and his chubby face had turned a pale blue.

"Oh, Jesus," he thought. "I n–need to call emergency." He said it out loud, but then realized the position he was in. A dead policeman in front, but shreds of marijuana and seeds in the house with two large bundles of unskinned plants behind the shed. The drying dressers were still in the sitting parlor, and potted seedlings under their gro-lights filled the spare bedroom. Who would believe there was no connection? He had to hatch a plan, and execute it fast, though *execute* was not a word he wanted in his mind at this moment. He should say something, Gar thought, to mark a man's passing, but nothing came, and he had more pressing needs. He looked skyward as if a prayer might be written there, but his memory couldn't salvage more than, "Who art in heaven?" It came out as a half-hearted question.

THAT WAS TWO HOURS ago, and he had pretty much cleaned the place up, hoping nobody would try to pinpoint a time of death. The water in the quarry was murky, and you could dump a whole apple orchard down there without anyone suspecting.

His idea was simply to say Moyle had dropped in for coffee but had been stricken—he figured it was the heart—and fallen dead at his feet. He would cheat on the time and get things straightened out so that no one nosing about would begin to exercise their suspicions. He was counting on routine incompetence to help him out. It would probably take close to an hour for them to get any emergency personnel out this far along the cresting James, which had flooded out the closest two bridges just a week back.

VACUUMING UP THE STEMS and twigs, Gar kept cussing Rusty, whose idea the mini-plantation had been. Gar had been fairly content scraping by with his bush-hogging and back-hoeing business, hoping for the big contract that never came. He liked living on the old place their father had used as a sporting cabin. He heard bluebirds in the morning, whip-poor-wills at dusk, locusts pulsing in the late summer with their call-and-response. Since he had no dog, deer would nibble his apples, even his first stalks of herb, but not so bad as to trouble him, and the peahens strutted around like so many surly servants, dropping eggs in the iris beds, sweetening the afternoons with their jungle calls, shitting all over the woodlot and turnaround. He kept the flock primarily for the ornamental cock, who would drag his train about in an ill temper but then for no evident reason fan out the feathers, displaying the metallic plumes with their bronze-greens and smalt blue, the eerie, eye-shaped ocelli for which the birds were known. He thought they looked like Aztec kings, or what Aztec kings should look like. Lynda had adored them and often volunteered to scatter their feed. Rusty had said he should pen them and superglue their beaks shut, but what did Rusty know about real beauty?

THE OLDER BROTHER, the bully and visionary, Rusty had originally found out by accident that Gar was cultivating a little plot of weed. Before becoming a professionally glib and enterprising real estate appraiser, Rusty had finished community college, tried marriage twice, raised kids and discovered all the answers. He was the schemer and charm merchant, a notorious gash hound with a wild history, and when he took the first toke of a number Gar was burning on the porch to relax after a day of ditching, Rusty said, "Great Granny, Gar, you grow this stuff? It goes in smooth as a christening. You could make a living with it by yourself, but *we*, old son, *we* could make a killing."

So Rusty asserted his authority and brought seeds and pamphlets somehow gleaned from the Internet, a folder on the state and federal laws, plus clippings that revealed the raid strategies and tip-off errors that marked the intersection between growers and enforcers. He had evidently ridden his Mac cursor into the virtual ganja underground and found it to his liking.

"Okay," Gar had said. "We'll g-give it a go," a little pleased that his big brother was impressed.

That was three years ago, and Gar had remained the reluctant but hard-working partner through it all, the quiet brawn. Now he had enough money in the bank to call himself stable, but his time was all devoured by the stealth and labor, and Gar didn't feel any cheerier for his affluence. He was still slow to speak and stammery—he'd tried everything from a blue racer snake in a jar to a cicada shell under the tongue to cure it—and he wasn't any closer to finding a steady woman friend than he had been when he left Virginia Tech with half an agricultural engineering degree, shackling student loans, his family's distress and an exaggerated affection for ACC hoops. There had been the unforgettable fling with Lynda, whom Rusty had called "bodacious," but she was long gone.

THE BUZZARDS MULTIPLIED and wheeled like the circle saw at a timber mill. Gar heaved the bundles into the water and burned oil as he pushed the tractor hard to get back to the house, the phone and the body of Hoyt Moyle.

The scene that kept flashing in his eyes was just last winter when he told Rusty he wanted to bail out. They had been sitting by the stove drinking beer while Carolina routed Tech again on the TV. He could remember that the smell of stoveblack was strong in the air, as he had rubbed the Fisher up just a couple of days before, depending on the mistakenly mild forecast that he could let it sit cold. It had been his father's prize purchase for the cabin, and he shook his head to think how shocked old Frank would be at the source of his boys' supplementary income. Rusty, he could tell, coveted the stove, and he was a man who got what he wanted.

"I'm n-not g-going to be g-gardening this spring, Rusty. We've m-made some m-money and enjoyed it, but now it's t-time for me to p-p-pull out and aim for normal life."

"And what about your brother, brother?" Rusty didn't raise his voice or edge it. As always, he was smooth as butter. His tone suggested disappointment.

"I depend upon the extra income. You know, Megan has needs, and Paige and Jimmy. Hell, I have needs, not to mention commitments. I've made purchases on time, and I'm into Lowe's in a big way for renovations and carpet. Am I just supposed to let them come and repossess the carpet, rip out the new paneling and knock down the garage? I'm sure you don't mean for that to happen. You know daddy would…."

"I don't m-mean anything except I'm g-getting out."

"A little selfish, don't you think?"

"Look, if you want to continue f-farming weed, I've g-got no objections. You can use the b-back lot and get to it by the creek road. I just d-don't want to have any m-more involvement. It's all lost its-its allure."

The crowd roared as the Tech swingman sank a long jumper, and Rusty stared at the TV and smiled.

"Allure hell. It's not that easy, bro. You are the sole occupant of this land right over the knob from the crop. Your house is the closest, and everybody who matters probably guesses you've in it up to your knees. Prox-im-i-ty. If anybody unneighborly ever spots the crop, you're in deep guano."

"N-no, I've thought of that, Rusty, but I t-trust you to see that it d-doesn't t-trans-transpire. You see, I kn-know how clever you are at devising strategies and m-masks. You've been the b-best concealment artist I've ever run across. Hell, man, you are a natural-born f-flim-flam."

"But you've liked it, too." Rusty sipped his Corona and chuckled, scratching at a tuft of his red hair like a sit-com actor. "Nobody took to rose rustling like you that year before you went to Blacksburg. You were the greenhouse bandito king! And you liked the way Darnell Barris came around when we had all those roses scenting up the place."

It was true that Gar had liked the rose rustling. And Darnell. When Rusty explained to him how the modern breeders were having difficulty approximating the compactness, confirmation, hue and scent of old-fashioned roses, they had decided it would be easy pickings for them to slip into disused cemeteries and public parks, even private gardens to snip cuttings or, in the best circumstances, dig up and haul off whole bushes. They scouted every small town in the valley, then raised the makeshift greenhouse. Their daddy was too stoned on pain pills and too immobile with emphysema to care about their comings and goings, and his new wife Reba was just happy to see that they had a constructive hobby. At first they only went for snips, stealing about in early morning shadows with their gloves and scissors, their glass bud tubes with a splash of water and rubber nipples. Gar wore a cartridge belt slung over his shoulder to slip the tubes into, so with his deep woods camo face and dark kerchief he did resemble some border ruffian. Grafting and rooting were his specialties, easy for somebody born with two green thumbs, and before long Rusty had become the front man, selling the grafts and even whole rose bushes at farmer's markets and swap meets as far away as Greensboro and Winston-Salem. So many elegant ladies and fastidious old-maid gents were delighted to purchase the kind of roses they had savored in childhood and yearned for ever since, and they never seemed to suspect that they were carrying on commerce with pirates. "Dixie Dream" the roses were named, "Scarlet O," "Midnight White" and "Pearl Peach." Gar admired the way Rusty charmed the spinsters and their prissy nieces. Envied him.

"Look, I'll strike a bargain, bro. We'll do it for one more glorious year, then quit cold turkey. One last hurrah. That will give me time to arrange my finances. Fair?"

Gar lost his resolve and managed only to half whisper that he'd rather just let Rusty go solo from here, but even then he felt he was letting family down again.

"Now let me remind you, Gar. You live here. I mean, you have basically shit in your own nest, and any mischief around these parts will come back on you. Listen, bro, we'll have to let our payola payroll boys down easy or the doggy deputies are likely to turn on us. Here's how I see it now. You and me are the ham and eggs breakfast here, you know. I mean, to get it on the plate, the chicken is somewhat involved, but the pig is committed. It's your land; it's your pot. You're the pig."

AFTER SCRAPING HIS BOOTS on the edge of the top step, Gar entered the front room and lifted the blue princess phone from its cradle, then dialed 911.

"Emergency. May I be of assistance?" The woman's voice was calm, professional, soothing.

"Yes ma'am. This, ah, th-this is G-Gar Thaxton on Route 4 near West Branch on the James River. There is a sheriff's d-deputy out here named Moyt, n-no, Moyle, and he is, well, is having what I th-think is a heart attack. He's all b-blue and b-barely breathing. Yes, M-ma'am. He needs help right, right away. An am-ambulance. No m-ma'am, I'm n-not sure how. Do I p-press on his chest and then b-blow in his mouth, then pump the chest again? P-pinch his nose? Okay. Okay."

He listened to the details for another minute and then hung up. There was no point in trying anything like that now, but he walked out to where the man now lay under the woodpile tarp. The dispatcher had called the procedure "the kiss of life." The pea hens were roosting on the rail over their abelia nest, and the cock was promenading about beside the garage, helping himself to the oyster shell chips the handbook said they need for protein if they can't get enough insects. The next kiss Moyle was likely to receive would be planted on waxed brow or cheek. He wouldn't feel a thing. The buzzards weren't fooled by the camo-patterned tarp and continued to gather and ring. Some had settled in an oak and seemed to grin.

AS HE STRIPPED DOWN and threw his work clothes into the washer, Gar tried to calm himself by talking to Rusty, supplying both his words and his brother's. This was the easiest way for him to have a satisfying conversation, as the stutter seldom afflicted him in solitude.

"All this work, and there's g-going to be hell to pay over an overweight, Duroc-faced cop's bad choice of a place to die."

"Chill out, bro. You've got time on your side, and anybody will be able to see that it was some kind of a heart attack. You'll be in the clear. Once we straighten this up and cash in, I wouldn't be surprised to see that Lynda come prancing back."

"It's just like the rose r-rustling. I knew our luck was about to turn then, too. But this time you wouldn't trust my instincts. And you know how d-daddy would feel about it all. He'd be ashamed to know we were mixed up in this."

"Kick back, old son. You've got to get your face ready." Rusty would have said exactly that.

"Who will feed the p-peas their Startina when they take me in? Who will weed the vegetables and pick the peach tree? Who will keep up the place? Mow? P-p-aint?"

"They won't even make you sit in the cruiser. You've got it made in the shade."

"What about all those little wounds the b-bird bills made? And I let it happen. I did it."

"Not your fault. Easy to explain. Just the facts, old son. They'll send Cassidy or Hayfield, people you know, who understand you wouldn't hurt anybody not wearing a Dook or Tar Heel jersey."

"Cute, Rusty, and easy for you to s-say. You're somewhere around the Star City f-fanning out a stack of fifties, probably cooling in some Best Western with a local p-pole dancer. I'm down here in the ham and egg breakfast."

He poured a cup of bottom coffee and winced at the bitterness. Then, suddenly, he thought of the shotgun behind the front door. It would be best not to have a firearm about, even if it hadn't been used. Guns always excite cops, even legal guns. Even dirty cops.

In a minute he was on his way back to the old well, and when he got there he pulled the Deere to the edge and dropped the Wingmaster pump into the darkness. The sun angling onto the pool made a tarnished coin on one edge of the water, and when the shotgun splashed, his stomach went queasy, and he raced the tractor along a row of sorghum planted as decoy, eager to get back to the house before the blue lights closed in. Looking across the shorn field he knew nobody with any real curiosity would be fooled by all his strategies. What he'd been growing was plain to see. He was a goner.

Perched on the porch again, Gar watched the whirling scavengers, nearly twenty now, and thought about the word. *Buzzard. Buzz. Gar.* He'd caught a fair share of the long fish in his day, and *garner* actually meant to collect or acquire. The gar fish had deadly teeth and an appetite for anything. More like Rusty than him. Garbage might be his name from here on.

Some words meant something, Gar thought, and he was at ease with them. Even *Sensimilla.* Even *flowerets, resin, stem.* He smiled to picture himself soaping the plants against fungus, culling the spored leaves and isolating the flagging plants. It always seemed strange that the males had to be eliminated to secure a good crop. You could make a crop with dual-sexed plants, and he had done it on a small scale, but he preferred the less artificial approach, the way God and nature intended. Lynda's name was a word in Spanish for anything beautiful. He said it, drawing out the vowel like his conversation teacher had.

The half-hearted sirens in the distance began to catch his ear. "Soon now," he thought.

*Rusty* was a good word, and *well, porch, plank.* But what was a Moyle? This was the second installment of a reverie he'd had the night before as he listened to the mass courtship of the cicadas. He had walked out just at twilight and found a hawkball on the ground under a dying mockernut. Probably a chicken hawk's throw—a tangle of feathers, wet fur and bones woven like wicker. Picking it up, he imagined the predator wheeling, then plummeting with lethal speed and precise talons. It had feasted in the hickory tree. He stroked the bark, then examined the pellet, which seemed a fetish spun by some granny woman casting a curse. He knew there was no curse here. This mess was all his fault, and Rusty's.

Witchery. Nobody really knew what that word meant. At least, nobody he knew. Like Moyle. What was a Moyle? Could a haint caller use a word like *Moyle* to raise a dead man? From his slat rocker, he mused on the meanings of words and silence. He wanted to freeze the words at their things, devoid of relation and action. He thought of the tractor's crankcase slobbering oil, the cutter bar blades gummed with pine sap and moss, rock-nicked, begging for the rasp file. Things knew when to stop, but not people. Machines were the safest, the pistons slick in their bright sleeves, brakes and ignition wires, the belligerent little spark plugs, even the fuel line clogged like a glutton's arteries but easier to clean. Or animals. He had to admire the pure lament of a peacock's scream, which meant exactly what it sounded like, meant the world was not at peace or safe. But *Moyle*?

These were the kind of thoughts that always troubled him at work on his Allis-Chalmers, dredging, plowing, hauling. Digging posts, the Bobcat auger would spin like some nightmare sex act. He had this kind of thought when he was untangling roots or swiveling a plant into good soil, tamping the pliant earth back smooth. Thoughts that would not help you understand. He wished, as he often had, that he was smarter or less smart. He didn't know which would be better.

Moyle. Nothing would bring him back. Not lies or regrets or clever schemes. The sirens were at the head road now, and he could see the dust pluming. The lights would be the color of the water heater's pilot light, of the peacock's neck and saddle. Maybe he should have driven Moyle someplace else, denied having seen the man. Maybe he should have thrown him into the old Cherokee and driven him to the clinic. It was too late now, but he was innocent, despite the smirking grill of the squad car. Inside the swollen lie he had worked for two hours to construct, he was innocent of this man's life, though he felt stained and guilty and lost.

It happened like a commando invasion, squad cars coming in at all angles ahead of the ambulance—state boys as well as the locals. He had time to take just one step forward and open his mouth to explain when he felt his arms jerked behind him and the cold bracelets against the skin of his wrists. He could hear the teeth clicking in their steel sleeves.

"That's him," shouted somebody. It was Joe Steve's voice.

"Gar, you in a world of shit." Joe Steve aimed his index finger at Gar and raised his thumb like a pistol hammer. "Pow, mother-fucker." The thumb dropped.

Then he saw Sheriff Driggers himself leaning over the body and peeling back the tarp. "Good God, what you shoot him with, Thaxton? A elephant gun?"

"Peafowl" was all he could get out, but he stammered on the plosive and sounded like a weed whacker engine. "P-p-p-p-pea-fowl."

He never even saw the medical team, as angry hands pushed him toward the whirling blue light of a cruiser. A female officer he didn't recognize but blonde and familiar-looking guided his head down so he could slip into the back seat, and when the husky woman stepped aside, Gar saw his royal peacock flutter up and light on the top of another county car, then strut toward the bubble, as if he thought its blue light a rival. Then the bird shook itself and spanned his bronze-green tail like a stage magician showing his encore trick.

"I'm guilty enough, I reckon," he thought. "Pig in the pokey."

Then he said it aloud, "P-pig."

"Shut your flap, Gar," said Laine's voice from the front seat. "You ain't close to the line. You've crossed way over, you murdering son of a bitch."

The radio was crackling, its static like bugs in the pines. The car smelled like old sweat and something else, maybe crime. He inhaled deeply, heard his wet breath and began stammering.

"B-b-but...."

"I said shut it." The nightstick slammed against the steel mesh.

The male bird let out its night call, *y-eee-ooo-i, y-eee-ooo-i*, startling the cops and EMS crew and seeming to freeze them in place, as if the world had stopped because they had all heard something bloodthirsty, something ruthless and haunting.

As the cruiser ticked gravel and swerved onto the road, it wasn't

Rusty's face or his daddy's that filled his mind's eye. Not even Moyle.

"Lynda, I m-miss you," he whispered, starting to sob, and in the rearview he could see the peacock cant his radiant head, spread his wings and rise.

# AGAINST A SEA OF TROUBLES

THE FIRST THING ELON left in the lumber stacker's seat was an old Bible open to a fierce passage in Revelations circled in red with a grease pencil. Since the evangelist types always came out in force this close to Easter, the operator, Bart Boone, and his cohorts didn't give it much thought, and he pitched the book into some trash-wood before he cranked up the logger's cherry picker and started stacking the beamwood on a flatbed.

ELON'S SECOND MESSAGE was a Reebok box containing a long strip of bag paper bearing the words THIS IS NOT A RATTLESNAKE BUT IT WANTS TO BE. Bart showed it to Billy Priester, who phoned the boss on his cell. They'd been worried about tree hugger activists since the development was approved by the county, but this was not the form they had expected protest to take. Mr. Touissant advised Billy not to get his skivvies in a wad but to keep a weather eye out just the same. Touissant was a natural-born coonass, his men thought, no matter how shiny his blue suit, so he still had the Gulf accent, a fishy whiff and a fair amount of fight in him. He was already rich, as his foreman said, and getting filthier by the hour with no reservations.

Philippe Touissant, or Smiley, as the papers said he liked to call himself, had been in the Blue Ridge exactly six years and had made a killing buying up farms and lumbering before he slashed the land into acre lots and threw up summer home bungalows. His workers didn't much cotton to him, but he had a way with the paper-pushers and vote-chokers. No complaint anybody could write to the local paper's letter column could so much as slow him down, as his crews cut roads and gouged out roughing stations for processing the towering hardwoods they dropped. The county commissioners couldn't stop him and the board of supervisors wouldn't. Touissant's, Smiley's, theme song seemed to be the alarming, high-pitched crack of live trunks, followed by the thrash through understory trees not ripe for harvest. From Barn Mountain to Sweet Berry Valley, from Walker's Run to Timber Ridge longtime residents has wakened to the artillery volleys of falling trees and known whose wallet was filling. The sight of his bright new Humvee cruising the back roads brought out curses all around.

WHEN BART COULDN'T TURN the motor over on a Monday, he ran through his troubleshoot list, backtracking both the electricals and the fuel flow, until he noticed a foreign grit and thickness in the line, then checked the diesel tank, which he found clotted with honey, and that brought out Touissant in the silver Hummer and Sheriff Sensabaugh in a chocolate-colored cruiser. Touissant emerged from his sparkling vehicle wearing a white cowboy Stetson, while Bart and Billy hid their snickers, but they knew these peculiar raider visitations were turning into serious business.

JUST BEFORE DARK, snow flurries scattered their flakes through the limbs of the Judas tree, where red buds looked like lipstick rubbed on, but badly, like a girl learning. Elon was reading a James Lee Burke crime novel by the window and listening to the silence in the wake of the day's timbering noise. The sky was mostly cleared up by midnight, and Elon stood in the yard relieving himself, staring at the full moon.

"That bullet must have flown hot and fast," he thought, "'cause it cut through everything the sky could offer and scorched a silver hole." It was the pistol in his denim pocket that turned his thoughts down that particular path.

"Alva," he had said over the chicken pie the day before, "it all hurts so bad. I know it's just a self-pity, but it feels like great grief, and I don't see how much longer I can bear it. The noise, the evil of it all. No man has the right to do this."

She looked down at the steaming food on her fork. "Yesterday they was shaking the ground so hard, I could see my tomato soup on the table shiver. It's not just a sound now, Elon, it's all around us, like weather, but we've got to get accustomed. Someday soon they'll be through treeing, and then it will just be nail guns and circle saws. Then things will be quiet again."

"We're talking a year, Alva, maybe two. I can't live with it. Sometimes I want to stop them, to shock them into stopping no matter what the cost."

"You've got to not, Elon. You've got to not."

"I believe they will listen to, I don't know, maybe blood."

"Good Lord, Elon, if you get into trouble again, there will be twice as few of us here to keep the place sane."

She had heard him speak this way only once in the eleven years they'd been married. It was just before he decided he'd had enough of Charles Burrits and took the ball bat to his pins. Elon had broken the man's knee because Charles would not vote union and had started calling Elon a "commie nigger shit rat" at the garage.

"I'll not stand for that," was the last thing Elon had said to Charles, whom he'd grown up playing music and fishing with.

It was an evening with blinding thickets of snow falling, and the removal operators were all on edge, knowing they'd be in the cabs of plows and salters and dumpers all night and into the next day, that the coffee and black pills would not be enough to keep them from frazzling. Elon had turned his scraper into the K-Mart lot and bought a Louisville Slugger, first one he'd held in ten years, maybe more. Back at the shop the next evening he went straight for Charles, who said, "Here comes Karlo Marx the red Russian."

He spent a year in county and five on parole, but he'd handled it well and now stayed clean, keeping his new job at Mary Baldwin College trimming bushes, mowing, blowing saddle-colored leaves and spreading chemical on the icy walkways so the college girls wouldn't break their necks on the way to class.

It went well enough, he and Alva living simple out there in

the woods above McCaskell's pasture, maintaining their A-frame, keeping a garden and studying their testaments with no particular urgency, watching movies on the silver disks and reading paperback books. He liked alligator books and birds, stories about farm people and bluegrass, too, though he never picked the mandolin up again, never so much as tuned it after he got back from jail. It reminded him of something he wouldn't speak of.

When McCaskell's big spread was auctioned off to Touissant, the land baron made public promises—no commercial timbering, no view sheds to suffer, wildlife corridors to continue undisturbed and the like. Everything the protesting neighbors wanted to hear, except the water table problem, with six wells gone dry already in the span of two years. He might as well have promised to fix that, too, as he broke every pledge with a smile, and his timber crews worked from sun to sun, sometimes even loading trucks by floodlight until Leno was well into his monologue. The strain and shudder of the heavy equipment ate away at the sleep of all the locals on both ends of the night.

Elon shook his head and went about his business, his mind compacting like an oyster around a piece of grit. He simmered and clenched, while things were getting worse at work, too, a new school president trying to run the college like the minesweeper he'd once commanded. Now they had to wear pinstriped shirts and trousers lighter than Levis. Everybody got more scrapes and scratches.

Elon came home angry to the whine of saws and the snap of trunks, oaks crashing into the underbrush and the earth suffering another tremor, then the winch dragging the casualties, straining its gears, the Godzilla-toothed grabber lifting and stacking. Where would the birds sing? he wondered. How would the deer and foxes survive? Would they crush all the ginseng and galax? Would he ever see a whole night's rest again?

He fumed and quietly grumbled, but when the lumbering crew set up straight across Red Road from his drive, he began to obsess completely, and Alva could no longer calm him. He placed his gray

Halloween alien at the edge of the drive holding a sign about the endangered water table:

WELL'S GOING DRY
BUYER BEWARE
MAPLE RIDGE WATER CONSERVATION ALLIANCE

His neighbors threw in with him and raised their own signs, but their tone when he spoke with them signaled they believed the war was over and the victors could clear cut and sell to hog farmers if they chose to, the signs just a farewell gesture to good sense and restraint.

THAT WAS WHEN he started to talk a little strange, to say he couldn't labor another day under the heel of a Cajun yahoo and still call himself a man. So the gun came out, though he was not supposed to have access, much less own one. It had been his grandfather's and had been used in union business a generation before. He cleaned it, scraped off the pitted spots, renewed the bluing, broke it down and oiled it over and over, until the smell was almost overwhelming.

"What are you doing, Elon? You'll drown in all this. That's not even a registered gun."

"Do tell."

One night she found him in the basement with a mallet and knife tapping Xs into the lead points.

"Oh, Lord."

Next day he shot a dozen soda cans off the back fence, while she watched, her arms crossed tight across her chest.

"They'll call the law."

"For what? No noise ordinance in the county, Alva. I'm no noisier than their yellow machines tearing good woods into a snaggled-up Hell. I am for sure starting to drown in all these troubles. I am going under, Alva. I've got to do something, swim, something."

He could see the tears slip down her face. The crews couldn't see him shoot, as his back lot sloped down to the old hay road, but he was sure the report of the .32 had the attention of anybody listening.

"Hunters," the workers would have thought, if they had heard the shots at all through their earplugs and air thickened by the roar of combustion engines.

Diesel fuel could pool on the ground as if from a leak, he thought. Toss in a lit stick of sap pine, cedar, and we'll just see one of those monsters blaze up against the evening sky, but he was afraid of setting the whole forest aflame, and where would that get him? Arson was not the answer, so he started toting the Smith and Wesson in his jacket pocket when he moved around his four acres. Sometimes he'd be perched in the La-z-boy reading his Roanoke paper and drinking white coffee, and she could see by the way he sat or how the jacket hung on him that he was carrying.

AFTER THE HONEY, the sheriff had been polite at the door, inquiring about strangers and unusual events, all the while sidling in on Elon's alibi—"fast asleep, captain."

"What time you start to fade?"

"Bout ten I expect. I got the drive to Staunton in the morning, you know. It takes some out of me."

Narrowing his eyes and shifting his considerable weight to the side, the sheriff had dropped hints that destruction of property was not a petty offense, that any man who's seen the inside of jail could guess what such mischief would win him.

"Don't I know, Lamar. Don't I know."

The sheriff winced at the sound of his first name, though he'd known Elon for thirty years and had scrapped and lifted a few with him back in the old days.

"You've got to admit that your spaceman down the drive makes you look a bit suspicious."

Elon was unshaken by his old running mate's piercing eyes. He was calm, his voice a honey itself, his consternation and regret at the thought of eco-terror as genuine as could be.

"You keep your peepers peeled, then, Elon, and let me know, you know?"

"Sure thing."

The whole time the weapon was weighing down his pocket and he was slightly smiling. Sourwood, he thought, best damn bee sweetening around, but even a John Deere gets thirsty for something better than fossil fool. There was no waste involved here.

A WEEK LATER, he had been quiet all evening, mulling over the torture he was going through, the sense of powerlessness. He was thinking toward "impotence" without confronting the actual word, and Alva interrupted him. She had been in the back room sewing most of the evening, taking advantage of the warm air to breathe the edge of spring through an open window.

"You need to see this, Elon."

A small owl, a barnlet, was hunched at the end of one of the raw beams that crossed the top of the room and served as racks for hanging assorted items. He was no larger than a tea glass, and his white face resembled a halved apple.

"He's just a chick. Reckon how he got in?"

"Flew in," she said. I was doing needlework, and I heard a kind of whoosh. When I looked up, he was clinging to the beamwood up there, waddling over to the shadow corner."

"What you expect he wants here? Mice maybe?"

"It's an omen is what it is. Owl in the house is a bad sign, Elon."

"That's an owl in the daylight. Indian legend. What that is, Alva, that's the soul. Look at those eyes. We'd best let him out."

"Let?"

It took a broom on one side and his trout net duct taped to a rake on the other, but it was easy enough, the bird too terrified to move or flap about. Elon took him out the sliding door and turned the net downside-over on the picnic table.

"Don't do any harm, Al," he said as he loosened the strings and lifted the net away. "I hope you can find a tree left to live in. I hope you can get by." The bird rose almost soundlessly and was soon swallowed by the dark or the waning moon.

NEXT MORNING, THE SKY was a blue blur with a streak-o-lean tint just over the eastern evergreens when Elon slipped out of bed. The big Homelite saws were not cranked up yet, but he could hear the loader's engine idling. From the upstairs window he could see something shining over at the work clearing, something big and silver. "Touissant," he thought, and hurried to get his trousers on. He was used to dressing to the smell of Maxwell House dark roasted, but he thought he'd just as soon do this without the stimulation. Alva was still deep in her dream refuge, so he gave her a light near-kiss before easing down the loft steps in his socked feet. Even the dog thought it was too early for a dew piss, so Elon had the ground floor to himself as he loaded up the Mr. Coffee, pulled on his gum boots and slipped on his denim barn jacket.

As soon as he opened the door, the air and the white ground told him it had been an unseasonable night. He had the length of a football field to cover between himself and the source of the low vibration, and he shuddered as he began the walk. Crossing the new-growth woodlot, he heard the slightly frosted sticks crackling under his soles, while a chickadee scratched and chirred on the empty feeder by the deck. The dogwood beside the tool shed had made its own blizzard, and a few jonquils joined the forsythia's quiet hallelujah. Petals on the ash and chestnut saplings caught the early light here and there among the leafless large hardwoods and spruces. One crabapple due north of the house seemed to flare with a white fire. He fingered the pistol in his pocket and thought "something—swim or something" as he walked straight toward the machine with its treads like desert tanks he saw on the TV.

There in the operator's seat sat the Cajun, smoking a little cigar, a yellow safety helmet perched on his head like a canary. He had a Hardee's go-cup in one hand and a gear knob in the other.

"Touissant," Elon called across the hazy morning. "You decided you was letting your henchmen have all the fun? Want to get into the actual wreckage act yourself?"

The big man was so startled he dropped his coffee and then howled as it splashed his trousers.

"Shit shit shit, mon Dieu! What manner of thing are you? You're trespassing, mon ami, and me, I can have the law on your ass in one phone call."

That was when Elon showed the pistol, not pointing it yet, not "brandishing" as the ordinances spelled it, just dangling it by his side, his wrist pivoting a little back and forth, the blue gun, barely visible, twisting with it.

The other man's cigar dropped from his lips, and his eyes, in the sparse light, grew wider, as if he needed to see sharper to believe it.

"You know what the last red words in the Bible's last book say?" He didn't wait for an answer. "*Surely I come swiftly.* Imagine that in red, and you can't miss the truth of it." Then he raised the gun, carefully pointing the barrel straight for Touissant's heart.

The Cajun tried to stand but clonked his hard hat on the ceiling of the cab.

"Please don't shoot me." He was shaking like a wet dog. "What have I ever done to you? What in God's name have I done?"

"Be. Be and destroy. That was enough, brother." Elon knew he had to do it now or lose his nerve, his concentration. The light was growing, and soon the real workers would be coming over the rise in their pick-ups. He didn't have anything, really, against them.

"Me, I'll do anything if you'll just let me be, mon frere. True now, do anything you say."

"You've already done everything." But before he could squeeze the trigger, which was cold and sharp against his finger, he followed the impulse to swing his arm to the right and stop when it was pointed at the Humvee.

"Here is my word," he said, as the revolver spoke the same syllable four, five, six times, sending glass flying and dinking big holes with rat-colored rims into the metal of the door and hood. Then he dropped the gun into the mess of peeled limbs and sawdust, did a neat about-face and marched briskly back toward the lights of his house.

"Does it feel lighter now? Does it seem less hard?" he asked himself, but he was numb with the understanding of what might follow. By now the dog would be ready to resume his routine, and Alva would be in her robe, wide alert from the shots and fretting, knowing he'd done something extreme. He didn't know how long it would be before the blue bubble would flash up the driveway, spraying siren noise and gravel, but he said out loud, "I want to sit back in the quiet at my window and sip one last cup of sweet freedom coffee, to be absolutely still as still till what happens next happens."

—Kevin Remington

R. T. SMITH was born in Washington D.C. and raised in Georgia and North Carolina. He was educated at Georgia Tech, UNC and Appalachian State and taught for nineteen years at Auburn University, where he served as Alumni Writer-in-Residence and co-editor of *Southern Humanities Review*. Since 1995 he has been the editor of *Shenandoah* for Washington and Lee University, where he serves as Writer-in-Residence. He has also taught in visiting writer capacity at VMI and Converse College. Smith's previous collections of fiction are *Faith* and *Uke Rivers Delivers*, which was published in LSU's Yellow Shoe Fiction Series. His stories have appeared in *Best American Short Stories, Best American Mystery Stories, New Stories from the South: The Year's Best* and *the Pushcart Prize Anthology*. His poetry collections *Messenger* and *Outlaw Style* received the Library of Virginia Poetry Award in 2002 and 2008. Smith lives in Rockbridge County, Virginia with his wife, the poet Sarah Kennedy.

9 781604 542097